I0685059

Leaving Michael

Leaving Michael

By

P.J.P. Tuffrey

Copyright © 2020 by P.J.P. Tuffrey

This is a work of fiction. Names, characters, organisations, places,
events and incidents are either products of the author's imagination or
are used fictitiously. Any resemblance to actual persons, living or dead,
or actual events is purely coincidental.

P.J.P. Tuffrey has asserted his right to be identified as the author of this
book.

All rights reserved. No part of this publication may be reproduced,
stored in a retrieval system, or transmitted, in any form or by any means,
electronic, mechanical, photocopying, recording or otherwise, without
the prior permission of the author.

First published in the U.K. in 2020 by Lulu.com
ISBN: 978-0-244-25542-8

Cover design and images © 2020 by P.J.P. Tuffrey

Connect with the author;
https://pjptuffrey.wixsite.com/free-download

For

Valerie Tuffrey

John Tuffrey

When the gilded cage your rock star father's made for you becomes a prison, where do you run to, and how can you hide?

Follow Shaun and Bodhi's journey from "Pleasurelands" to Los Angeles and find out why the gilded cage can never be their true home.

Shaun, a mixed race Brit has been P.A. to Michael Michael, his fellow Brit and world famous rock star for as long as he can remember. But now, with Michael's intersex child Bodhi begging him to help him leave Michael's vast estate, Shaun has to make the hardest decision of his life; to keep living a lie, or to follow his heart...

A fascinating and thought provoking meditation on the nature of fame, the nature of gender and the nature of happiness!

If you love literary fiction with a wide conceptual reach that leaves you feeling enriched by the end of it – you'll love this book!

Chapter 1.

This is the letter I'd like Bodhi to read;

'Bodhi, if you had listened to any radio station at all on that day twelve months ago, you'd have heard a playback of the desperate 911 call that started the whole media frenzy we're both still caught up in. You'd have heard a panicked female voice, hoarse with fear telling the operator that your father had collapsed, and that he wasn't breathing. You'd have heard the operator asking for an address, and you'd have heard the voice screaming back; "Jesus, its Michael's place! Everyone knows where it is, for God's sake get an ambulance out here quickly!"

If you had watched any T.V. news station bulletins on the following day, you'd have seen the red striped ambulance enter the gates of "Pleasurelands" behind the Police C.S.I. cordon. You'd have seen the "Do Not Enter" tape flapping in the breeze, separating the news reporters from the medics pushing the wheeled stretcher into the property, and you'd have seen the heavy faces of the investigators swapping comments with each other behind the shields of their raised hands.

If you had followed any of the links that appeared online the following week, you would have seen the leaked Police Department photographs of the bedroom where your father died. You'd know that a filthy, uncared for clutter of discarded gadgets and unworn clothes filled every frame. You'd know that compact discs and sheathed vinyl in precariously balancing rows were covering the corners and the edges of his floor, and that bottles of pills and prescription medications on his bedside tables, were stacked up in towers gathering carpets of dust next to his photographs of you.

But even if you hadn't listened to the radio on that dreadful day, when, two weeks later the toxicology reports cleared the Coroner's desk, and Michael's body was released for his funeral, you surely must have heard the headlines announcing on the hour every hour; "Death by Dependency on Prescription Medications", and you couldn't have stayed unaware of it.

Even if you hadn't watched the television on that day afterwards, when the squabbling over the details of his Will eventually spilled over, and endless talk shows on every channel launched wild speculations for us all on the consequences of Michael's sudden Opioid death, again, you must have known about it.

And even if you hadn't in fact clicked on any of the links in the week after your father died, when that whole stack of Michael's hits re-entered the charts, and tributes to him blew up everywhere on the Internet; well, despite the insignificance, in the broad scheme of things of one solitary man's death, the reality is, that no matter if you Bodhi, are living in a Buddhist temple on a hill with hardly a laptop to be seen; you surely could not now be still un-aware of the fact of your father's passing—and yet you haven't got in touch with me at any point in the year since, even though everyone's going crazy with speculation, and all I need to know is; why not?'

Yes, that's the letter I'd like Bodhi to read more than anything, but for all the times I draft it out, swapping the words around for a better effect; here I am sitting comfortably in my titanium wheelchair, drinking the cups of coffee that my girlfriend Hailey helps me drink, and I still don't even know where to send it. If I could give it to the postman across the street with his Velcro shoulder bag to deliver, I surely would. I hear him as I sit by our living room windows every day, clacking through

Belsize Park's unlatched gates one by one. He stops to chat with a neighbour sometimes in his north London accent, and even takes letters from them to post himself, though he shouldn't. Maybe he'd take mine. But it wouldn't help, because I simply don't have an address I can put on the front. Bodhi is completely lost to any letter I can send.

Again and again Hailey tells me that I should just; 'Let it go'. She shrugs her slender shoulders, and reminds me with a quick kiss on my good cheek that Bodhi's unknowable location will stay unknown to me no matter how much I want it to reveal itself.

'You need to get on with your life, babe,' she says, 'you've got to forget about him, or her...or whatever he was. You need to concentrate on getting back as much of your mobility as you can. I don't want to be sitting here reading magazines all day and nursing you, you've got so much more living to do, and I want to be a part of it.'

I love her dearly that she does, but the fact is I hear people telling me to 'let it go' all the time. The physio says; 'let go of trying to be the person that you were, Mr. Adefumi...accept the reality of how things are for you now, Mr. Adefumi'; the psychologist says; 'let go of expectations about the future, Shaun, try not to be unrealistic.'

I hear it so much of it, I'm not even sure what 'letting go' means anymore. Sure, it's kind of Hailey to care, but as the months have gone by I just can't forget what happened to Bodhi at all.

What Hailey doesn't understand, because we haven't been together long enough, is that having watched over the child of the most famous man in the world for half my fifty years, it isn't just that I grieve for having lost contact with him. What matters more is not knowing whether the choices he made before we parted company have found the successes they deserve. That's what matters—and the fact that he was intersex, or inter-gender doesn't have anything to do with it at all, he acted like a boy, and whether he entirely looked like one or not made no difference to me, it never did.

'You should imagine the boy prospering,' Hailey says, 'and then you'll feel alright about the fact he isn't around anymore.'

'I do,' I say to Hailey, 'and it helps for a while. I see him stretched out unrecognised, somewhere nice…somewhere safe. Maybe on a Los Angeles beach, not so far from the places I helped raise him in. I see him with his blond hair stuck messily to his almond coloured brow, the warm wind drying him of his untroubled sweat. Or I see him in the road less wildernesses of Northern California, camping out with friends under pristine skies.'

'So, it's all good then…'

'Yes, but then the worries come back that it's a different blue than the Santa Monica sky that's surrounding him, that it's a blue-grey coldness instead and he's lost in misadventures in Detroit or Dayton, or someplace like that. I worry that his life has become a meaningless thing to him now, and worst of all, that it's my fault if it has.'

'Why,' Hailey asks.

'Because it was me and only me,' I say, 'who said his farewells to Bodhi, and that day twelve months ago was the last day when anyone knew where he was.'

'It's the wound to your head that's left you so stuck with your obsessions and your memories,' Hailey says, 'but tell me what happened with Bodhi anyway. I'll stay silent, you can take your time. Tell it the way you want me to hear it, and imagine I'm not even here.'

I tell her it could take hours, days even and she says; 'well, we're not going anywhere, are we?'

In my silence, Hailey says; 'its okay my love— you don't have to torture yourself. You don't have to do this. Whatever it was that happened, it wasn't your fault.'

'But it was, Hailey,' I say. 'You know, even the first thing he asked me in the truck stung me; he asked me why I'd given him the name "Bodhi". It was as the great gates to "Pleasurelands" disappeared into the distance in my rear view mirror.'

I can hear Hailey settling down on the couch behind me.

'We'd been driving south towards L.A., heading out of the Sierras and away from "Pleasurelands." We were inside a battered old Chevrolet Pickup. If there hadn't been so much for us to share about the place where Bodhi had grown up we might have sat there silently, watching the black road dither into the distance with our windows down, and the hot dry air enveloping us. We might even have looked forward to the future. But it hadn't been like that, there'd been so much to share, and so much he wanted to know—so much, that I rack my brains now to think whether there was any place where what I did, or didn't say in sharing it all, made Bodhi go wrong...'

Bodhi sat twisted in his seat, looking towards me. Strands of his shoulder length hair were sticking to the beads of sweat on his soft cheeks.

'Bodhi means wisdom, right?' he said. 'How am I supposed to know anything about wisdom, Shaun? If you hadn't called me Bodhi, none of this would have happened.' He wiped his forehead with his fingers. 'You should have called me Chris or Junior, or even Ocean or Sky or something.'

'You realise I'm probably going to get sacked for driving you away,' I said back, 'and this is all you're worried about? I haven't even had a chance to tell my girlfriend that I won't see her till later.'

'I wish it was the only thing I'm worrying about,' he said tightening a buckle on a tattered green rucksack I'd given him.

I shifted my grip on the sticky steering wheel. 'Who says it was me that called you anything?' I said.

'David told me.'

'Everything your cousin David says is a lie,' I said.

'Yes, I kind of realise that,' Bodhi said, 'but what else am I supposed to go on? I've got to believe something.' Bodhi set his full rucksack down into the foot well of the truck. He shifted on the torn vinyl of the trucks' passenger bench seat. 'How did it happen then, that I got my name?'

The ancient Chevy's engine churned over the sound of his anxious high pitched voice. I checked the rear view mirror again to make sure no-one was following us, flicking my eyes from the road in front to the road behind.

'What does it matter now?'

Bodhi paused before speaking again;

'My father's not going to sack you, Shaun. You've worked for him for too long. But I don't know what's going to happen next. What if you have a heart attack? What if you get killed by a meteorite, falling out of the sky? Anything can happen. You're the only one I can trust to tell me what's true. I don't even know who I am, I don't know anything.'

'You know almost everything, Bodhi, really you do,' I said.

But of course I knew that he didn't.

I took a deep breath; 'It should have been straight after you were born that you got your name, just like anyone else, but as usual your father had other ideas. Anyway, what happened was that your mother stormed out of the house with you in her arms. You were only tiny. This was from the house they had in Laurel Canyon, in Los Angeles.'

'Did you talk to her?'

'I was in bed when she left. My girlfriend at the time Nicki, she had her head on my chest keeping me there.'

The wooden fence rails I'd fitted to the flatbed of the pickup years before had been rattling behind us, and I looked in the rear view mirror again to make sure they hadn't been rattling loose.

'What happened?' Bodhi demanded.

'Your mother, Mia had driven off in her white Porsche Carrera— something she hadn't done for months because of the pills she'd been taking. She'd managed to negotiate the freeway, and then the busy four way stops of back streets off Sunset Boulevard without having an accident. She'd booked a room in a hotel with one of those old, brick sized MicroTAC cell phones which she always carried with her in the car.'

Bodhi looked at me blankly, he'd never seen one. I explained to him that it was just an old phone and he shrugged his shoulders and waved me on. 'What she ended up with,' I said, 'were rooms on the eighth floor of a luxury hotel about a mile from your parents' house. If she'd been thinking clearly, she could have booked the room when she'd got there, but obviously she hadn't been. She'd turned the keys over to a valet. It was the Beverley Boulevard Hotel. The valet was called Dante.'

'Did he drive off with the car or something?' Bodhi said. His face was contorted with confusion, but as innocent as it had always been.

'No, nothing like that,' I said. 'The valet and a hotel porter had tried to help your mother in with you and the baby things she was carrying, but she'd ignored them, struggling past without saying anything. They hadn't tried to help too much, they said, because she was obviously very wealthy, and she hadn't seemed too interested in what their ideas of assistance were. Though, to be honest, it sounded to me like they were just regular guys and didn't want to end up carrying the baby.'

Bodhi ignored me; 'Where was Michael? Why wasn't my father with her?'

'They'd had an argument, that's all. It was no big deal, or at least it didn't seem like it was. He'd driven himself away from home in a rage. It was the slamming doors, which woke me up. It turned out he'd got in a car and ended up driving furiously along the highway to the coast.'

'Why do you say furiously?'

'Well, eventually he crashed, that's why. But I'll get to that.'

'What happened next?'

'A phone call came to your parent's house. I was still in bed, but because Konrad, your father's P.A. had just been fired, I'd had to answer the call myself. It had been from a receptionist at the hotel that Mia had taken herself to, to say that there was a distressed lady, standing on the balcony of her room and calling out for your father.'

I had needed to concentrate as an articulated semi-truck pulled onto the dusty highway ahead of us, it was full of tomatoes, stacked up so high that from time to time one or more would fall out, and land in front of us, splattering like tracer fire.

'I thought it was a prank call; another journalist trying to get together tit-bits for a story, it used to happen all the time,' I said to Bodhi.

'What did she say?'

'She said; "Hey, I had to work hard to get through to you. Okay?" something like that. I let her keep talking for a bit. I figured I could always put the phone down on her. But then she said her friend's aunt worked for Michael, and her name was Maria, and she worked as a cleaner...and then I realised I knew who she meant. So I took the rest of the story from her, and told her not to call the Police.'

'Why not call the Police,' Bodhi asked.

'You don't know anything do you,' I said, and Bodhi stared back blankly at me. 'Because if you're famous, even a little bit, and you call the Police in L.A., someone in the Police department will pass the info on to a journalist. You can be sure of it.'

'Why?'

'They'll be getting kick-backs from a tabloid,' I said. 'You might as well call the papers yourself. Which Michael wouldn't have wanted. Anyway,' I added, 'the receptionist was asking for Michael to come and talk to this woman; your mother, Mia Heywood, because she sounded like she knew him very well. I thought she'd been clutching at straws really, but I gave her the credit for trying, and so I told her that your father of course couldn't come, because he was out of the house, and, unlike your mother who just loved having one, Michael never kept a cell phone in any of his cars because they weren't reliable enough, and so he was uncontactable. The receptionist seemed disappointed when I told her that, and to be honest a bit desperate. So, after I thought about it for a bit I told her I knew Mrs. Heywood myself, and I'd come instead.'

I pulled out and passed the truck in front of us. The road ahead had been sucking us forward, and I'd had to watch my speed. Being stopped by the Police with a missing person on board would not have been good for either of us.

'You went to see my Mum, Shaun...'

'Yes. I drove to the Beverley Boulevard Hotel as quickly as I could. The valet, who turned out to be Dante, wasn't too happy to have a bunch of keys thrown at him, but he caught them, and then he did the usual thing of glaring back at me suspiciously. What the attorney said, in the Courtroom, because they left no detail unquestioned, was that he was; "weighing up the actions of Mr. Adefumi against the other indignities his day was likely to bring him, and considering in his mind whether the dark brown shade of Mr. Adefumi's skin tone meant he didn't actually need to help him at all." Or in other words he was probably just being racist against me, but that was par for the course.'

'I don't know what you mean,' Bodhi said.

'No, I know you don't,' I said, and had it been any other blonde, blue eyed kid I'd have been offended, but Bodhi had had a very sheltered upbringing. I smiled at him, and Bodhi smiled a confused smile back. I continued; 'after I got inside the hotel, I explained to the receptionist who I was, and after she'd passed me on to one of the hotel managers, I went up to the eighth floor. The young manager came with me, he had the keys in his hand. I remember he wanted to know all about Michael, even while we were going up through the floors; "What's it like working for Michael? How did you get the job? Is it because you're English, like he is?" I suppose it was reasonable, I was only dressed in old clothes; an out of date tour t-shirt, jeans. I probably didn't look like part of anybody's entourage.'

'Where was my mother?'

'Are you sure you want to hear all this,' I asked.

'If I don't hear it now, when will I ever?' Bodhi said.

I looked from the road in front of me over to Bodhi. He was waiting for me to speak. I looked back to the road.

'We reached the eighth floor, and—Riccardo; that was his name,' I said, 'Riccardo took me to the Presidential suite and opened the door for me. He told me to call him if there was anything I needed, so I thanked him and walked in. I could hear a baby crying—that was you, so I walked in further. There was a Gucci handbag lying on the floor with its contents spewing out, which I remembered had seemed ominous. Then the lounge opened out in front of me, and then I saw your mother. She was standing on a balcony that looked out over the whole of L.A. She was framed against the dark blue sky.' I looked over to Bodhi; 'you didn't have a name yet, but you were wrapped tightly in swaddling clothes in a basket that rocked gently in a breeze, on a decorative iron table beside her.'

'Did she say anything to you?'

'She was standing with her back to me. I called out; "Mia!" I'd been too startled to keep quiet. But no, she didn't move, she didn't say a word.'

'What did you do?'

'Nothing, I wasn't sure what to do. I was just standing there watching the warm updrafts rippling the curtains. I wasn't sure whether to rush towards her, or just stay standing there. Your mother was a very elegant woman. She was also kind of fierce. I didn't know whether she would have turned and held me like a younger brother if I'd reached her, whether she would have played with my curly red hair like she used to after she met me. She used to call me her 'brown Irish teddy bear', and then she'd hug me until I blushed.'

I looked over at Bodhi. He was paying attention to me as though I was telling him things that were actually important. It seemed to me that I was just dredging up old memories, and painful ones at that.

'Your father had told me I was to help her with anything she wanted. That was what he said when I met her for the first time,' I said.

'When was that?'

'About six years earlier,' I said, concentrating on the road.

'Anyway, you're standing there in the hotel room...'Bodhi said, after I'd been silent for a while.

'Yes, and I didn't know how she would react, so I didn't do anything at all,' I said. 'She might have sighed and flinched if I'd given her a brotherly touch on her shoulders, like she had since she'd got ill, and that would have been okay. But she might have started screaming abuse at me instead, and I couldn't afford to have anyone hear that, not coming from a wealthy white woman in L.A.'

'Why not?'

'Don't worry about it,' I said, 'the point is; if I had tried to ease her back into the shade of the room, would she have allowed me? I didn't know. The vastness of the empty space in front of her seemed to be calling to her, but I couldn't decide what to do. And then, Mia took away my choice anyway.'

'What did she do?'

Did I need to tell him everything? The memories played so easily in my mind; how she lifted her leg up to the height of the railing on the balcony, and the wrap-around of her skirt fell away until the seam stopped it from parting any further. How she raised her leg higher, even against the stitching. How, for a bizarre moment, as the threads snapped stich by expensive stitch I had been worried that she was damaging an expensive dress, despite the fact that it was becoming clearer and clearer before my eyes that she was threatening to damage not only that, but the very body that wore it. But did I need to tell him that?

There was a turn-out ahead, I pulled into it and we parked. I turned off the ignition, listening as the engine spun awkwardly to a stop, and then cleared my throat. 'Your mother climbed fully over the railings. She was standing on the outside of them, holding on,' I said. I looked at Bodhi. 'If I could only have heard her say something, I could have cheered her up,' I said. 'It wouldn't have mattered how sad she sounded, but she just didn't say anything. I wondered if she was bluffing. The ledge was wide enough for her to stand on, so she wasn't in any immediate danger. If it had been a cry for help, I could have been that help. There was, even at that point nothing that had needed to go wrong, it could all have turned out okay.'

Bodhi nodded.

'I could have calmed her down inside her rooms, I could have thanked the girl at the reception, assured her that there was still no need to call the Police, or say anything to the Press, and then I could have driven Mia home, called her sister Marcelyn, waited for Michael to return. I could have sorted everything out. I've always thought I should have said to her; "don't move Mia, keep a hold and I'll be there, everything will be alright", but before I could reach her, half walking, half running, she took you, Bodhi out of your basket, held you in one arm close to her chest, checked your face, gathered in the cloth around you, and then looked up from you straight into my eyes. I can't get the images out of my mind.'

'It must have been horrible,' Bodhi said, putting his hand gently on my shoulder as a tear trickled down the side of my nose.

'I froze,' I said to Bodhi, 'holding myself motionless because I didn't want any movement to provoke her. You know, there hadn't been a trace of emotion on her face, she had looked at me for long enough that she couldn't have failed to see the emotions on my face, but she hadn't spoken, she hadn't tried to speak, there hadn't been even a moment of a muscle twitching that I could have taken as the outward sign of some inner struggle. There had been a hundred forms of "No!" written on my face, but still she hadn't said anything. And then she simply released her grip.'

'She shouldn't have done it.'

'I shouted "no!" but it was too late, she had fallen. I couldn't reach her. It was as though the space between us had to stay constant; the closer I threw myself at her, the further from me she became. I couldn't have grasped her hand had I been faster than the speed of the gravity that propelled her to the ground. I couldn't have reached her baby,' (her baby!), 'to snatch it from her had I been travelling at twice the speed of gravity. She fell, you fell, and anything I might have done, or said was too late, too late.'

'She jumped from a balcony, with me in her arms,' Bodhi said.

'You did know that, Bodhi. Didn't you?'

'David told me,' he said, looking down at the dirt encrusted foot well of the truck, 'but he told me so much stuff, I never knew what was true and what was a lie.'

'That's your cousin for you,' I said. 'But what I'm telling you is what happened, because I was there. Are you sure you want to hear more?'

Bodhi nodded.

'The next thing was, I threw up on the balcony, again and again until my stomach was empty. I didn't dare to look down, I went back into the dark of the hotel room, and sat on the bed with my head in my hands. Sometime later, it can't have been as long as it felt like it was, the smart young manager who had let me into the suite of rooms burst back in and rushed to the window. I don't know what he thought he was going to do. Maybe he thought Mia was caught on a snag, dangling there, and he was going to rescue her. Maybe he thought he could rescue the reputation of the hotel—after all they'd decided to give the room early in the morning to a woman who must have been, at least to some extent visibly distressed? I don't know. I remember he asked me; "are you alright", and I wondered what I was supposed to say, when someone asks you that? And then he asked me; "That isn't going to get you sacked, is it?" I had to force myself not to shout at him. But looking up I could see the confusion on his face; he didn't know what to say, he was only young. He opened and closed his mouth a few times, but then there was a crackling over his Walkie-talkie, and hisses and pops, and, I don't know, he gathered what he needed to do, and left me alone.'

'So that's how it was,' Bodhi said, 'there was nobody to help you?'

'No, so I wandered eventually, dazed, down to the parking lot, collected my car and drove back to your father's place.'

I cleared my throat, and rubbed my eyes. 'We'd better get going again,' I said. 'If your father wants to find us, it won't be that hard. We'll need to get more distance between you both.'

I started the red, rusty Chevy again. It was stick shift, and the parking brake was stiff, but the road had been quiet, and we re-joined the highway, coughing out fumes from the back of the truck.

'I was still alive though,' Bodhi said, 'didn't you know? What happened to me?'

'That was the happiest thing ever,' I said. 'I got back to Michael's, and the first thing I had to do was tell my girlfriend, Nicki what Mia had done. She didn't want to leave me on my own, but I warned her that the Press would be swarming, and for both our sakes she needed to go out, and stay out for the day. She had dance classes to go to, or something like that. She was a dancer. Then Marcelyn phoned. She had her cell phone in her car and called soon after Nicki had left. Marcelyn had been on her way to her physiotherapist, she'd left David with the nanny. I think she'd just got there. She guessed what had happened.'

'How,' Bodhi asked.

'She'd heard something on the radio, a news report. They were calling Mia the "Boulevard Hotel Jumper" at the time. They didn't know who she was, or if they did they weren't allowed to say because her identity hadn't been confirmed. Marcelyn said; "tell me it can't be Mia they're talking about, Shaun. Please." Her voice was shaking. She started crying, I could hear her, and she blew her nose. I made sure she was off the road, and I could only tell her that I was sorry, and that I had got there too late. She had a good sob, and when she'd calmed down, she asked me how Michael had taken the news, and I had to explain that your father was out, on the road somewhere. "You'll have to break the news to him", she said—which was a horrible thought. But then I realised he may have heard it on the radio too, and even though they weren't saying who the lady was that jumped, the fact is Mia had used that hotel a lot, so it wasn't a random place, and of course, she had been very ill for a long time.'

I looked over at Bodhi. I was worried for him. Will any of the other clothes in his bag fit him better? The jeans and T-shirt I've lent him don't look right on him; he almost looks like a girl, with his long hair and puffy man-boobs. Does he have enough dollars in his jean pockets to buy any more clothes? How is this whole journey going to work out for him?

'Marcelyn told me they had taken Mia's body to "Mercy Medical Center" in L.A. That was what they had said on the radio. Of course the body hadn't been identified, and really I should have stayed at the Hotel to do that when the ambulance had come, but I'd been too dazed by the whole experience. Marcelyn had said; "You shouldn't blame yourself, Shaun. Mia is my twin. I need to identify the body myself", so I left her to do that.'

'I still don't understand though, why didn't you find me and take me with you? Didn't I matter to you at all?'

'It was a weird combination, Bodhi. Marcelyn hadn't said you were alive, I just assumed you weren't. It was only when I turned the T.V. on and scanned through the channels for something to distract myself with that I started to think about you. But, Jesus, I didn't want to think about you. I mean, for God's sake, who would jump with a child in their arms? I felt sick to my guts. But there was nothing on T.V. so, I ended up watching the local news reports, and there was one with this big cleaning lady. She'd been out walking, taking her children to school, and she said she'd heard a gunshot, so she'd ducked, pulled her children towards her and tried to take cover. But then she'd seen Mia, and it was all a horrible mess, but the reporter kept asking her questions, and then this woman said she heard the strangest thing...'

'Which was?'

'...which was you. A baby crying. So she looked around and saw you, a screaming baby, still wrapped in a blanket, red with blood and bits of Mia. I jumped off the sofa, because I couldn't believe what I was hearing on the T.V. She said the baby was wriggling and screaming its head off, and she said you must have bounced. And the reporter said; "What? Bounced?" "Yes, bounced", the cleaning lady said, "from off of its mother's chest", and landed just a few feet away.'

'I suppose that was pretty amazing,' Bodhi said, looking away from me, out of the window of the passenger door.

'My head started spinning with how unlikely it was. I was sure you had both died. It was impossible. But yes, you had bounced from the chest cavity of your mother, and you had survived, unharmed, completely unharmed. Mia's body had protected yours. It was a miracle.'

'Michael didn't know though.'

'Your father didn't know anything. My first thought was to let Marcelyn know. I still hadn't been thinking straight, so when I tried to contact her I couldn't, she didn't have her phone on—well, of course she didn't because she was at the hospital. So I jumped into a car again and drove there. I wanted to let her know she could find you, as well as her sister. Foolish really.'

'Why?'

'Because without the suitable proof of connection to the deceased they wouldn't let me anywhere near Mia's body, and I couldn't find Marcelyn either. But I was able to find out from a nurse that you were healthy, and then I drove back to your father's place.'

I eased the speed down cautiously to 55 as we approached the black and white of a Patrol car lurking on the other side of the highway. What was it doing there? I wondered, is it waiting for me, will it pull out after a while, turn and follow me. Is its radio abuzz with the message; 'All vehicles, look out for a black male, approx. 200 pounds, five feet nine inches, driving a broken old red Chevrolet Pickup; California plates. White male, twenty years old, in the cab with him. Possible abduction. Please copy.' Or was it just that it was the end of the month, and the Police department needed to make up its funding shortfall by trapping speeders? 'Better drive slower,' I thought to myself.

'Your father however, had indeed heard the news reports on the radio,' I said to Bodhi, 'and unfortunately he'd crashed his car on the freeway. Fortunately he was okay, but some Officers of the California Highway Patrol had needed to take him away from the site of the accident in the back of a Police car.'

'Was he hurt?'

'No, he wasn't, but he was in shock. I met your father at the gates to his house about an hour later. I got back from the hospital just as he arrived. A Policeman was still doing his best to comfort him, but he looked distracted, as though meeting the Great Michael Michael couldn't possible mean he was meeting a man whose wife had just jumped from the eighth floor balcony of a hotel with his baby in her arms.'

'What did you say?'

'I told him and his colleague that it was okay to leave, and that I'd do my job and look after Michael.'

'How did Michael seem?' Bodhi said, lifting his feet onto the side of the rucksack lying flat in front of the torn brown leather seat.

I reset the milometer. I should have done it earlier, as soon as we had left. I wanted to know how far we had gone. How far I had taken Bodhi, how far I had to return.

'What did he say, Shaun,' Bodhi asked.

'You have to understand, Michael loved your mother very deeply. She was the love of his life. And then all of a sudden she was gone. It was a terrible shock for him. His head was in a bad way, I mean, he was so dizzy when he got back, he could barely stand up. I shouldered him over to a couch and sat him down. We waited for the Police cars and intercoms to fade into the distance. Everything fell into a silence. And then he groaned at me; "Why didn't you stop her from jumping? You were with her, weren't you?" I didn't know what to say, I didn't know how much the Police had told him.'

I could feel my grip on the steering wheel tightening, I had to peel my fingers off, and readjust my hold.

'I told him I couldn't reach Mia on the balcony, but then Michael said; "What did you do, wait until she was over it before you moved, or anything?" Before I could say it wasn't like that, he stood up and paced around the lounge. He shouted at me that I didn't need to be so polite, he said; "You could have run, Shaun. You could have grabbed her by the hair!"'

A row of Pine trees by the side of the road strobed sunlight over Bodhi and me while we drove on. I remembered that back then I had followed Michael, stepping in and out of the bright sunlight that flooded in from the small courtyard that bordered his lounge, shading my eyes from the brilliant flashes reflecting off a pool which rippled under the splashing droplets of a fountain.

'Michael was angry,' I said to Bodhi, 'he just needed someone to take it out on. After that he asked me why I didn't talk more to Mia, when she was over the balcony. He thought I could have talked her down. But you see, I couldn't have done. I tried to tell Michael that the whole thing played out in seconds. But he wasn't listening, he only wanted to say; "You're so bloody silent, Shaun". Well...it's not like he didn't know me,' I said to Bodhi, 'I'd been working for him for ten years by then.'

I ran my hand over my face. It was a warm morning to be in a truck with no air conditioning.

'I wanted to say to your father; "Michael, you don't need answers from me, do you. You only want to be able to tell yourself that you've asked the right questions." I wanted to say to your father; "Michael, you know perfectly well why Mia killed herself. How much I need to squirm while you pretend you don't—that's the only question bothering you, isn't it?" I wanted to say to him; "Michael, you think being able to maintain your sense of moral superiority is the real reason you're paying me, don't you. Not that I run around fixing your broken promises and healing your mistakes." But I didn't say any of those things to your father.'

I just added them in my mind to all the others words and phrases I'd carried around, and hadn't unburdened from myself.

'Anyway, your father was still confused; "Couldn't you have stopped her from leaving here with the baby?" he said, "Where did you think she was going to go? You must have thought something was wrong? You shouldn't have let her go." I told Michael I didn't want to stay awake all night with my girlfriend Nicki, following the to's-and-fro's of his argument with Mia. I told him that we shut the door of our flat on him, and we tried to get some sleep. I was trying to tell Michael that the next thing I knew was him driving off, but before I could, your father accused me abandoning Mia when she was at her lowest ebb.'

Bodhi stayed silent and I looked over to him for some sympathy, but it hadn't been forthcoming.

'Michael knew the state of mind Mia was in when he'd left her that morning,' I said, 'how was I supposed to know? He had left her. He had left first, before her. I didn't know that. I was asleep. I told him Mia must have driven off while Nicki and I were asleep. I told him the baby wasn't crying—it couldn't have been crying—so how was I supposed to know what her intentions had been?'

I wiped the sweat off my face. The memories were making me hotter than the air.

'Michael had started crying, hiding his head in the crook of his arm. If it hadn't been for real it could have been in a music video. He was such a good actor.'

'I know,' Bodhi said.

'Anyway, I told your father Marcelyn was at the hospital, and that as soon as they had checked you out, you could come back to his place with her.'

'Was he happy about that?'

'I wish I could tell you he was overjoyed, but you have to understand, Bodhi, it was Mia he had lost.'

Bodhi nodded, and looked out of the side window again as I kept talking.

'"What am I supposed to do with a baby, here?" he said.'

'He didn't care that I was alive?'

'Maybe the Police had told him already, I don't know. Maybe it wasn't a surprise, me telling him. Maybe that wasn't actually the first time he had heard the news. I don't think you can judge your father just because his response to the fact that you were alive, was to wonder what he was supposed to do with you.'

'I guess.'

'He wanted to know where Mia was. The police hadn't told him, or if they had, Michael had been in too much of a daze to remember it. I told him what Marcelyn had told me. And as soon as I'd done that, Michael picked up the car keys that I'd thrown down on the table in front of us, and he started to stride towards the door. He was going to go straight to the hospital morgue. I grabbed him around his waist, "Michael, you can't go there," I said. He threw my arm off, but I wrestled him. "Michael don't. Don't go now. Trust me" I said. He kept twisting in my hold...I told him to leave Marcelyn to identify the body, that he didn't have to do that, but he still struggled. He just wanted to see Mia. I told him he couldn't go there. I told him that the hospital would be crawling with journalists, because the hotel would have leaked the story to the Press. "How would they even know Mia was mine?" he said. I thought he was going to punch me, but then he just told me that I'm hopeless, and I shouldn't have mentioned anything to the hotel. He didn't realise that the hotel had called his house because Mia was calling out for him.'

Bodhi nodded.

We were reaching the town of Littel. I stopped at a junction, then turned right. A row of businesses were spaced out in front of us on both sides of the highway. A drive through coffee parlour. An auto repair shop, a Rite-aid.

"'Don't go to the morgue, Michael. There's no reason for it" I said, "You don't want to see her like she is. Remember her, but don't make the way she looks now the memory." That stopped Michael in his tracks. I remember I told him; "it was a long fall, and there was nothing to break her fall, except the hard ground". At that point,' I said to Bodhi, 'your father finally broke down in tears properly. He pushed me away. He turned his back on the door, dropping his keys. Instead of trying to leave, he reached for a drawer that slid out from the end of the big oak dining table we were still standing by. He took a bottle of pills from it that he must have had hidden in there, and then, without a word more to me, he disappeared along the marble slabs of the floor, walked up the open sided staircase to the top floor, and closed the door to his private rooms upstairs.'

I eased the gristle in my neck against the greased up headrest behind me.

'It was weeks before I saw him again. Not properly anyway. He simply disappeared, he was inconsolable. I hadn't realised how hard your mother's death had hit him. He kept himself in his rooms, he didn't speak to anyone, not even Marcelyn, and he only took meals if I left them for him on a table outside his door.'

'Didn't you call a doctor?'

I laughed; 'There was no point.'

'Oh, it would have been Dr. Tzu,' Bodhi said, turning round towards me in his seat,

'Yes, Dr. Tzu. That's why I didn't call a doctor. I could have called another one, but he wouldn't have seen them. He was dependant on Dr. Tzu. He was addicted to her, or to what she prescribed him anyway, and he had been ever since Mia had introduced him to her.'

'She's really scary,' Bodhi said, untying his rucksack, 'she has a pill for everything.'

'She would have ground them up and fed them to you if I hadn't got the Cooks to tell me. I threatened to cut her throat in the middle of the night, if they ever saw her messing about with your food. We weren't the best of friends after that little conversation.'

'I didn't know that,' Bodhi said, looking suitably shocked. He started rummaging in his rucksack. A T-shirt came out, I could see the cord that tied the top closed was caught, and he was struggling to reach inside.

'What are you looking for,' I asked.

'Soap. If I haven't got any soap, how am I going to wash my clothes?'

I shook my head.

'You're worrying me now,' I said to Bodhi. 'You begged me to help you leave "Pleasurelands." You begged me to help you leave your wife Diamond, and your baby son too. I told you I couldn't help you, but you begged me. Now I have helped you—but what am I helping you to do? I tried warning you how unprepared you'd find out you were, didn't I. But still you insisted you had to leave, and you insisted you had to leave now.'

'It's okay,' Bodhi said, 'I'm just asking.'

'Bodhi, Nicki will help you get on your feet. I'm not saying she'll do your laundry, but she'll show you how to. It's easy. Don't worry about it.'

'But I've never met her and I don't want to ask too much of her. What will I do if she can't?'

'Find a public laundromat.'

'How will I know how to use it?'

'Are you sure you still want to do this,' I asked; 'leaving "Pleasurelands"?'

Bodhi sat back in his seat; 'Yes, Shaun. I do. Let's keep going.' He took a deep breath, and pushed the T-shirt back in his bag. 'Tell me more about what happened after my mother died. My father can't really have been left so alone, can he?'

'But he was,' I said, relaxing into driving again. 'He shouldn't have been, he had thirty years' worth of contacts in the music business to turn to. He should have had friends pouring in day after day, visiting, calling, writing... But they didn't. He was too famous, even back then. He didn't have friends, he had admirers. And once Mia had killed herself and had tried to kill you, all of a sudden there didn't seem to be anything for anyone to admire anymore. People were afraid of him, basically. Maybe that's what admiration really is.'

'Michael had you though, Shaun.'

'Yes, he always had me.'

'What did you do?'

'I kept doing what I'd always done; rising early to make sure that the zones on the security alarm were turned off, letting the Cooks come in to set the house up for breakfast, checking Michael's diary in the office, playing back the voicemails from the answerphone—though after Mia's death, there was only a succession of apologies and cancellations to note down for Marcelyn.'

We passed a business called 'Kyle's automotive shop', and I suddenly realised that in the rush to get Bodhi out of 'Pleasurelands', I'd forgotten to put the spare tyre in the back of the Pickup. We'd better not get a puncture, I thought to myself.

'The inquest and the funeral came and went, but your dad kept his dark glasses on and stayed as quiet as a monk,' I said to Bodhi. 'Eventually, there was one recording on the tape that was worth listening to, it was an important sounding old man saying; "Grieving with you for your loss Michael, stay strong, we're all keeping you in our hearts here, etc. etc. our deepest condolences, Senator so and so". It was the Governor of California. He had a very recognisable voice, and your father must have heard it from his rooms, because he came down to investigate. I'd been drinking coffee with Nicki in the office, so I had to usher her away to some utility rooms. Then I played Michael the message again. He was a lot less impressed than I thought he would be. Or maybe he just concealed it well, I never know with him. He was stoned. He was smoking some of the "medicinal marijuana" that Dr. Tzu had supplied him with, along with her usual tranquillizers. He was barely dressed, I remember. I had to wave the Cooks away from the kitchen in case they were offended. He only had a bathrobe on and he hadn't tied it around his waist tightly enough. Also, the two Cooks were Latino and, well, they were good workers so I didn't want to lose them.'

Littel ran out of shops, and the road wound on.

'I offered to get back to the Governors' office, and thank him, but Michael just peered over the top of his dark-glasses, and said; "I hardly know the guy, and he doesn't know me. I played him a private show for his inauguration, and now he's a fan-boy", he called the Governor of California a fan-boy...Anyway, he went on to say that people remember meeting him, like it's burned into their consciousness, but at the same time he hasn't a clue who they are. And there was something very true about that.'

I checked the fuel tanks on the dashboard, reminding myself that for the two tanks, only one gauge worked. I thought to myself I should have refuelled in Littel while I'd had the chance; the old Chevy was a gas guzzler.

'But it must have meant a lot to the Governor,' Bodhi said, 'having Michael play for him.'

'Yes, especially since it was years since he had done,' I said. 'So, anyway Michael was at least out of his rooms, and I wanted to keep him talking. He told me he remembered when he and I had met, and we went through that memory again...'

'How did you and my father meet,' Bodhi asked.

'Another time maybe,' I said, hesitating.

'Okay. But you know, there may not be another time,' Bodhi said. I looked round at him. There was a serenity to his demeanour. He was serious, but relaxed at the same time. I felt a fatherly rush of pride that he'd grown into a man at last.

'I will tell you, but I have to get the order right, Bodhi,' I said. 'We're going to have to stop at some point. I'm going to have to let you out, and you're going to have to walk away. What then? Some parts of the story are always going to end up untold.'

Bodhi nodded.

They always do.

'Okay, so, after your father came out of his room, we had a coffee, and he said; "What the hell am I going to do?" He seemed like he was having a nervous breakdown or something. He put my arms around him and pulled himself into my embrace. We rocked together in the sunlight with his beard itching into my face. I shouldered his head with my hand, pushing against the weight of him leaning onto me. Our sweat mingled. He smelled of honey. I told him that everything would be alright—you know, the usual thing—what else are you supposed to say? But he doubted it. It was as though he was drowning inside himself. I never saw him as unsure of himself as he was that day. Never, not in all the thirty odd years I've worked for him,' I said, looking over to Bodhi. 'I remember I looked out across the garden we had. It seemed to be bursting with life. I looked out over the horizon to the city below, sprawling in the blue grey haze of its own smog. And I remember I suddenly felt so useless. I felt like I was letting this incredible, "Great Man" down. "What about the boy, Shaun?" he asked. He let go of me and wiped his forehead with the back of his hand, flicking away tears from under his sunglasses, pinching mucus from his nose, "How am I going to bring him up, without Mia?"'

I looked back at Bodhi briefly, as we chugged along through a widening landscape towards I-395, gauging his interest, assessing his tiredness. 'So, you see, he really did care about you,' I said. 'Once he'd had time to take in everything that had happened.'

'I know,' Bodhi said, seemingly unconvinced.

'"Marcelyn will keep taking care of him" I said to Michael, 'she'll keep loving him the same as David. They'll grow up together, they can play together, David's only a year older", but your father said;

"for how long? What happens when the boy finds out Marcelyn's not his mother but his aunt? What happens when the boy finds out David isn't his brother? What happens when David finds out he isn't his brother, huh? What happens then?" He shook his head, as though he was losing an argument with himself; "can you imagine finding out that this little boy who gets a part share of your mothers' love doesn't actually have a right to it?" he said, "and if you manage to kick him out of your life, you can have your mum all to yourself? Well, wouldn't you try?"'

'He was right, there' Bodhi said, and I nodded.

'Michael went on,' I said, 'he asked me; "What happens when the boy has to hear what his own mother did to him, how can he stay sane when he hears what Mia did?" He was looking at me to contradict him, but I couldn't find any words. Any moment, I thought, he's going to wake up and realise that I wasn't the right man for him to lean on; that he would remember the girlfriends who flocked to him and call them, that he would remember the guys who'd always been trying to measure themselves against him, or the hangers-on who just wanted to bask in the golden light of his presence. Surely they would be the ears and the shoulders he'd settle for, I was thinking. But Michael went on; "I'd go mad if it was me, that much suffering is unbearable" he said, "he'll go mad. That's what's waiting for him." It was as though phrases from a loop of thoughts were slipping out of a sack he'd had them held inside,' I said to Bodhi, 'ideas snarling around like small dogs twisting and whining to escape; "If he goes mad, I'll go mad. There's no way out of this, Shaun," Michael said; "My life has spun itself into a spider's web, and I'm caught up in it. Sooner or later there's a spider of madness that's going to come and stick its fangs in my neck, it's going to paralyse me and feed on me."'

Bodhi stayed sat facing the road while the story unfolded, his eyes cast down towards the dirt covered foot well where his bag of clothes was stuffed.

'I didn't know what to say to your father. But I had to say something. So, basically I told him to build "Pleasurelands",' I said to Bodhi. 'But I didn't realise it would work out like this.'

'What? You told Michael to build the place I've just had to fight to leave?' Bodhi said, 'the place that left me living in a parallel world; a padded cell?'

'Well, looking back I feel guilty about it, of course. I know it's been difficult for you, and I'm sorry. But I had no idea it was going to work out like this.'

'Wow.'

'Take it easy on me,' I said, 'it was a difficult time for your father too. You're not the only one who's had hard times in their life. So, yes; I told Michael he could be the best daddy a boy could ever have, that he could build you a palace, Bodhi, and fill it with everything you could possibly want. I told him he had the money, I told him to think how lucky you really were, that his son could have everything he could ever want. He was worried to death that you would go mad if you found out what your mother had done to you. I told him that you didn't need to know what Mia had done. I just said what I thought Michael needed to hear, I didn't think he would take it so seriously. I mean, I just told him the story of the Buddha, basically. It was him who got me into Buddhism in the first place, it was his idea. He messed about with it, I thought he knew what I was talking about. I thought he would use the story to help himself keep going. But he took it literally, like he'd never heard it before...and I told him how lucky he was, to be able to do all that for you, and he listened to me. "The boy doesn't have to go mad,

Michael, and neither do you. He doesn't have to know exactly what happened. He doesn't have to know exactly what his mother did. Not until he's grown up and old enough to make sense of it," that was what I said to him.'

'Shaun, you gave me an impossible life!'

'And now I'm making it up to you,' I said.

Bodhi looked up at the grey lining of the cab, and exhaled in frustration. 'Why did it matter so much to him? I mean, not every man who loses his wife ends up doing something as extreme, and as weird as building a massive estate like "Pleasurelands" do they?' he said. 'Why Michael?'

'I don't know,' I said, 'although not every man has money like your father. Not every man can.' I paused, and Bodhi sensed it;

'You're not telling me everything, Shaun,' he said.

'I really don't know,' I said, 'but maybe it was guilt. They had an argument, and it didn't come from nowhere.'

'What argument? Who?'

'Your mother and your father. It was Konrad's doing, the P.A. he'd not long sacked. He'd only worked for Michael for, I guess a year, maybe. He'd taken over from Louise as Michael's Personal Assistant. Michael had got him from someone else on his recording label, a country and western singer, I don't know who.'

'What about him?'

'He turned out to be weird. Really nasty. He followed your father in his spare time. He tracked him. Stalked him I suppose. He went to the places Michael went when Michael needed to relax, places your mother didn't know about, places Michael wouldn't have wanted her to know about. They were Private clubs and dark special Bars, and private houses too. So Konrad found out, and then he let Michael know that he'd found out. He was getting ready to blackmail Michael, is what it comes down to. It was very unfair; the fact is your mother was ill with depression and had been for several months. It was hard for Michael. He needed to relax, he needed company.'

'He was having an affair?'

'Yes, but it was just a lightweight thing. It was no big deal.' Bodhi looked at me quizzically, and I had looked at him back, 'I'm sorry, but it wasn't.'

'How did my mother find out,' Bodhi asked. 'Why didn't it stay secret?'

'It was eight weeks after the day you were born. You weren't expected to survive the delivery. Your mother had had miscarriage after miscarriage, stillbirth after stillbirth. It was driving her mad, or, it had driven her mad. So you were born, and you were alive, and you were healthy. Mia was overjoyed. Your father was overjoyed. And then, later on in the same day, Konrad had another little disagreement with Michael over the phone, and Michael chose that moment to sack him. On the spot. He'd had enough of Konrad's little weirdness's. And then in revenge, eight weeks later, Konrad sold his story—which in itself shouldn't have been a big deal, maybe a few lurid headlines and everything would have gone away. However, it wasn't like that. It wasn't like that because Konrad—the vicious bastard—was using a film camera to secretly film your father meeting with his publicist. He filmed them kissing and cuddling in her house in Malibu. The creep was stood behind a sand dune on the beach shooting through the plate glass picture windows that looked out from her rooms over the ocean. There was no doubt who it was on the footage—so of course the networks went crazy for it, and it was all over the T.V.—so there was no way your mother could avoid seeing it. And that was all it took for them to have that monster argument.'

'My father felt guilty for what my mother had ended up doing, as a result of the affair he'd had becoming public knowledge—that's what you're saying?'

'Yes.'

Bodhi thought about it. 'That's not enough, Shaun,' he said. 'Not enough to make him build "Pleasurelands". Not enough to make my father surround me with friends who weren't my friends and to marry me to a girl called "Diamond". He could have got over it.'

'He should have got over it, but he was taking God knows how many pills a day from Dr. Tzu, and smoking dope. He was regularly coked up to his eyeballs, and he was drinking whiskey by the crate. He didn't get over it, he could have done, but the point is; he didn't.'

'Was he insane?'

'Call him insane if you want, how should I know? But he was, is, the biggest star in the world. What passes for madness may pass for genius, but all people want is music to dance to. And he makes it.'

'And I can go to hell in his slipstream.'

'You're not going to hell, Bodhi,' I said, 'you're going to Los Angeles. Nicki has a flat in West Hollywood, there's enough people there that you can fade into the crowd as quickly or as slowly as you want.'

Bodhi pulled a small wad of dollars out of the back pocket of his jeans and started counting them. 'Was it because I was a mixture?' he said. 'Part boy, part girl?'

'That your mother tried to kill you? No. Nobody knew anything about that for years, Bodhi,' I said, 'not until you were much older, in your teens. It was never obvious, and it was never a problem.'

'This is five hundred dollars, right?' Bodhi said, changing the subject.

'Here, take this,' I said, giving him my bank card from out of my wallet. 'You can go to any bank and key in the last four numbers in reverse. You can take money out of my account until you get yourself sorted. Don't worry how much, you can pay me back when you've made your fortune. Just don't give the number to anyone else.'

Bodhi looked at the piece of plastic I'd given him, turned it round and read the numbers, then added it to his dollars and put them back in his jeans.

'Listen; you reminded Michael of Mia,' I said to Bodhi. 'That's what he said, the day he came down from his rooms to listen to the Governor of California on his Answerphone. He said you were his little Prince, and he would think of her, every time he saw you. And he was happy about that because he never wanted to forget his wife. That day, for the first time since you had been born, he took an interest in you—he was asking about you, he wanted to know where you were, and I told him you were with Marcelyn. He said he should see you, and I agreed with him. We took a walk together in the garden that he had in Laurel Canyon. I remember it, because while we were talking a butterfly landed on the head of a marble Buddha statue Marcelyn had put in the garden. It was a Monarch butterfly sitting on the head of a Prince. Michael saw it, and that was when he said you were his little Prince. He said to me that you had meant everything in the world to Mia, and that now you meant everything in the world to him. It may sound impossible to believe. But it's true, it's the truest thing I know, Bodhi. Your father's love for you had no bottom, it was as deep as the ocean.'

I met Bodhi's eyes briefly before I turned my head back to the road.

'As we were talking, Michael took his dark glasses off,' I continued. 'He'd been wearing them constantly since your mother died, it was like he had been afraid that anyone who saw his eyes would see his guilt, would see his shame. But now he had a plan—to build you a palace and fill it with everything you could possibly want—and now it seemed like everything would be alright, and so he could reveal himself again.'

'That was what he seriously believed?'

'I had no reason to doubt it. I had no reason to persuade him to do anything differently, because at least he was making a move in the right direction—I just didn't know he would take it all so literally.'

'And I still didn't even have a name?'

'Okay,' I laughed, 'so, I said that to your father, and he said; "Oh, he'll choose his own name when he's old enough. He'll name himself. That's what Mia agreed". "Did she", I said. I doubted it. But even if she had agreed, I said to Michael; "what name do you think he would choose at the moment? "Sorrow", or "Tears?"'

Another little town was approaching; 'Freedom,' altitude; three thousand, four hundred feet, population; six hundred and seventy.

'After a few moments Michael broke into a smile and slapped a big hug round my shoulders, "I'll call him Buddha, after you, Shaun" he said. And I said back; "No you won't!" I wriggled out from under his arm; "you can't call him that". "Don't tell me what I can and can't call my own son", Michael said, "there's loads of footballers called Jesus, why not Buddha?" So I had to tell him that it would offend people, and that it would always offend people until you, Bodhi, were grown old enough that you could change it to something else, which of course would be the same as leaving you to choose your own name in the first place. "I don't have to listen to any shit from you" your father said to me, so I said; "why not call your son Bodhi, meaning Wisdom? And that shut him up. "Bodhi sounds cool" he said, "Okay, Shaun, I'll call the boy Bodhi", and from then on, he did.'

Bodhi was looking tired. He ran his fingers through his golden curls, leaned his head back onto the headrest and closed his eyes.

'Why don't you get some rest,' I said, putting the radio on low.

Chapter 2.

We rumbled on through Freedom. It seemed a fitting town to pass through with a young man starting out on his own way beside me, and I felt like saying that to him, but Bodhi had his eyes closed, and I decided to leave him. The radio station was KDO something and it turned out to be a religious station. It was playing 'Christian Contemporary music to soothe your soul and praise the lord', and I didn't want to listen to it. I switched through the channels. It was an old radio and I had to spin the dial station by station: KIBT; Country and western. KSVW; Sports and Public Broadcasting. KVXM; Religious again. KSBP; Pop and rap. KRRS; Rock and Soul. That one reminded me too much of Michael so in the end I turned the radio off.

Bodhi opened his eyes. His face was relaxed. For a moment I could see the child in him still, and I felt like we were a father and son taking a trip to the beach. But we weren't. I wasn't his father and he wasn't a child—he was twenty one years old, and the previous forty eight hours had been testing for both of us. I figured he would be as worried by what his father might be doing now as I was. After all, against Michael's wishes, and even without his knowledge, we were spiriting away his only son from 'Pleasurelands', the only home Bodhi had ever known, and with his unlimited resources, if Michael had decided to find us, and punish me, he would do so very easily. Not only that, but we were leaving behind Bodhi's wife and his baby son too.

'You know Michael can flip moods like a light switch, don't you?' I said, 'I've seen him do it so many times. I'm amazed I've survived working for him for so long, Bodhi.'

'It can't be all bad,' Bodhi said, after thinking for a moment; 'being able to change moods quickly. It must have helped him after my mother died...'

'Yes, I suppose so,' I said, letting my eyes stare far along the road into the distance. 'It had been an awful time. We'd still been under siege from the media; him—for sure, but his staff and me too. Marcelyn had had to sack several members of staff for selling secrets about Michael, and I kept on getting staff resign on me. So between the two of us we couldn't hold on to anyone to cook, clean, manage or maintain back then that Michael could trust. The hassles were daily.'

'What was it to do with Marcelyn,' Bodhi asked.

'She was your father's manager,' I said, 'she'd been his manager for four years at that point. It was four years since we'd left the U.K.'

'I thought she was looking after David?'

'She was doing that as well, or at least her nannies were. And she was looking after you too,' I said, 'until your father started to take an interest. But it was very difficult for her. She had gossip-mag freelancers camped outside her home in Santa Barbara trying to rake up even the tiniest pieces of news that they could sell about Michael. They were sleeping in their cars in wait for her. So while your father had been hiding away like a recluse, she'd been fending off endless harassment from photographers trespassing over the sand dunes at the back of the house she had, even though the beach was private. And they were all trying to capture pictures of the baby that your mother had failed to kill, i.e.; you. It hadn't been surprising at all that Marcelyn decided to move back to Michael's Laurel Canyon place with you and David. Even though it had been a lovely beach front house that she'd had.'

'But I thought you said it was hassle there too?' Bodhi said.

'It was. We were too close to the public road, and telephoto lenses could keep us under constant scrutiny, but at least we had proper security. Anyway, even with the bodyguards it was obvious Michael had to get away from there, we all did. It could have been a nightmare, trying to find somewhere suitable but fortunately your father had a very reliable agent called Hal Kardanglian working for him. He was Armenian, a big fat guy, always had to have a seat to rest himself on. He did Michael a real favour and found him a property for sale on the south-eastern edge of the Sierra Nevada, about a hundred and fifty miles north of L.A. It was lots seven to ten of the Williamsburg Holdings, an old cattle drover's ranch. So Michael bought it straight away, and it was an amazing place. To be suddenly living on three thousand acres of gorgeous ranch land in the foothills of the Sierras, in the best of California; that was amazing to me. Not just that it was dry and warm, but that it had riverbanks full of Pinyon Pines and giant Sugar Pines, and Madrones on the valley slopes; I couldn't have imagined a more beautiful place.'

'And that was "Pleasurelands"?'

'...And that was what became; "Pleasurelands",' I said; 'and that's what we're leaving behind now.'

Bodhi nodded, and looked at the road in front of us as though to see if he was missing anything. Then he dropped his chin again and stared at the floor. 'There wasn't anything there when you got there?' he said.

'There were a few ramshackle old farm buildings,' I said, 'grotty, rotting, dusty little houses. And that was the first thing we did— demolish them all and put up some temporary buildings; some chalets for us, and some cabins for the security guards. After that the real work began. Your father had some definite ideas about what he wanted, which was hardly surprizing really. He drew up the plans and gave them to Hal, who hired architects, and they turned your father's felt tip sketches into actual plans that the contractors could work from. From that, the building work began. They put up the new entrance gateway, the great Limestone posts and iron gates and the high wall that led away from it in both directions.'

'Keeping everybody in, so they couldn't escape,' Bodhi said.

'Keeping everybody out, so they couldn't get in,' I said.

'And then they put the chain link fence inside, topped with razor wire...'

'"For security," your father said.'

'And cameras on top of each of the posts that held it up?'

'For more security,' I said. 'The guards sat in the offices I designed for them, and they watched the video feeds all day. You can't imagine a more boring job, Bodhi. But at least it was boring. If we hadn't had the fences and walls they'd have had actual work to do and we would have had to pay them a lot more. As it was, no one could ever enter or leave the property without us knowing about it—which is why we need to get some distance between us now.'

'But the big geodesic domes weren't there,' Bodhi said, 'it must have been a building site for years.'

'Yes, it was. Hal did a great job; authorising the payments when the builders' charges came due, settling disputes with the planners in Littel, smoothing down ruffled feathers on site; but it went on for years. The land did become a building site; there were giant tracked excavators spreading trenches like tributaries of a chaotic river, lines cut snaking downhill to sewage tanks, uphill to water tanks, all buried beneath the surface, and pipes laid to them. Then there were trucks coming one after another pouring concrete by the tonne until floor slabs appeared, and after that the smell of burning metal for week after week as grinding discs cut steel joists fresh from the forges for roofs, floors and window supports. But before you knew it shapes appeared above head height; twenty feet high, thirty feet high. And where only empty spaces had been before there were rectangles, pyramids and domes emerging. And for a while the estate looked like a landing colony on Mars.'

There were crossed flags on the shoulder of the highway ahead to indicate maintenance work, and past them, a road sign for I-395 fast approaching. I checked my fuel tanks again, and watched as my speed dropped for the workers in hard hats and sun protectors covering their necks, as they walked purposefully around between their own back-hoes.

'All the building work and the noise must have stopped my father from making any music,' Bodhi said. 'He can't have liked that.'

'He didn't seem to mind,' I said, 'maybe it was just what he wanted. He certainly seemed to enjoy helping with the work, or pretending he was helping with the work; chatting away with the carpenters while they hammered up framework and partitions or laughing with the plumbers and electricians. It seemed to give him a kick drinking coffee with the labourers; you could see it on their faces...'

'What?'

'The sense of amazement that they were actually working alongside the great Michael Michael. And them with their dirty hands.'

'But the domes though...'

'They came last,' I said, 'after the rooms and the kitchens that the cooks and cleaners needed in the staff quarters near the creek. And after the maintenance buildings had gone up, and the houses for me and Nicki, and for the nannies. Michael's house, and his dance studio and recording studio, and Marcelyn's house. The domes went up last, but they were worth the wait. You were almost four by the time they were finished. Can you remember?'

'Just about,' Bodhi said. 'I've got a vague memory of lorries coming, and grass being laid out...'

'...In the central courtyard. Yes,' I said. 'Tens of millions of dollars your father spent on those domes. Glass and steel geodesic domes as high as the sky and as wide as football pitches, and not just one, but five of them. It was amazing just seeing them going up, never mind getting to kit them out with the circus funfair rides and arcades and the giant swimming pool with the wave machine.'

'And the moto track,' Bodhi said.

'And the ice rink,' I said, laughing; 'of all things in the middle of California; an ice rink and a ski slope.'

We left the construction zone behind on the highway, and the ramp approached to join the Interstate Freeway. I asked some more of the truck, and with a puff of black smoke it responded. We rounded the curve of the ramp, slipping onto the empty lane. The road was still quiet, a truck in front of us and a couple of cars catching us gradually in the lane to our left. On the other side of the freeway there were the usual couple of giant semi-trucks glinting chrome at the sky as they made their way by. Bodhi straightened himself in his seat, but seeing nothing to interest him, he looked back towards me.

'I used to worry about the cost,' I said to Bodhi. 'But Michael wouldn't hear about it. He'd say; "what do you think I'm worth, Shaun? Who do you think owns the rights on my music? Do you know?" His face would go manic; "Me, Shaun, I own them, that's where the money comes from, it rolls in like the tide. They never stop playing my songs on the radio and the T.V. The money just pours in. Don't worry about the money, Shaun," he'd say; "don't worry about anything." Then he would smile again.'

We had been driving for a couple of hours, and I was getting thirsty. I thought about where I could take a break, and then I remembered a rest stop we would reach in a few miles.

'You were growing up as the last dome was being kitted out,' I said to Bodhi, 'the one with the zip wires and the climbing wall. Michael wanted it all finished so you could enjoy it. They were both glad by then that the endless noise was coming to an end; him and Marcelyn. Marcelyn in particular. She used to leave you with the nannies she'd hired, and David too.'

'She had a whole roster of them,' Bodhi said. He breathed in deeply, stretching his arms and back as far as the cab would allow him, pushing against the stained and dusty flock lining of the roof.

The truck coughed a puff of black smoke, and we stuttered for a hundred yards or so. I checked the dials on the dusty dashboard until the engine settled down again.

'Everything was going so well,' I said, 'The buildings were finished, Michael was steady, Marcelyn was doing okay...and then, just as I was thinking about branching out and maybe starting my own business; you had that incident with David, and you nearly drowned.

'It's one of the first things I can remember,' Bodhi said.

'You were four years old.' I glanced at Bodhi, 'I can still smell the musk of your wet clothes and your fear to this day.'

'He had my shoe,' Bodhi said. 'David had taken it; he wrestled it off my foot. I did my best to kick him away from me, but he was too strong. He overpowered me. Before he could get the other one off me I'd run away from him. But he called after me, he chased me and then he waved my shoe in front of me. He would stop and say; "here you are", but then, just as I would be about to take it back from him, he'd snatch it away again and run further. I was crying I guess.'

'It was midday, sometime early May, there was still snow; you could see it on the distant hilltops. But there had been a lot of snow melt and the creeks were full. I had told the nannies to keep you away from them. Both of you, David as well. But then the little creek near the staff building overflowed, the little one that usually just fed the ornamental pool near Marcelyn's house, and there was some flooding beyond the car park that the Cooks and cleaners used. I guess I should have done something about it, cleared it away somehow, built a berm and cut a ditch. But I hadn't. And then one of the Cooks came running over to the staff accommodation building. I was mending an air conditioning unit; they were always breaking down. It was Catalina.'

I asked Bodhi if he remembered her.

'Yeah. She was kind,' he said.

'Well, she was screaming; "Bodhi is in a pool behind the car park, drowning. Help him, help him." I told her to calm down, her apron strings were flapping and she'd looked like she was going to trip up over them while she was running towards me. She was out of breath, because she was a big lady, and she shouldn't have been running at all. "What did you say? What pool?" I asked her, "the one that appeared after the rains, behind the car park, the new one" she said. "Come on, Mr. Shaun. Come!" So I put down my drill and began trotting in the direction of the car park. But I was thinking while I was going there that there wasn't a pool. It was only as I reached the corner of the car park that I realised what Catalina was talking about. It was an area about the size of a tennis court, and the water could only have been about a foot deep. Now, you understand Bodhi, I wasn't a father, I wasn't your father. I'd had nothing to do with you up to this point, I'd left you to the nannies, they were perfectly capable, a bit too posh for my liking, and I didn't know why Michael, or Marcelyn rather, had hired English nannies, but they had and I had no real problem with that. As I say, I was doing maintenance work. I was happy with that, but then all of a sudden I realise that the baby your mother and father had both fought so hard to create was apparently drowning and the whole tedious battle they had been through even to have you conceived could come to an end in a moment. Really it should have been Michael racing to save you, but he was in his studio in his house, I could hear the blast of feedback and the sound of keyboards. So I kept running, I'm really running now, brushing along the side of the parked cars, crashing against a wing mirror, tripping against a badly angled tyre, and then, just as I'm running toward the overhanging branches of a Madrone tree and I'm watching out that I don't take my eye out on the gnarly flaky wood, what do I come across but David running in the opposite direction toward me, laughing—I asked him; "where's Bodhi?" but he didn't answer me, he just cried back; "Fuck off, fuck off."'

'Really?'

'I was so shocked I let go of him and watched him run away. He was only five years old. Then I heard you, or I heard something; a splashing maybe. But I turned and I could see you; you were in the water, you were face down. I thought you were dead. I've never been so panicked in all my life.'

'I don't remember this bit.'

'I threw myself at you, I just dived in head first. I actually landed on my chest. The water wasn't so deep, but of course, you were only small and it was plenty deep enough for you. So I hauled you out with one hand and lifted you onto the bank of the little pool and brushed the hair out of your eyes and the bits of grass that had caught on you, and all the time I'm praying that you're not dead and that you're going to breathe again, but you're not, your skin is cold. And then I'm thinking what the hell do you do for the breath of life? How do you do chest compressions on a child? What am I supposed to do?'

'You must have been really scared,' Bodhi said.

'I was terrified. I took your shoulders and started shaking them, and slapping your cheeks. I was willing you back to life, and the worst thing was; you looked so serene, so at peace, and there I was disturbing you because I, I, not you, I couldn't bear the thought that you were dead. So now I'm crying with all my heart, crying until I'm exhausting my own breathing and I'm feeling tingling in my face like I'm going to pass out, and then, just then, as I gasp one more breath into my lungs, finally, you do the same, and cough and splutter back into life. You wailed and cried again, gasping and sucking in lungful's of air. There was so much fear in your eyes, and there was so much love in my heart, and so much fear in me too that I felt like I was being welded to you by some sort of cosmic welder. And then you reached your little arms out and put them around my neck and hugged your face against mine, and I just sobbed like a littler baby than you were. I cried my eyes out. You were clinging to me like a little monkey might have done and I was saying; "it's alright, it's alright", and hugging you away from the water's edge. You wrapped your legs around me as I carried you away, resting your wet cheek against mine so trustingly it felt like glue bonding me to you, like araldite.'

'I don't remember any of this, to be honest, Shaun.'

'In my arms you melted like warm cheese around a piece of toast, and then your desperate crying faded off to burbles and then to silence.'

'I remember Catalina carrying me.'

'I gave you to her. She caught me up as I walked back with you across the car park. "Is he alright Mr. Shaun? You give him to me." She knew what to do. I'd never held a baby before, so I gave you to her. I was in shock, come to think of it.'

'I remember the sense that something had happened that was wrong, that's all. But then I remember you tried to leave me—and I wasn't happy about that.'

'I wanted to find the nannies and give them a bollocking. Catalina told me they were with Marcelyn in her house, and she had been shouting at them. So I found a phone and called them, but I had to come back into the kitchen with the phone on the lead because you were crying again, even though the big old Cook had you squashed against her bosom and balanced on one of her big fat hips. I remember, I was waiting for the phone to be picked up, it was ringing and ringing, and then you just looked at me and reached your hand out silently, and, you know, it was as if, in the stillness of the unanswered phone call you were saying to me with those big blue eyes of yours; "never forget what it felt like to have me cling to you, and I will never forget what it felt like to have you rescue me." I remember that as clearly as anything.'

'Liza came in and asked me what I had been up to, didn't she.'

'Eventually, yes, she did. She didn't seem to realise the enormity of what had happened at first, so I told her that you had nearly drowned. She was apologetic, but it turned out it wasn't her fault and I guess what she felt was professional relief. It had been difficult for her. Marcelyn had insisted they both be there with her, Annie and Liza, even though they had told Marcelyn that nobody was watching you. "She's power crazed, if you ask me" Liza said. Which was disloyal of her, but probably true. "Aren't we paying you well enough?" I asked her in return, but she came back with; "too well. The college warned us about situations like this." After a moment I said, "Why don't you have a word with Michael?" but she just said; "why don't you", and walked off out of the staff building with you, holding your hand. And I had no intention of saying anything to Michael.'

The rest stop came into view a couple of hundred yards away, and I was glad. My bladder was full, and I needed to splash some cold water from a rest room tap on my face. I needed to find a drinks vending machine too. There was the usual mix of executive saloons and Pickup trucks in all of the parking bays. I parked up in one and Bodhi and I jumped out. There was a good green area with concrete benches and trees surrounding it, and the trees were shading some of the benches at least. By the edge of the grass there was a yellow metal sign with bullet holes in that read 'Beware of Rattlesnakes.' Beyond was the toilet block, and I made my way there.

Funny how a small thing can change your life, It could have been so different otherwise. I could have owed no loyalty to anyone, I could have had no responsibilities. I could have cruised through these last twenty years. I could have had a lot more fun, that's for sure. But instead I had Bodhi to watch out for.

I bought six bottles of water from the vending machine and walked back to the truck. I popped the hood and checked the oil. Bodhi had been sitting on a bench, staring around at the sights; simple things like a family with its dogs chasing each other, and a broad middle aged couple straddling their massive motorbike to head off again sunburnt on their road trip.

Bodhi came back to the red Chevy. He had the size of an adult, but there was a softness in his shoulders. He needs to toughen up, I thought to myself, he needs to get to a gym, or do some proper manual work for a bit, some garden labouring or some building. Maybe he can get a job on a farm somewhere.

Just as we were about to hit the road again, the earth started shaking beneath us. There was a small earthquake, a precursor perhaps. The motorbike couple had been looking surreptitiously towards us, but the shaking distracted them. I was glad to have Bodhi out of sight. If he'd wanted to disappear, that had been fine by me, but what I hadn't wanted was some rednecks making a scene because they'd heard something on the radio that I hadn't heard, some report saying; 'News just in; the son of Michael Michael, the originator of great tracks like "Don't leave me baby", and "You know it has to be me" has apparently been abducted and may now be under the control of a former employee of our favourite recording artist, a vicious man who goes by the name of Shaun "killer" Adefumi. Members of the public are warned not to approach them if they see them but to dial 911 and report them immediately'. I worried that anything was possible with Michael angry.

'How long until we get to Nicki's house in L.A.' Bodhi asked.

'It's a flat that she has, not a house. Don't expect too much. And it's very good of her to agree to take you in, seeing as I haven't had much contact with her since soon after that incident in the pond.'

'Okay.'

'Its maybe four hours until we get there,' I said.

We settled back into the rhythm of the road; the constant thrum of rubber on hot tarmac, the infrequent Doppler effect of cars passing us on our left. I handed Bodhi a bottle of water and he drank it. I drank mine, dropping my eyes back down to the road after every gulp, trying not to let the truck slip onto the shoulder of the highway.

'The thing I've always wondered,' Bodhi said, turning to face me, 'was why David never bullied me after that? After I had fallen in the pond. Was he sorry it had happened? But he never said so. He never spoke about it again, it was like it had never happened at all. Did he change? But people don't change really do they. Was there something else?'

'After your father got to hear about it? Yes of course there was something else,' I said. 'He'd picked up on some kind of disturbance and later on in the afternoon he got me to pop in and see him in his studio. He'd been drinking, and he offered me whiskey. He was insistent, but I hadn't wanted to, and he let me off. He didn't always, you know, but if he did let me off without joining him he'd want me to make it up to him some other way. He'd want me to do him a favour, and that's how it was on that afternoon. "Have a look at the tapes and find out what actually happened earlier, Shaun," he said.'

'What did he mean?'

'What he meant was; I'm really pissed off that Bodhi got wet in the pool—fortunately no one had told him you'd nearly drowned—and I want to make use of the incredibly expensive surveillance equipment I installed in all of the buildings when I built this place, to have you find out what David actually did.'

'So is that what you did?'

'Very reluctantly, yes.'

'Didn't you want to find out what had really happened? To me?'

'It's not that simple,' I said to Bodhi. 'The whole thing about the surveillance equipment was a crazy set up. Michael had been paranoid about intrusion onto "Pleasurelands". He'd been paranoid about the possibility that somebody might try and photograph you when you were a baby, because you have to understand that for many years after you were born there was incredible pubic interest in this little tot who'd survived a fall from the eighth floor of a hotel balcony. But it wasn't just photographs from some over enthusiastic paparazzi that your father was worried about, it was the possibility that there might be an attempt to kidnap you, like Getty's son, the oil billionaire...' Bodhi shrugged his shoulders. 'Well, anyway, Michael became massively concerned while the buildings were still being put up. He took me to one side and told he wanted everywhere monitored, day and night. I told him he was crazy, to his face—I could still do that then, but he was serious. He said; "don't you think they want to kidnap him, those scumbag labourers? Can't you see them eyeing up their chances, remembering where the locks are, looking out for the weakest entry points? I don't trust them for a minute. What would you do, if you were slaving your arse off for the peanuts these guys get paid? What would you do if you needed money in a hurry, huh? Do an honest days' work, or kidnap Bodhi and demand huge amounts of money from me? They know I'll pay the ransom, I'd pay it straight away. I'm not a miser, am I? No." I could hardly get a word in when he was on a rant like that; "These guys working here are trailer trash, they live in trailer park slums with rubbish strewn everywhere; they're not much better than homeless vagrants. Believe me," Michael said, "we need security. And I'm going to get it fitted." I told him we already had security guards night and day, but that didn't work, he said; "they're the ones who sell the information on in the first place; about where the cameras are, how to break in, what to steal. All they're good for is sitting around in a cabin stopping people from wandering in through the front gate."

A Yellow Corvette shot past us, maybe late for a meeting in Hollywood, I thought to myself. Bodhi hadn't noticed it, they were all the same to him, fast, slow; just another car he doesn't know how to drive, I figured.

'Your father told me what he'd planned; "I'm getting cameras and microphones put covertly into the ceilings of every room by specialist contractors working for me secretly," that's what he said to me. "They'll be hidden in the wall cavities too." I was outraged; "what, mine as well?" But no, it turned out he only meant everywhere except his, mine and Marcelyn's rooms. But still, I thought he was losing his mind. So I asked him why he was doing this, and he said that he wanted the whole estate to be monitored at all times. "I want everything taped onto video, that's my plan, and then all the tape decks and banks of filled up video cassettes will be there for insurance; there for the great what if.'"

I checked Bodhi's face for some kind of recognition, does he see where I'm going with this? But his body language was inscrutable.

'We had an argument,' I said to Bodhi, 'We had a big argument. You know, Michael doesn't like to lose arguments, and he mostly never does. So, the next thing he said was that he wanted me personally, to view the footage. He wanted me to be able to check the fences on the C.C.T.V. at any time he wanted me to. He wanted me to be able to monitor, in detail the various sectors of the estate, at any time he wanted me to. He wanted me to be able to listen in to the conversations in the staff quarters, watch the movements in the lounges, and yes; the bedrooms too. "Oh, don't worry, it's not like you're going to get to see anything you haven't seen before, Shaun," he said, "God, you've seen a lot worse I know..."'

'What did he mean by that,' Bodhi asked.

'I'll tell you another time,' I said, and he raised his eyebrows.

'Michael said he didn't want staff smuggling in hookers or friends, or who knows what, and thinking they'd get away with it. "It's my estate, it's my building, my rooms," he said, "They're my beds, damn it. Why shouldn't I know what my staff are using them for?" I remember I asked him, once more whether it was even legal—which again was my mistake because he just snorted and said; "who gives a fuck whether it's legal? Anyway," he said, "it is legal because this is my land and I make the laws here!"'

The sun had risen and the temperature had been rising too. I checked the gauges on the dash, all we need is for the engine to overheat, I thought to myself. A pair of Red tailed Hawks circled over the road near the top of my windscreen, flashing their plumage with each swoop and turn, distracting me.

'But you haven't told me why David didn't bully me again, the way he did when he took my shoe and I fell in the pond,' Bodhi said.

'Yes, and that's just the point; you didn't fall in the pond.'

'Didn't I?'

'No. I'll get to that. The thing is, Michael made me check the surveillance footage. It was the first time I'd had to, and I was pissed off that he had won the argument over whether any of it had been necessary. But I did check it. I went over to the security office and I gave old Charlie a shock. He hadn't been expecting me to come by, which was fair enough because I hardly ever did. He dropped his feet off the desk and threw his newspaper down. "I've got some work to do," I said, and sent him off to have a walk.'

I asked Bodhi if he had ever seen the office I was talking about, and he shook his head.

'There was no reason why you should have done,' I said. 'It's a standard set up in there; a stack of colour monitors that stare back at you.

There's about twenty of them; three vertical rows, seven or eight screens wide. And they just sit there. Occasionally one screen pulls your eye to it with a person walking past, a cleaner, or a delivery driver, but for the most part it's just a bank of still pictures stacked up on top of each other. Really it's a desperate job for Charlie; sitting there and watching them, and I'm glad it suits him because it certainly wouldn't suit me.'

The hawks were following us on the freeway, I could still see them in my rear view mirror.

'Anyway, the video recorders used to sit under the desk. It was an old system back then, its all-digital now, but this was nearly twenty years ago. They were piled up in whirring stacks. You had to reach in amongst a pile of cables snaking across the floor to make sure the video you were going to play back was the right one, but once you'd done that, then you'd take the remote controller on the desk and select the right input; wind the tapes back to the beginning for the monitors that were fed by the cameras you wanted to see, which in this case was the one nearest the back of the staff car park, and start watching. The screen carries numbers on it when you go into playback. It's a time stamp; day, date, hours, minutes and seconds. So back then I chose the time, stopped the playback and held the screen. That let me look back at what the cameras had seen, rather than just what they were seeing.

'You were like a god then, Shaun. Sitting there, able to watch the past.'

'Yup, a real control freak, because there wasn't anywhere the cameras couldn't see. Which was why I hadn't wanted any of this set up in the first place.'

'What did you see?'

'I saw David first of all, running along the side of the flooded pool, turning and waving a little leather sandal with a metal buckle. He was laughing, or it looked like he was—to be honest, the camera angle was pretty wide, and the quality wasn't that good. But I could see him running back and forth, and then you came into view chasing him. You were lunging forward and jumping up to try and reach your shoe, but he wouldn't let you have it. Then David ran on underneath a few overhanging branches, and it must have slowed him down because you caught up with him and manged to grab your shoe. But he didn't let go of it to start with, so the two of you were pushing and tugging. Finally, you won, David let go, but just then, and I couldn't believe my eyes when I saw this, but David waited until you had turned to face him, and then he shoved you as hard as he could in the chest, with both his hands and pushed you off your feet so that you fell back into the pool with your arms spread wide like an angel and splashed into the pool.'

'Oh!'

'Exactly. Not what I'd expected to see at all. And then, to compound the matter, rather than wait by the pool, or walk in—because he must have known that it wasn't that deep, rather than do that and rescue you, the little bastard just ran off. And that was when I caught up with him and he told me to fuck off. I could just see that at the edge of the video feed in the security office. After that, obviously I knew what came next because I'd been there.'

'I didn't realise,' Bodhi said.

'No, and I couldn't tell you. There was never a time when it would have made sense to tell you. You were still too little, you were growing up, and then, then you were a teenager and it was too late. But I knew, I had seen what had happened, and I knew myself that I had to keep an eye on you, because Marcelyn wasn't going to, after all David was her son.'

'Did you tell Michael?'

'That's a good question. I thought about deleting the tape. I was worried about what your father might do, I was worried about what effect it might have on him; he was paranoid enough already. But in the end, I felt like I had no choice. I copied the evidence onto another tape and I gave it to him.'

'What happened?'

'It was pretty predictable to start with. Marcelyn called me into her house the next day, sat me down on one of those immaculate white Chesterfield sofas she always had, and told me what Michael had said to her a couple of hours earlier. She was distraught actually. It didn't look like she'd even bothered to brush her hair, not on her weaker side anyway. Any kind of shock always made her spasticity worse, and she'd got a lot weaker since David had been born, but that morning she looked truly awful. "Please, Shaun. You've got to help me," she said. And that was a first, because she'd been pretty cold to me ever since your mother had died. "Michael has gone crazy," she said; "he's told me to send David away. He must know I can't do that. You've got to make him see sense." Obviously, I had no way to do that.'

'David didn't ever go though, so you must have been able to do something,' Bodhi said.

'No, he didn't go, that was true, because in the end I persuaded Michael that you needed to be home schooled.'

'Okay,' Bodhi said, 'that explains why I didn't get to go to school like normal people do.'

'You are a normal person, Bodhi,' I said, though we both knew that he wasn't. 'A lot of children get schooled at home, it's not that unusual.'

'It's stupid, and they shouldn't let parents do it; they lock children away in their world not ours.'

'Well, I thought it could work for you, after all money was no object.'

Bodhi was unimpressed. 'Anyway, why didn't David have to leave?' he said.

'Okay. So I figured, after persuading Michael to get you home schooled, that you'd need friends coming round, otherwise you'd be all alone, and Michael wouldn't have wanted that. And then, if you were going to be here with lots of other children playing in the domes that he'd built at enormous expense, it wouldn't have made any sense making David leave. So, in the end that was what persuaded Michael, and he forgot about sending David away.'

'And I got to lead a weird life,' Bodhi said.

'It didn't start out like that,' I said. 'Michael was enthused by the idea of having other children come round to play with you, he loved the idea. He told me to make it happen. But that was the easy bit. Don't forget, we were in the middle of nowhere, the nearest actual town was twenty miles away. We were surrounded by farms and small little towns that didn't have a school, so to find children who could actually come to play with you I had go and get them myself. I literally had to drive round very morning, pick up the children from house to house and bring them to "Pleasurelands". And then, in the afternoon, when they were all tired out, I had to take them all back again. Every day, for years. Do you see how much work I made for myself?'

'Why did you do it?'

I paused. Should I tell him all this? I wondered. How much is this going to help him, and how much is this going to hurt me?

'There's a sign coming up for Los Angeles,' Bodhi said, 'on the highway in front of us. How much time have we got, until there isn't time for you to tell me anything at all?'

'Its hundreds of miles away,' I said, but Bodhi had a point.

'Look, I'm not a perfect person, okay? It doesn't reflect well on me, but Marcelyn made me promise,' I said, sighing. 'She persuaded me.'

I pointed to the bottles of water on the bench seat next to him, and Bodhi opened one for me.

'The fact is, Marcelyn had been completely tight lipped about who the father of her child was ever since she had announced she was pregnant—which, incidentally had been at the worst possible time. But there she was in her lounge pleading with me to help her, and yet when I asked her who David's father was...not a word. I mean, I thought it was no big deal. I thought she could trust me, of all people. She might not have liked me, but we'd been through a lot together by that point, and there was no good reason why she shouldn't have told me. Also, I figured if I knew who the father was, it might help me to understand why you were so different from him. Okay?'

Bodhi nodded.

'Well, she still wouldn't tell me. So I started to get angry. "I'm not your fucking slave," I said to her. "Treat me like a normal human being, it's not so difficult." But nothing. So I walked out, or at least I started to, and I guess Marcelyn realised I wasn't joking. "Come back, Shaun," she said, and I could tell from the tone of her voice that something had changed in her, and so I did. I sat down again and Marcelyn; she swallowed, she licked her dry lips, she stretched out the spastic clench in her weaker left arm with her right hand, wiped some strands of sweat wet hair out of her eyes and said; "it was Michael, alright. Are you happy now?"'

'What?' Bodhi said, shocked.

'Yes, you are as good as brothers, David and you because your father is the same and your mothers were identical twins, except of course they were anything but identical, which is what your aunt said to me as soon as I'd stopped laughing.'

'You were laughing?'

'Out of shock. I didn't expect to hear Marcelyn say what she'd said, any more than you expected me to say it just now...but then she fixed my eyes with hers, and said; "do you have any idea what it's like, Shaun, to understand someone else from the inside?" and I went quiet. "To know what they are thinking, what they are feeling? Do you? What they want, how they are going to react, how they are going to respond? We were identical, Mia and me," Marcelyn said, "I knew her and she knew me. Do you have any idea what it's like, for your whole life, to see every eye in a room, every head, turn to look at someone who isn't you, but who could almost be you? Do you?" That's what your aunt said. She said that your mother had never looked down on her, that she had always supported her. She said she had always treated her as an equal and had always understood how it felt for Marcelyn when every man's eyes in a room automatically span towards her, and never towards your aunt, except in pity or disgust." Of course David and you are brothers,' I said.

'But you must have been an idiot for not realising it sooner,' Bodhi said. 'I mean, surely there had been clues? You must have seen Marcelyn and Michael talking to each other in special ways, sharing glances, spending time together? How could you have missed that? You were with them all together, all of the time.'

'Just let me finish,' I said. 'I wanted to say the very same thing to Marcelyn, for precisely that reason, but I'd realised as soon as she'd told me, that if Michael was the father of David, then there was no way he was going to press Marcelyn to send David away, and all Marcelyn had to do, if she was so set on David staying—and she obviously was—was to tell him herself. But before I can get so much as half a sentence out of my mouth, Marcelyn said; "but Michael doesn't know he's the father, and you mustn't ever tell him, Shaun." Which made me laugh again at the utter ridiculousness of what your aunt was asking me.'

'Why did she say that?'

'These are things about your aunt I shouldn't really tell you.'

'You can't not tell me,' Bodhi said. 'You made the decision to keep me at "Pleasurelands", you set me the trap for the life I was to lead until I pleaded with you to help me leave...this very morning. You have to tell me. You owe me this.'

This is karma, biting my backside, I thought to myself. Yes, I had no choice.

'I couldn't believe what Marcelyn was telling me,' I said to Bodhi. 'It made no sense. Of course I told her that, I said; "how can Michael not know he's the father, how can he not guess that he's the father. Surely he must have had some doubt in his own mind; that after he had slept with you, and somehow you got pregnant, that it was likely it was his? It's not that hard to imagine. It's not going to come to him out of the blue like some sudden shock. He's not really going to be that surprised, Marcelyn." But she dug her fingernails into my arm hard enough that it hurt, and said; "because he wasn't there." He wasn't there? The words were like words you'd hear after fifteen Brandy's; they didn't make any sense at all and they were making my head spin.'

'How could the baby have been Michael's, but he wasn't there?' Bodhi looked at me as though there might actually be a way that this could be possible. He was waiting me for me to say; Oh, I didn't tell you about remote pregnancies did I? Silly me, that was something your home tutors and I left off the curriculum accidently.

'Well, he wasn't there, as it turns out. Marcelyn had done something desperate, and it had been hard for her to tell me, and she hadn't been able to tell anyone else. I guess it had been eating her up inside, it was easy to imagine that it had been. "I took his semen from their bed sheets," she said. She was shrinking in front of me. She was trembling. She was afraid and lonely, and in that moment—what could I do? I could have blackmailed her for life with that confession that she'd just made. I could have controlled her. I could have used her to exercise control myself over Michael. The great Michael Michael. I would have been a powerful man myself if I had done that. Maybe I should have done. Maybe anyone else would have done...'

'But you didn't because you are a good man,' Bodhi said.

We were approaching a long sweeping bridge that curved elegantly above the floor of a valley below. At the bottom there had been a river breaking white water over rocks in the middle of the stream. A cutting through hills to our left had steps tapering it back to the top, and making it look like a giants staircase. There was a welcome rush of cooler, moist air over our faces.

'Your aunt had humiliated herself, in front of me. But only from fear that she would have been shown to have humiliated herself in front of Michael, and the memory of her sister. I couldn't do it. I couldn't take advantage of her. I felt pity for her. I don't know, I'd heard enough about "compassion" from the odd Buddhist monk I'd spent time with, I couldn't ignore that. Maybe my practice had been weakness. Maybe...anyway, enough maybe's. So I said okay to her. I told her that I would find a way to persuade Michael to let David stay with her at "Pleasurelands" without telling him that David was actually his own son. It seemed like madness, and maybe I became mad at the same time. But that's what I did.'

'It's a big secret to hold inside of you,' Bodhi said.

'Yes, and one way or another our secrets eat us up and shape us like cancer. But that's what life is. Live long enough Bodhi...you'll discover it.'

'I don't have any secrets,' Bodhi said.

'You will have, the moment you step out of this truck,' I said. 'If someone says to you; "hey, are you Michael Michael's son?" you'll say "No, not me." You'll have to, otherwise they'll start looking at you like you're fresh meat, like you're a pile of loose dollar bills just waiting to be claimed.' Bodhi's smile dropped from him. 'And there's nothing wrong with that. Just look after yourself is what I'm saying, and learn it quickly.'

Bodhi scratched his armpit and looked at the floor of the truck. I looked back to the road.

Chapter 3.

'So, you got me home schooled, and there were a lot of other boys and girls for me to play with,' Bodhi said eventually.

'And...David stayed on at "Pleasurelands",' I said.

'Yes, David stayed on at "Pleasurelands",' Bodhi said, 'which was fine because it didn't make any difference to me. I could run around the grounds with everyone else. We could play hide and seek and there was so much space to explore I could run for hours and hours and no-one would find me. And for years, that's how it was.'

'I was glad about that, Bodhi,' I said, 'like I say, it was a lot of work for me.'

'But then something changed.'

'Well, things are always changing, aren't they?' I said. 'What's the problem with that...'

'Because when you're young,' he said, 'it seems like things aren't going to change, not ever, and you get used to them.'

Bodhi twisted in his seat and sat looking at me while I drove.

'The thing is, I was happy with how things were,' Bodhi said, 'but then that film got made at "Pleasurelands", do you remember? And something changed afterwards. There was no way to understand why, or even how, but something did, I'm sure of it. It was like there was a distance afterwards, between me and everyone else. I ended up like an alien from outer space inside my own head. All the boys and girls...Carrie, Cilla, Petey, Jonno, Sherrie, Wayne, and Suzie Jones of course—it felt like suddenly they were different. And if the truth be told, Shaun; I never felt the same after that.'

While Bodhi was speaking I could see that the hills we'd been driving away from for the previous hour had shrunk into the distance and the flat valley bottom that our route out was winding through had widened. Now the freeway ran parallel to those hills, and the full majesty of the Sierra Mountains was revealed as far north and south as any short glances away from the road could comprehend. They seemed to be ranging up to the sky to hold it down to the earth. I could see their peaks still snow covered, and their glacial whiteness's. I could see their jagged grey and brown angles stacked against each other like a giant wall that rose above me, ominously. They seemed to be telling me; you are not here now, you are somewhere else, and you must think carefully about whether you really want to come back.

'So what was it,' Bodhi said, 'what was it that had changed?'

'Look—the years had rolled by and we'd all got into our various grooves,' I said, shifting in my seat. 'It was really nothing to do with you...But there was a lot I wasn't seeing, and it was only when that documentary crew came that I realised it.'

The traffic was starting to get heavier on the Interstate highway and I checked my distance from the truck in front. Instead of empty lanes beside us, now there were occasional Pickups and family cars passing by.

'I should have appreciated,' I said, 'that even after things had quietened down at "Pleasurelands", even after David had been allowed to stay and other children were coming, that it would still be wrong of me to stop worrying about you. But that's what I did; I stopped worrying about you. I was busy of course, but what spare time I had I was just whiling away chilling out with girlfriends, that kind of thing. And so was Michael, and so was Marcelyn. None of us were really thinking about you very much.' I glanced apologetically at Bodhi, 'the problem was that, like you say; you were a happy child. Nothing seemed to get to you. You never seemed happier than when you were exploring the woods and riverbanks, watching the birds and enjoying nature. Isn't that true?'

'Yes, I loved it,' Bodhi said.

'You used to come and go to my house, you remember? I even let you do meditation with me at one point.'

'Yes, that's right.'

'So everything seemed fine. And by the time you'd reached the age of eight, or thereabouts, your father seemed fine too. He'd recovered his creativity; he was putting together new music...getting videos together. He'd even started talking about putting out a new album, and that was when the documentary crew got involved.'

'Okay.'

'But the whole thing just crept up on me unawares. The first I knew it was happening was when Marcelyn called me into her office and told me to make sure the buildings were all looking their best, because a film crew was coming. "Are they coming to film the buildings?" I asked her, but no, of course not; "Michael's going to go on a new tour," Marcelyn said. She was beaming from ear to ear, or you know, ear to nose anyway. She sounded triumphant, it was as though she had managed to make this happen all by herself, and she was so proud she didn't care who knew it. "Wow," I said, humouring her, "a tour? What, Michael's going to do a few shows somewhere local?" because that's what I thought it would amount to, but; "No, no, no. It's going to be a world tour," Marcelyn said, "just like the old days, only this time it's going to be even bigger, because its practically ten years since his last tour, and there's so much demand for it." "Double wow," I said, a little bit stunned; "So the film is going to be promotional material then?"

"Yes, they're from a T.V. network, it's going to be syndicated worldwide and I don't want anything to look bad for them.'"

I glanced across at Bodhi, we were in a part of his past that should have made sense to him.

'The documentary was going to be about your father,' I said, 'and his life and career. It was going to be the main publicity for the tour they were preparing, and that meant it was a big deal. Michael's tours cost millions and millions of dollars to set up, and the profits could be astronomical, but the fact is; there was risk too, a lot of risk. The stakes were high.'

'Okay.'

'Do you remember any of this?' I said to Bodhi.

'I only remember some strange guy being interested in hearing about the Otters in the river, and the nests of Black-winged Phoebe's that I'd found,' Bodhi said. 'He asked me lots of questions about them...and there was a woman with him, with blonde spiky hair and a clipboard.'

'That was Lizzie, she was the producer. It was George the interviewer who did the damage.'

'What do you mean?' Bodhi said.

'Well, it turned out he shouldn't have been asking you anything at all. It was part of the deal Michael and Marcelyn had agreed with the production company beforehand. I only found out because I got to see the film soon after it was finished. George had sent a copy through for approval, and it was watched in Michael's private cinema in his house. I set it up for them, so of course I could hear their reaction to it from the projector room as it played. At one point there was a big shouting match with George on the phone, and part of what was said was that George hadn't had permission to film you for the documentary, which I didn't know anything about. Michael called me out of the projector room, and I said that to him right there and then, that as soon as Lizzie and George—and there was a cameraman and sound guy too—as soon as they had arrived, Marcelyn had told me simply to help them in any way they wanted.'

'I never saw the film,' Bodhi said.

'No, of course you didn't,' I said, 'Michael and Marcelyn wouldn't have wanted you to. In the end they weren't happy that anyone saw it, even though just about the whole world did.'

'Why? What was in it?'

'A lot of things,' I said. 'It wasn't all bad, by any means. The finished film started with shots of the grounds. I think they'd had a helicopter do some aerial shots; the whole estate looked incredible. Then George had done a voice over saying how brilliant it was to be able to interview Michael just as he was putting out his first new album for a decade, and how interesting Michael's life had been, and how revealing it was to have the chance to compare the day to day life of an immensely successful 'creative' with the content of their new work, or something like that. Then the camera did cut-away's from the two of them talking; Michael and George, to focus on the gold discs hanging up in the background of the shot—your father had done the interview in his studio—and also the statues in the awards cases against the walls; the Oscar for best original song...the Grammies...the glass pyramids with "AMA" cut into them. It was all very well done, but then the interview headed off into areas that Michael hadn't been expecting.'

'How do you mean?'

'George started asking questions about the children around 'Pleasurelands', and that was when I started to realise that I might have misunderstood Marcelyn. She had definitely said; "Show George anywhere he wants to go, make sure he sees the domes—they're really exceptional after all..." but she hadn't thought it through. She'd probably thought I knew what to do. But I didn't, I was clueless, I'd lost my street-wise edge, I was innocent. That was how George ended up interviewing you. It was complicated,' I said to Bodhi, 'you see, George was a handsome man...you remember?'

'I remember he looked like he had too many teeth for his mouth,' Bodhi said, 'and I couldn't understand everything he was saying.'

'He had an Australian accent,' I said to Bodhi, 'which, by the way Marcelyn loved. But, yes, he was a handsome man, and he was very charming. In fact, he was so charming that your aunt was bowled over by him. It turned out that George knew perfectly well what he was doing; he was flattering her. He'd say; "How is my gorgeous Marcelyn today?" because the filming took a week. Or he'd say; "You're looking beautiful today, Marcelyn...have you done something with your hair?" and so on and so on, and your aunt fell for everything he said, it was downright embarrassing. Michael didn't see any of that, so he couldn't say anything, and it wasn't for me to try and point out to Marcelyn how easily she was falling for him. I guess her disability meant that she just wasn't used to having men flatter her, not handsome men. Or maybe George was particularly good at it. But the end result was that she wanted me to help him, and she didn't give me any boundaries. So when George said; "Hey, Shaun, mate, can we see the inside of the pods today?" I said sure, and I showed him the domes. The cameraman, Tony, and Jerry the sound guy came along as well as his producer, so perhaps I should have been more guarded, but even though Tony had his camera on his shoulder, I thought it was for carrying around, and I didn't realise he was going to be filming all the time. I remember I actually asked him whether he was going to be filming, but before he could answer, Lizzie, the producer with the spiky hair and the super confident manner said; "Oh, it's only for filler material, Shaun. Don't let it worry you." And just then some of your playmates came into shot, and so I didn't think any more of it.'

'Who came into shot?'

'It was Carrie and Sherrie, I don't know. I think it was them. I couldn't concentrate because George kept distracting me; "How long have you worked here, Shaun?" he asked, "You don't mind if I ask you some questions do you? It's going to take a long time to see everything here isn't it, it's quite a big place." I said it was fine, and I told him it was eight years since we'd bought the property, and I'd been there since the start. I didn't see any reason not to answer his questions—after all Marcelyn had told me to.'

'But you were proud of the fact that you'd worked there for so long,' Bodhi said.

'Yes, and George probably realised that too; "You must know this place very well, Shaun. I bet you know how the kids we can see running around get to be here." Which of course I did; "Oh, I bring them from the town myself," I said, and I remember George raising his eyebrows and tilting his head, to encourage me to keep talking. So I did; "I drive the six miles into the town of Littel every weekday morning and collect whatever children show up, just as Michael wants me to." Lizzie smiled when I added; "Once I'm there I keep a route so regular my S.U.V. could be a school bus if it was painted yellow." Then I said; "I stop in the same places, parking up briefly and sounding my horn, then boys and girls run out of the wooden shacks and trailer-homes they live in, screaming and hollering to meet some of their friends in the back of my little coach. Then I give them juices and snacks while I drive on to the next pick up point, and after the last child is collected I zip back to

Pleasurelands and unlock the domes one by one. Then Marcelyn sends off David and Bodhi to join them, and once they're all assembled I supervise their play." "What do their parents think about that," George asked, and I explained that the parents were mostly in a bad way; "you know, it's a very poor area, George; there's a lot of homelessness, and there's a lot of drug addiction. We just happen to be on the outskirts of much of what's worst about rural America," which George nodded to. And I remember seeing Lizzie making notes on her clipboard too— which made me feel important. "It's not exactly Beverley Hills, is it," she said, with a wink and a knowing smile.'

The truck in front of us was a milk tanker. Its body was chromed, and the end of the tank was shaped convexly so that as we approached it the front of our truck reflected in its imperfect mirror like a toy car. It was mesmerising, but I had to concentrate on what I was telling Bodhi:

'George said; "that's quite convenient for Michael really, isn't it—that you bring children here," and at the time I wasn't sure what he meant. I was leading him and his crew around the funfair dome, trying to make sure they didn't fall over things as they walked backwards talking to me. Then Lizzie asked how long the children had been coming to "Pleasurelands", and I told them since you were four and David five, and she said; "You must have needed a full size nursery with so many children about," and I said; "No, we used the rooms in Michael's house, upstairs, to start with. We were always having to change them out of wet clothes, but now of course we don't need to do that anymore, the children can change themselves; they don't need us helping them to the toilet or washing them or anything." And Lizzie was scribbling away as fast as she could, and Jerry, the cameraman was looking into his viewfinder, and just as I was starting to get interested in what Tony, the sound guy was doing with his bag of recording equipment, George distracted me with another question; "So tell me, Shaun, how many registered nursery staff did Michael have working here?" I told him the truth; "None. We did it all ourselves. Michael was very hands on, if you know what I mean." "I bet I can guess," Lizzie muttered, and I remember hearing that, and just letting it go—even though it jarred, but it all made sense later as we saw the film.'

'I thought there were lots of grown-ups helping us,' Bodhi said. 'Weren't there some ladies speaking Spanish, and the Cooks too? Didn't they help with getting fresh clothes?'

'Yes, they did, Bodhi. But the other women were from the cleaning staff.'

He nodded as a small piece of the jigsaw of his life fell into place.

'I said that to Lizzie; that we had help we could call on, but then she just started shaking her head to herself. I still didn't realise what she was thinking. "So there were just the two of you then; you and Michael, with occasional help from cleaning ladies, all day with a group of, what four or five children?" George said. "Oh, no; there were at least ten children, if you include Bodhi and David," I said, "but Marcelyn did help too sometimes, if her health was up to it. We weren't being heroic."'

I looked over to Bodhi, 'I'm telling you this now, but I didn't ever tell Michael or Marcelyn that I had had that conversation; they'd have killed me.'

The milk tanker took an off-ramp and left the Interstate. The sun was starting to feel hot in the cab and I took a drink from the water bottle in my cup holder, finishing it.

'Lizzie asked me if I had records of who your friends were, and where their parents lived. She said it might be nice for her to go and visit them, and I imagined that she wanted to hear how grateful the parents were for the chance for their children to be playing with you and David, in Michael Michael's magnificent estate. I assumed George would feed it into the documentary, I thought I was helping Michael and Marcelyn. I told her that no, we didn't keep records because there didn't seem much point, that the children came and went day by day depending on who I could find in town, and that it was all a bit informal. I added that sometimes I couldn't take the children home anyway because their parents weren't to be found, or else they were crazy on Crystal meth. Then George asked what we did if that was the case, and I told him that we had them sleep over. And George said; "Where?" And I told him in Michael's house. "Doesn't he find that a nuisance," George asked, and I said; "No, Michael really loves having kids around." Again, I should have realised from the look on George's face what he was thinking, but just then a pair of water balloons burst near us, and Lizzie started asking Jerry and Tony about their equipment—because of the risk of water damage, I guess.'

'What had happened?'

'Four boys—I can't remember who it was, although one was David—they screamed with delight and ran off from behind the helter-skelter.'

'That was the orange and white striped tower under the centre of the dome, before Michael took all the funfair rides out and put his Dinosaur collection in it?' Bodhi said.

'Yes, that's right,' I said. 'Then two girls ran past us chasing the boys, and one of them was Suzie Jones, who stopped and said; "We'll get them for you; they're really bad." And Lizzie, the producer quickly said; "Thank you," taking a hold of Suzie's arm and pulling her so that she was in front of the camera; "What do you like best about it here," she asked. "Michael's got a hairy chest!" Suzie said screaming with laughter. God knows why. Then she ran off towards one of the funfair rides, and her shouts and laughter blended into the fairground tunes blaring out from the pipe organ. I mean, thank God they didn't put any of that into the finished film,' I said to Bodhi, 'but that was what they saw—and straight away Lizzie pointed out to me that the girls were both topless, which I had thought seemed reasonable enough because it was always very hot inside the dome, and they were only eight after all; but she seemed to think they ought to have been better dressed. If I'd been given another moment to think about it I might have realised what the angle was that George and his crew were arriving at, but before I could, George distracted me again; "Which one of those boys was Bodhi, Shaun?" "None of them," I said, "Bodhi doesn't usually play in here. If you're looking for Bodhi, you'll find him wandering through the fields of Bluegrass, birdwatching or following the Otters by the pools." Which is how he and the film crew knew where to find you.'

'Okay,' Bodhi said, 'now that makes sense. I thought he was just looking around the grounds because he liked them too, and then they all bumped into me by chance. But I can see it wasn't like that.'

'No. They were definitely working out an angle for their documentary, and, I'm sorry to say, while we were still walking around the funfair dome I was making it easier and easier for them; "Doesn't Michael get worried about something happening to Bodhi," George asked. "Some of those kids with David look a little...rough don't they?" "Yes, some of the children are probably being ill-treated," I said, "It's a real shame." "You bet," George said, "What do you do if they get too rough?" "I stop bringing them and get some fresh children," I said. I remember George looked shocked. I just thought he was a bit slow.'

I looked out of my driver's window and laughed at my own stupidity.

'I didn't realise what I was saying,' I said to Bodhi, 'or at least, the impression it was giving him. George was looking at me askance, so I added that Michael was only too happy to see new faces in his gang because he didn't favouritize. That if the whole of the current group of kids were replaced one by one with newer children, he didn't mind at all. And Lizzie said; "No, I'm sure he doesn't," and just to round off my idiocy I said; "It's like a shot of energy to Michael every time a new kid comes, because they're so happy to meet him. He laps it up like a thirsty kitten." Then George gave me a matey hug and said; "Thanks, Shaun. You know what; I think we've got enough background shots now," and they all turned and left the dome, and to be honest, I only felt worried at the time that I hadn't been able to show them the best parts of it.'

'They probably came and found me straight afterwards,' Bodhi said.

'Yes. Though I didn't realise they'd talked to you at all until the film was showing in Michael's house.'

'Was it all about me then, the film?'

'No, not at all, don't worry,' I said to Bodhi. 'After the opening conversation—George asked your father some obvious questions about the sense of loss he must have felt after your mother's death, and whether that had found expression in his new songs—then he went into a long spiel for the audience about how Michael had grown up in London, just after the end of the Second World War, and he started asking him questions about his relationship with his parents, and Michael said something interesting about playing on old bombsites when he was small and how his own mum and dad didn't have any money and so forth...at which point your father told me to fast forward the film a bit because it was getting boring, so I got up and I did and then I came back out of the projector room and sat down a few rows behind them, but it wasn't long before I wished I hadn't.'

'Why?'

'Because straight away I could hear George on the voice-over asking whether your father's own childhood had contributed to the choices he had made at "Pleasurelands", particularly in terms of the way he had a lot of children around to play with you Bodhi, in what he called; "Michael's amazing geodesic fun domes." That didn't please your father. He said he didn't know why George had gone off in that direction, that he had thought George was going to stick to asking about Michael's own career highlights, and that he had told George himself specifically not to ask about you at all, which of course was embarrassing for me, so I started shrinking in my seat. But it got a lot worse. It should have been a straight forward pop music promo, but instead it was starting to look like a serious documentary: George kept asking about the children. He was hinting that there was something improper about the way Michael used, what George called; "vulnerable children from vulnerable families," and your father started getting angry on the film. He was saying; "this is my house, my home. I can do what I want. I'm giving these children a chance to enjoy the most amazing facilities that they're ever going to see, they're not going to enjoy opportunities like this anywhere else around," but instead of cutting that part out, George had left it in. Michael was getting furious; "What the fuck is he doing?" he said out loud. "It's an offering to the local community," Michael said on the film, defensively. "That includes having them stay here overnight, unaccompanied?" George asked sarcastically.'

'Why was George hinting that there was something improper?' Bodhi said.

'Well, that's a long story,' I said, 'I mean, Michael has money, and appetites...'

'Is he a bad man?'

'He has done some things that aren't good,' I said, 'as we all have.'

'Was this how the documentary went out? Did people see this? It sounds awful, it would have hurt him. It would have hurt my father. But I didn't know anything about it, so nothing changed afterwards, as a result. Not too much, did it?'

'No. And yes. He defended himself. On the film, Michael said; "You know George, these questions are ridiculous! Get back to the music, that's what you're here for." Then in the cinema in his house he shouted; "Bastard," at the screen. Marcelyn asked him if she should call George the next day, but Michael shouted; "No. I want you to call him right now! Get him on the phone." Which she did, putting the phone on speaker, and when George answered he said; "Hello Marcie, how lovely to hear your voice again, how are you," which was kind of funny. Though the mood darkened pretty quickly; "What the fuck are you playing at, George?" Michael said, and George laughed.'

'He laughed?'

'Yes. He'd made his decision. That was clear. He said; "Michael, we've edited the footage we took and made an editorial call that the documentary benefited from including parts of the interview that you're probably talking about, whether you want them used or not." So that was that. And in the background now, on the film there's a section that you featured in, a piece that started with a long shot fixed on you sitting cross legged like a Buddha underneath a giant incense Cedar watching a Dragonfly flit in front of you. The camera lingered on the gold skin of your arms and your blonde, sun-bleached hair, and the voice-over said;

"Bodhi is a young man who really loves nature," then there was a closer shot.'

'That was what I was doing when I saw them the first time. I was meditating, like you. Then George saw I had something in my hand and he asked me what it was, and I told him it was a Harlequin bug with bright yellow wings, and if I squeezed it too hard it would make a really bad smell, and he asked me what I was going to do with it...'

'And you said you were going to let it go. He put it in the first version of the film, and everyone would have fallen in love with you Bodhi, if it had stayed in the final version; you looked so calm, sitting there, and so kind. But Michael was getting madder and madder; "Get Hal Kardanglian on the other line," he said to Marcelyn, and she started struggling to her feet, but I fetched her the phone from the corner of the cinema to save her the trouble. "George, if you don't listen very carefully to my instructions you are going to have my lawyers down your throat—got it?" "Oh, Michael, don't make threats," George said, "We can work this out, okay; like gentlemen."'

'I didn't realise they were filming me,' Bodhi said, shaking his head.

'No, of course you didn't, and none of its your fault.'

I changed my grip on the steering wheel, stretching out stiff fingers.

'So, what it came down to eventually was a deal,' I said. 'Michael didn't want footage of you in the film—he was too sensitive to the memory of your mother, and of her death, but at the same time he also didn't want George suggesting, or implying, that there was something improper about his relationship to the other children around the place. So George countered by saying that he felt everyone was still so interested in how you, Bodhi were developing, after all that had happened to you and your mother, and that he couldn't leave it out of the finished film, but that he could offer Michael an arrangement whereby he would withdraw the suggestions of improper behaviour with the other children if Michael was willing to let him use that footage.'

'Of me?'

'Yes. Though Michael was furious; "You can't use the footage of Bodhi, and you can't use the other parts of the interview either," he shouted. But George said; "We can run it all through the lawyers if you want Michael, but think about it; the more fuss you make, the more interest there is, and what are you going to end up with? You're going to end up with all the allegations that have ever been made against you in the past, lumped together with the fact that you have young children in your home, not always fully dressed and roaming around unsupervised." Which was bit of a hammer blow. Then George softened a little; "Look; I don't particularly want to put all that stuff in the film, because as you say quite rightly, the children are coming from disadvantaged backgrounds and as far as I can see they're not actually coming to any harm here. But; I do want to include the footage of Bodhi, because it's of great interest to the public, and anyway, it's beautiful footage."'

'So what happened,' Bodhi asked.

'Michael wouldn't agree. Marcelyn was on George's side, she kept saying; "Just let him use the footage of Bodhi, Michael. What does it matter? You can't let him broadcast the other stuff, even though it's only rumours, it'll damage your image, and it'll cost us money." But in the end, he cared more about keeping the footage of you, Bodhi, away from the public than he did his own reputation.'

'That's terrible.'

'Yes. It hurt Michael, for sure. He'd been betrayed by a guest in his own house. But that wasn't quite the end of it. He'd got Hal

Kardanglian on the other line that evening, and Hal was able to put enough pressure, eventually on George and the network that the film didn't get aired until after Michael had completed his world tour, which was an enormous success. So, it wasn't all bad.'

'Good.'

'But when it did come out, like I said, everyone saw it, including all the residents of the town of Littel. So, then they stopped their children coming to "Pleasurelands".'

'Ah, because of the allegations?'

'Exactly.'

'Now, that makes sense,' Bodhi said. 'But the boys and girls started coming again soon, didn't they. So what happened? Did the allegations get cleared up? How did my father prove his innocence?'

'It wasn't that simple. He didn't prove his innocence, he took a different route,' I said, looking across at Bodhi, 'he ignored them. He ignored all the allegations. He just decided you needed friends, and so, given that the tour had made huge amounts of money for him, he decided eventually to start paying the parents to bring their children to "Pleasurelands" themselves.'

'He paid them?'

'Yes, after the families stopped letting me take the children to "Pleasurelands" in the usual way, after a few weeks of no children coming, Michael told me to go around, speak to the parents and offer them money.'

'So, from then on the boys and girls I had around me to play with were being paid to be there?'

'Yes.'

Bodhi sighed and looked vacantly out of the Chevy's window beside him. 'Oh God. Okay. Thanks for telling me this, Shaun. Things make more sense now.'

'I'm sorry, Bodhi,' I said. 'I tried to persuade Michael not to do that, but he wasn't listening to me. For a while I had to be very careful around your father, it was partly to do with what was in the rest of the film. I didn't think he was really watching it, but the words and pictures must have seeped into his consciousness.'

'What was it?'

'George was asking you whether you played much with your cousin David, and whether he looked after you because he was a year older than you, and you said no, and then George asked you whether I looked after you, and you said that I did, and that sometimes you even did meditation with me. Well, I knew there were going to be problems as soon as I heard that, and sure enough, just after Michael had told me to kill the line to George, and had thrown open the exit door from the cinema in the semi darkness; just after he had shouted; "I've got such a fucking headache," to himself; just after I had started wondering whether I was going to get let off the hook for everything I'd said to George; just after that—Michael turned, quietly and said, with exaggerated composure; "And you, Shaun: don't you ever do meditation with Bodhi, ever again." Which is why I never did.'

'But I did it on my own,' Bodhi said, sinking into his seat. He looked down at the foot well of the old truck. 'I'm getting hungry,' he said, in a flat monotone.

'So am I,' I said. 'Scan the horizon and look out for a signpost for a place to eat.'

Bodhi sat quietly looking around at the sides of the road, and while he did I thought about all the payments I'd ended up making to local families; one hundred dollars here, one hundred dollars there...everything in cash, sometimes to the mother, sometimes to the father—it depended who was the drinker, or who bought the drugs. 'Don't talk to me if you haven't seen the money...you'll have to sort it out between yourselves,' I'd say if their other half had wasted all the cash, but there'd be more for them the next week anyway. I've spent how long paying bad people to do bad things? I wondered to myself. Too long, that was for sure. But at least they had to bring their children to 'Pleasurelands' themselves—that had saved me some work. Leave your mobile phones at the gate. No cameras, no tape recorders.

'What about that place ahead,' Bodhi said, as a sign for a 'Carls Jr.' poked over a line of straggly Oaks on a ridge that we sped towards.

'That'll be too busy,' I said, 'and too full of people who might recognise you. But there'll be another place near it, we'll drive around and see.'

I turned off the Interstate, did a slow rolling stop at the junction and turned right, pulling eventually into the parking lot for a non-descript looking Bar stuck in the middle of nowhere. It was just the sort of place we needed to be at.

We got out the truck. Bodhi jumped, and I eased myself out with a painful stretch. Then we walked past a row of Harley Davidsons glinting in the midday sunlight, entering 'King Kong's Bar and Diner - biggest burgers you'll ever see'.

We walked up to a counter, where a gaunt, toothy old Latino guy said; 'Howdy,' and we ordered our burgers. The windows were high up in the walls of the Bar and the light they let in was filtered by thin curtains that had long since been forgotten about by whoever had put them up. It was dark, and the Bar was cool. An old air conditioning unit blew air in by the corner near the rest rooms, and above the counter a T.V. had sports playing.

I sat down with my back to the wall facing in, letting Bodhi sit with his back to the few regulars who glanced in our direction as they ate their burgers, shot pool or drank their beers.

'I don't understand why my father let that film you were telling me about be broadcast, if he knew there were things in it that would hurt him,' Bodhi said. 'Why not, like Marcelyn said, let them use the footage of me? It was unimportant. There wasn't anything to it, it didn't hurt me, even if I saw it today...tell me if I'm wrong, but I can't see how it would hurt me now?'

Bodhi looked to me to contradict him. I shook my head.

'Why then?'

'Your father wanted to be in control. I guess he figured he could insist the network refuse to broadcast the film, even though it was finished. Maybe he thought he was so important that he would be able to ruin George and get the film destroyed? But in any case, he knew perfectly well that there were already accusations against him. Several, not least an incident on his tour bus fifteen or sixteen years before. He knew that, and I knew that.'

'What was that about,' Bodhi asked, 'an incident on a tour bus?'

'It was just the usual rock and roll things,' I said.

Our burgers came, and they were large alright.

'I don't know what that means, Shaun.'

I opened up my burger, pulled a piece of pickle out and closed it up again.

'Bodhi, this part of your father's life is not nice. There's a dark side that most people never really get to explore because, basically they don't have the chance...I mean, they don't have the money or the influence over other people. But your father of course does, and there were times when he used that to its fullest extent. And now he spends time and money keeping it secret.'

'Okay?'

'And you're asking me to tell you about it.'

'Because I'm leaving him, and I'm leaving you,' Bodhi said, with a steely glint in his eyes. 'So tell me what I need to know,' he said. 'This burger's big, but it's not going to take half an hour to eat, so for God's sake, just tell me the things only you can let me hear.'

I could see Bodhi was going to be doing the eating, and I was going to be doing the talking. But the burger wasn't what I needed anyway, and I threw it down on the polystyrene tray it came in.

'It was nineteen eighty two,' I said, 'it was one of the last tours Michael did before he met your mother. In fact, it was part of the reason why meeting your mother became so important to him. We'd been touring on the east coast and we'd started heading into the mid-west. It had been a great tour; sell-out crowds, record attendances, you name it. There'd been a film crew with us then too. I mean, there were always photographers and rock journalists with us at some point of the tour; that was part of the game. Michael was happy to play up for them, but the rest of the band, and the road crew too, well, we couldn't relax. So it was getting a bit tense in the tour buses. It was Steve Brillstein, Michael's manager before Marcelyn, who made us put up with the film crew; we didn't have any choice in the matter. We were three weeks into the tour by the time the film crew felt they had enough footage to leave us alone, and that was in Des Moines, I think. In Iowa. The next concert was to be two days later in Chicago, Illinois, and before that we had a long drive east. To compound the frustration everyone felt, a quirk in the scheduling meant we were heading back on ourselves; by rights we should have been heading further west, through Nebraska and on towards Denver, Colorado.'

I grabbed a couple of fries and scooped up some mayo.

'I was only eighteen years old. I hadn't known Michael for more than a few years. He trusted me, for various reasons, but I was expendable, back then I guess. So if there was something he wanted, I kind of had to do it. And something like that came up on the tour bus after we'd finished the concert in Des Moines. It was early in the morning and the guys were still too hyped from the previous evenings' performance to sleep.'

Bodhi was looking at me impatiently, as much as to say; come on, get on with it!

'Okay, so basically they wanted me to find them some girls.'

'To play around with?'

'Yeah. Only...'

'What?'

'Young girls.'

'Underage?'

'Yeah.'

'And you did?'

I sighed. 'Well, yes. But it wasn't that simple. We'd arrived in Chicago late morning the following day. It was a horrible day, there was a vicious wind and the city dust was stinging in your face. The road crew went straight into set-up mode for the next concert, hurling flight cases down ramps and into loading bays for the auditorium, while Michael and his band started checking out the sight lines and sound arcs and that sort of thing. So I slipped away, bought a local newspaper, and got a taxi to a school I read about on the South side that was having some sort of open day. I got there and then, it's like I'm having a nervous breakdown. I mean, what was I supposed to do? Start waving tickets at these beautiful blue-sweatered black girls flashing their shining aubergine thighs from under pleated maroon skirts? They weren't much younger than I was.'

'You liked the look of them yourself,' Bodhi said, between mouthfuls of burger.

'You bet. And I felt sorry for them. I felt guilty for what I was thinking. And I felt worried about getting arrested if I tried telling them what was expected from them, in exchange for the tickets I had in my back pocket. So I was basically wandering around like an idiot, banging my head with my hand and leaning against the chipped school railings. And you know, there were a lot of folks there who weren't school children; there were parents and older brothers, and I'm thinking; if I say the wrong thing here I'm going to get the shit beaten out of me. Or am I going to get arrested? There was a Chicago Police car nearby that blinked its blue lights. I could feel the driver's eyes on me, and there were school-run pick-up trucks and sedans parking, so I turned and started to walk away. In my head I'm cursing Michael and thinking to myself; I'll give all this up and become a monk. This is just plain wrong, because at the time that was what I was thinking about.'

I took a couple more fries, and a drink of Coke. Bodhi was looking at me intently, his burger held in both hands in front of his face.

'To be fair, Bodhi,' I said, 'it wasn't your father alone who was pressuring me to do this, it was the other band members; Aaron, Vince and Benjy. It was their idea.'

Bodhi nodded.

'So, I guess that stopped me from completely walking away. And who knows, if I had gone back and said I'd failed, maybe they would have said; "Hey, Shaun, you daft twit. We were only joking anyway. We didn't think you'd actually try and get four virgins for us..." But, anyway, just as I'm walking off, there's this cute girl with straightened hair dyed almost blonde and she calls out from behind me; "Hey, bro', is that a Michael Michael shirt?" She danced around in front of me to block me—a very sensuous girl. She says; "I've not seen that one before, is that the newest one?" I told her it was. "How come you've got a new T-shirt already? Did you see him in New York?" I told her I had, and Philadelphia too, which was true of course, and then she said; "Wow. Hey, are you English?" "Yeah, I work for Michael." "Oh my God!" she said, "I'd die if I could meet him. Can you get me into tomorrow night's show?" I was thinking to myself; run for your life, you silly girl. You don't know what you're going to be letting yourself in for, but then I thought, well, it's her life, not mine... so I said yes, I could get her in, and then she looked over her shoulder to the other side of the street, grabbed my arm and pulled me away from the sidewalk, into an alcove where a giant wheeled garbage bin with a green lid sat slanted to the wall. "My friends are over there and I don't want them to see us," she said. "They'll want to come and see Michael too, but they're so dumb; they don't know how it all goes, baby. They're immature, but I'm not. I know how it goes." And she looked me in the eyes with a stare that seemed to speak of a life time of experience, and I knew what that looked like. So I thought to myself; yes, she knows how it all goes alright.'

I looked at Bodhi, and I could see he hadn't a clue what I was talking about. None at all. But he had asked for me to speak, and so I would.

'She was pretty, Bodhi. She really was. I gazed at the softness of her teenage skin, the perfect curve of her eyebrows, the cheeky dimples of her smiling cheeks; I was taking in the loveliness of her before Michael or any of the other band members could themselves, I was convincing myself that one girl this nice would be enough for all of them. And then, as though she could sense what I was doing...she slapped my face as hard as she could! Just like that, out of the blue. "But if you're fucking lying; I'll knife you bro'. I'll slice you open," she said.'

'Really?'

'Oh yes,' I said, to Bodhi. 'So I quickly pulled a ticket out of my back pocket, and gave it to her. "This one's a back-stage pass," I said. "Hold on to it and don't give it to anyone else, got it?" "Yeah, baby, yeah," she said. She was called Cha'relle. I told her where to meet me after the show and I'd let her into the backstage area; "What happens then is down to you," I said.'

'Was she happy,' Bodhi asked.

'Put it this way,' I said, 'she stepped in towards me, and I flinched a little, because I thought she might want to hit me again, but instead she smiled, and then she licked my face... She worked her tongue up my cheek to my flickering eyelid, and then laughed and walked off with a dreadful glint in her eyes, and a dangerous sway to her hips. I tell you; it wasn't me who was the predator.'

'I can believe it,' Bodhi said. 'So then sometime later she sold her story, like they all did, and people said my father liked young girls?'

'Not exactly,' I said, finishing a bite of burger. 'The next morning, after the concert equipment was all packed away and the buses were getting out of the arena, the girl with the skin like shining aubergines was still with them. I saw her get on the bus with the musicians. We had a six hour drive to Minneapolis, and having spent the first few hours of the new day helping a guy called Andy dismantle the sound rig, I joined him, and Ian and Mike, I think, on the road crew's coach, which then sped off, following Michael's out of Chicago. I could have been feeling down, but Aaron had whispered to me; "You did well!" as he'd got on the bands' bus, so I was feeling pretty good. I was probably still in Michael's good books, if you know what I mean. I got some sleep, as best I could. The coach was rocking and twisting through the city roads, then we rumbled along on the Interstate. Finally we pulled into a rest stop at a quiet section of I-94, surrounded by forest. The sun was low in the sky, but it was obviously morning, and I guessed we were stopping for fuel. But we weren't. The door of our coach opened suddenly, and a burst of cold fresh air blew in, and then a second later Benjy, Michael's keyboardist shook me by the shoulder, saying; "Shaun, we've got a problem, you'd better come. Quick...""

'Where to,' Bodhi asked.

'The other coach,' I said. 'I hauled myself out of my seat, dragging the blanket I was still wrapped in along the floor of the bus until it fell off me on the stairs down to the door. I didn't have any shoes on so I was hopping around puddles on the tarmac. I hauled myself into the other coach and as soon as I did Vince, the drummer said; "That stupid fucking bitch went mental, Shaun," and he handed me a bloodied shirt; "She went for Michael, he's at the back, he needs some first aid.""

'Wow, was dad hurt?' Bodhi said. He had almost finished his burger, and wiped his mouth with the back of his hand.

'There was a trail of crimson droplets on the floor of the bus. They led to your father, who was crouching by the rear window, supporting his left arm with his right. I could see straight away there was a long gash across his left cheek, and I knew this would be a disaster if it was deep.'

'God...'

'Exactly. "Where is she," Michael asked. His voice was tremulous. Well, of course, I didn't know. But Aaron said; "She's run off, she's somewhere in the rest stop, I've looked around but I can't see her." Benjy said; "She'll have hitched another lift, that skanky bitch." I asked your father what had happened, and Vince said; "She fucking flipped," then Michael said; "I don't know, I was asleep. The next thing I know is I'm getting smashed with a microphone stand." I tended the wound on his face. It was mercifully superficial, and I told him so. Then Michael asked me; "Where did you manage to find that psychopath?" Which, to be honest, at the time was a bit of a strange question, so I just said; "What do you care? You got what you wanted. Anyway, what was she even doing on the coach?" "Oh, what do you think she was doing on the coach, Shaun," Benjamin said, "don't be so bloody naïve.""

'What did you do, Shaun?'

'I covered Michael's cheek with a dressing, Bodhi. I said; "Just as well I only found you the one girl though, hey?" and your father kind of liked that, he said; "You're the cocky one all of a sudden, Shaun, aren't you!" with a grin that stung him instantly into a grimace. "You've no idea what you missed out on, mate," Vincent said, and he pushed a Polaroid camera into sight on the blood spotted fabric of the bench seat along one side of the tour bus.'

'What did that mean?'

'What it meant was that when, a few seconds later, there was a blip on a siren, Benjamin, who had been talking to the driver of the coach who didn't seem to speak much English...Benjamin knew that the Polaroid camera was in plain view and he then tried to signal to me to hide it.'

'Why?'

'Because the siren had come from a Police motorcycle, and the rider, who stood his silver machine on its stand, rapped his truncheon on the bi-fold doors of the bus and forced the driver to open them. The coach of course went suddenly completely silent. Vince was panicking to get rid of the joint he was smoking, which was pointless because the whole bus stank, and Aaron started trying to hide underneath some seats. "Stay where you are guys," the Cop said. At which point your father put on his best British accent and said; "Officer, you're a very welcome sight, very welcome indeed. Please, come forward." The Cop strode slowly towards us, nostrils flaring. As he saw Michael prostrate on his bench, he eased his mirrored dark glasses off and held them with one of the arms in his mouth. "Michael Michael?" he said. You understand, Bodhi, the tour buses needed to travel incognito, so it's not like we had Michael's name emblazoned on the side or anything.'

'Yeah.'

'Well, the officer said; "I'm a great fan of yours," and your father asked him his name, and he said; "Ramirez," and your father said; "Officer Ramirez, I'd like to report an incident, that just happened on this coach a few moments ago, that involved a sadly delinquent young lady..." but he tailed off as Officer Ramirez slowly reached for the Polaroid camera sitting on the bench seat in front of him, examining it and then scanning the seats for its printouts, which he found in a small pile tucked loosely into the crack between the back and the cushion of the chair, right next to Michael. This was all quite funny really, now I think back to it. "You're touring at the moment, Michael," Officer Ramirez asked, as he looked at the photos.'

'What was on the photos,' Bodhi asked, innocently.

'Cha'relle, naked apart from her school skirt round her waist, with three white, flash bleached bodies connected to various parts of her,' I said.

'Oh, right.'

'It was the first time I had ever seen Michael afraid. He was really worried. He stood up, still holding his arm so that he was face to face with the Officer, and said; "Look, man; the bitch is completely mad, okay?" There was a tense silence. We all held our breaths on the coach to see how the gun toting bike cop would react. Had Michael read him correctly? Then, holding the photo up, in front of Michael's face, Ramirez said; "Yeah, I'd be pretty mad." Then Michael started pleading; "She was crazy to start with Officer. Look; girls...you've got to understand; they beg me for it!" "I know this school uniform," Ramirez said, "its Perkins elementary. You know the girls who wear this are 8th grade?" Michael shook his head. "That means she was thirteen years old."'

'Too young,' Bodhi said.

'Too young,' I said back. 'Ramirez asked; "Where is she now?" "She ran off towards the cars and trucks parked over the other side of the rest stop," Vincent said, nervously. The whole thing could have got really nasty, but then a voice crackled on Officer Ramirez's radio; "Officer Ramirez, do you copy?" He answered; "This is Ramirez." "Could you respond to a 10-110" or whatever the code was "...on North settlement road?" "10-4, on my way." Then he said to us that the code was for a juvenile disturbance, and the road was about half a mile away. He took a card out of his rear pocket, added a phone number to it and then handed it to Michael; "What shall I do with her when I find her? Let me know how much it matters to you, Michael. It might need quite a lot of careful consideration," he said winking.'

'What did my father do?'

'He nodded, and I guess he paid him a bribe later on. But first he told me to get him a Jack Daniels. "I've got such a fucking headache," he said.'

Bodhi had finished his food, I didn't want all of mine so I pushed it towards him. He was hungry, but before he started on it he asked; 'What did this have to do with Michael meeting my mother?'

'There's a whole lot of other stuff I haven't told you about. Rock and roll stuff. This was just the first time he hadn't gotten away with it. I guess he realised that he needed to settle down. If this story had made its way into the papers, he might have lost a lot of public good will. He was taking too many chances with that already. Then, there was a publisher's party for his autobiography, in New York, it was actually a couple of years later, but the timing was right, and that was where your parents met. Michael had been just waiting to meet someone suitable, and your mother certainly was.'

'I want to know more about that,' Bodhi said, but just then the old guy who had served us our food brought the bill over. I nodded to Bodhi; 'give the man the card I gave you.' Bodhi started searching his pockets, first the back, then the front. He couldn't seem to find it, or remember where he had stowed it.

'Is she gonna give me a Credit Card?' the old man asked, 'because we don't take them, you know.'

Bodhi found the card and looked round. His hair fell away from his face and he looked at the old man.

'No, he's going to give you a Debit Card,' I said, and the old guy mumbled something about long hair making it difficult for him, and that he had bad eyes anyway. He took our payment, and we went to the rest rooms and left the Diner.

Chapter 4.

Back on the road in our old red Chevrolet, I tried not to break wind too much. The window was open, and Bodhi didn't seem to be noticing anything too bad, so I settled back into my driving rhythm and relaxed. Bodhi was quiet. He had folded his arms across his chest as soon as I had turned the ignition, and had seemed to be holding himself in ever since. The freeway settled down into a gentle drone.

Eventually Bodhi unfolded his arms; 'How did my father meet my mother,' he asked.

I looked around at him. 'Honest truth is I don't really know,' I said. 'I'd been looking after your father's place in Regents Park, in London, with the place to myself while Michael and Louise were away in New York.'

'Louise was my father's P.A.?'

'Yes.'

'What were they doing there together, were they lovers?'

'God, no,' I said. 'They'd been there for the publication of some book about him, a biography full of photos. You've probably seen it.'

'No, I don't think so.'

'I remember the book because it had one of me in it, as a blur in the background as Michael was struggling through an airport somewhere being mobbed by fans. Anyway, they'd been there for a few days in New York, and meanwhile; there I was living in a multi-million pound flat in Regents Park...'

'Why was that such a big deal,' Bodhi asked.

'Because it was only four years earlier that I'd been living in a rough old hostel in Hackney, just a few miles down the road. It was bliss for me, I can tell you.'

'So, they met at a party...'

'And that's about all I know...the phone rang, Louise said; "Michael's met someone here and he wants to impress her, she's slim, sexy, she's maybe half Japanese, and he's really fallen for her. Can you get to the mansion in Warwick and set the house up for tomorrow, he wants to show it to her." I said; "No, Louise. I don't know how to," and she said; "Don't be stupid, its easy, just hire some cooks and waiters from the agency, the numbers' in the book and look after them when they arrive." I said to her; "Why don't you come back and do it yourself?" and that was when it all became a bit clearer...'

'What did?'

'What your mother would be like.'

'In what way,' Bodhi asked.

'Because it turned out that your mother had insisted that Louise stay in Manhattan and do some sightseeing, and not accompany Michael any further because, basically she and Mia had fallen out with one another straight away. I could sense that in Louise's voice as soon as she started telling me about it. They were just not compatible personalities; Louise was professional and prim, your mother on the other hand, she was rich, hot as molten lava—and she knew it—and not accustomed to being told what to do.'

'So you got a promotion, really,' Bodhi said.

'Well, I hadn't thought about it like that,' I said, 'but yes, I suppose I did. So, I set the house up as Louis had said, and a day later, in walks your mother into the grand hall at "Oak House", with Michael, both arm in arm in their dressing gowns, and Michael does indeed have a crazy goofy grin on his face, like he really has fallen madly in love with this girl. And she told me how her father is a financier from the richest part of Rhode Island, or your father did—I can't remember, but it certainly all made sense.'

'That was my mother then?'

'Yes.'

'If Louise didn't like her, did you like her? Would I like her?'

'You'd love her, I'm sure you would,' I said to Bodhi. 'As for me; well, that didn't matter one way or another. I'd gotten very used to seeing staff come and go, confusing the fact that they were close to Michael as meaning something more than it did. I was just staff, not your father's friend, and I was very happy to help him in any way I could. Liking or not liking your mother didn't come into it. Though, for sure she was bossy, but that was just her nature. Then...just behind them, after I'd met your mother, someone else walked in and your mother said; "Oh, this is Marcie, my twin sister."'

'They'd all travelled together?'

'Yes, they had,' I said. 'And straight away I could see that Marcelyn had a limp, and a crooked smile, and that she wouldn't say very much. And straight away I knew she and I were going to get along a lot better than your mother and me.'

'Although you're not getting along very well now,' Bodhi said.

'True, but I've told you why that is already.'

I looked over the freeway to yellow parched hills that rolled into the distance. Soon, I thought, there will be the outskirts of the city, and city life, and all that comes with it.

'And then they were happy together; my father and mother, for years and years,' Bodhi said, 'until...'

'Yes, you know the rest,' I said.

Bodhi sat quietly as fields of half human looking cacti came slowly into view; tall green succulents with sharp pointy leaves the length of your hand. Amongst them, almost in disrespect to their surroundings, dark metal see-saws pumped oil up out of the ground.

'What I want to know is, how did my father keep telling himself that falling in love, getting married, having children and all of that made sense? After what he had been through, how did he manage to convince himself that keeping on making meaningless music would help people,' Bodhi asked.

'What?' I said, taken by surprize.

'She was his wife, he loved her, you said so. I mean, I never knew my mother so I can't say I loved her. I'm sure she was very nice—well, apart from the fact that she tried to kill me—but I'll take it like you said; that she was very nice, until she was disturbed, unhappy, unbalanced even. But to my father, if he loved her, couldn't he see...'

'What?'

'Couldn't he see the need to let go?'

'Of what?'

'Of everything. After she died. To renounce his past, to stop doing what he still does; selling a lie in his songs; kidding people that everything is going to be alright, even when people die; that romance makes everything better, that it heals every hurt? I mean, he never remarried, so he must have learned something...'

'Listen, your father doesn't live like a monk, I can assure you of that, and never has.'

'So why can't I? I mean, why can't I not live like him? Why didn't I get that choice when I was growing up?'

I had to sit back in my seat and think about what Bodhi was saying.

'How did my father come to think that it had to be the way for me that it was for him in life? How could he give me no choice?'

'He gave you lots of choices,' I said, uncertainly.

'Then why did he make me marry Suzie Jones?' Bodhi said.

'He didn't make you...'

'He absolutely did, Shaun. And you helped him.'

'Look, I don't know about that, it was complicated,' I said, adjusting my grip on the steering wheel. 'Let me back track...the thing is, after that film got made, after it got shown on T.V., people started to make fun of your father. Did you know that?'

'No.'

'Well they did. There were jokers making jokes about him and they didn't care whether they hurt him or not. It was as though they thought Michael was fair game and they could mock him whenever they felt like it, even though they were still enjoying his concerts and buying his albums. It was unfair and it was painful, and it took a deep toll on your father. How would you like it,' I asked Bodhi, 'to have people make fun of you?'

He shook his head.

'You wouldn't. No one would, but he couldn't avoid it. Except in his head he had to avoid it, so he started drinking more and taking more and more of the pills that that evil bitch, Dr. Tzu supplied him with.'

Bodhi looked shocked, and I shrugged back at him.

'Shaun, you're making excuses for him.'

I huffed, tutted to myself and looked out of the windshield at the road ahead.

'Bodhi,' I said eventually, 'I'm not getting angry with you, because there are things I know that you don't; and as hard as its going to be for me to tell you, there are some things I need to let you know about yourself right now.'

It was Bodhi's turn to huff like the wind had been taken away from him.

'First of all; don't forget in all of this that after the documentary, when the children your father paid—or rather I paid—came to play with you, their parents were signing non-disclosure forms so that whatever they, or their children experienced at "Pleasurelands" remained secret. You might be amazed that any of them signed them, but they did because they wanted the money and Michael paid well. But the point is there were contracts in place—so when Michael decided he wanted only girls to be your friends, all I had to do was wait until the contracts expired and replace youngsters like Wayne and Pete with more girls.'

'So what, that's nothing new to me,' Bodhi said, 'Marcelyn said having other young men around David made him too aggressive.'

'Yes, it did.'

'And you remember how much unpleasantness there was at that party, with the kart racing in the Moto Dome...'

'Your sixteenth birthday, how can I forget it—I thought I was going to have to call the Police once David started kicking off. But anyway, it wasn't for that reason that Michael made me bring only girls to be around you. It was for a different reason altogether.'

Bodhi sat leaning on the dashboard, one forearm on the hot plastic, the other on his knee.

'You remember when your father converted the old funfair dome into a house for his Dinosaur collection?' I said.

'Yes, I helped Professor Schmidt put the hydraulics on his new Triceratops skeleton.'

'That's right. You'd grown out of the funfair by then, and you spent several months helping your father redesign it, and a good job you did with the dome too. But while Michael was bullying the Professor to set his prized new fossil up so it could shake its head from side to side— which he really didn't like having to do by the way—Dr. Tzu was running some tests on a sample of blood that she had managed to trick me into collecting from you.'

'Okay, but where's this going?' Bodhi said.

'You had slipped in the Dino dome and cut your hand, and Dr. Tzu had been at "Pleasurelands" for a check-up for Marcelyn. Somehow their conversation had got onto your development...like I say, you were sixteen at the time, and Dr. Tzu, unbeknownst to me had decided to test your D.N.A.'

'And how did that involve you?'

'I took her a sample of your blood for her... I had a hundred other things to do than try to work out what Dr. Tzu was scheming for. This was six years ago. She said she just wanted to make sure she knew what your blood type was, for her records and could I get her a sample; "even a bit from a cut on his hand would do," she said. I should have realised she knew full well you'd slipped and cut yourself only an hour before.' I glanced across to Bodhi; 'I hadn't realised that you were starting to be in real danger. I was off having a good time with Nathalie, my girlfriend...so I wasn't really thinking about it.'

'Okay?'

'So, some months later Michael called me into a meeting in Marcelyn's Office and I hadn't twigged at all that this was what it would be about.

'What was it about?'

'He was sitting behind Marcelyn's desk, with papers spread out in front of him. "Shut the door behind you," he said. Marcelyn was resting on the sofa by the side wall and Dr. Tzu was perched on the arm of a chair opposite. The blind over the window was pulled down for privacy, and the fluorescent tube above us was buzzing away. It was all a bit awkward. Then Michael picked up two of the papers and waved them at me; "What do you think you're doing taking blood samples from my son?" he said furiously. Obviously, I didn't know what he was talking about. "You got Bodhi's blood for her to test," he said, pointing at Dr. Tzu, and then she started trying to explain herself, saying; "Mr. Heywood, I only ran the tests on Bodhi's blood because Marcelyn was worried about his proper development, she told me to do them. You're both my patients and it's my job to look after you," or something like that. Then Marcelyn said she had been worried about you for a while, and when Michael asked her why she didn't say anything before, Marcelyn changed the subject and started talking about David having a difficult time, which didn't get much sympathy from your father; "Face it, David isn't a child anymore he's a grown man and he needs to stand on his own two feet," he said, to which your aunt replied that David had just been expelled from college for selling methamphetamine to some of his fellow students.'

'I thought he'd passed all of his exams early, that was what he said,' Bodhi said.

'Well he didn't, but he got away with staying on at "Pleasurelands" because your father was blind-sided by the results of the testing Dr. Tzu had done on you.'

'Which was what?'

'Very simply, Bodhi; Dr. Tzu said the blood results showed that you, Bodhi have both XX and XY chromosome pairs.' I looked to

Bodhi; 'Do you understand what that means,' I asked him. Bodhi went quiet and there was a long pause.

'I had to research this myself,' I said; 'When a man and a woman have a baby, the sperm adds either an X—female—or a Y—male—chromosome to the X in the egg. This determines the genetic sex of the embryo. During the first weeks of development, genetic male and female foetuses are anatomically indistinguishable, then, at around eight weeks of gestation, the embryo starts differentiating. But when there's both pairs of chromosomes that you have, it doesn't all go to plan and the baby ends up a little bit in between.'

'So what you're saying is; I'm a little bit in between?' Bodhi said.

I paused, to let the enormity of what I had just told Bodhi truly sink in.

'Then what David told me was true; that I am neither one thing nor another,' he said, staring at the road in front of us.

'What is true, is that you have the best of both worlds,' I said, putting my free hand on his shoulder. 'But, yes. Technically you are, what's called intersex; an hermaphrodite.'

Bodhi licked his lips and swallowed quietly.

'Your father said straight away that he hadn't wanted the tests done,' I said to Bodhi, 'and I was concerned about the question of consent too, because, obviously, no-one had asked you, and you were over sixteen years old then.'

Bodhi was quiet, and I couldn't blame him.

'To be honest, it explained a lot of things for me,' I said, 'unimportant things. But the question then was; should we let you know?'

'Why wouldn't you let me know?' Bodhi said.

'Because what didn't you already know? It was your body, you saw it every day; you washed it every day. It functioned for you perfectly well. In what sense was there a problem that you needed to know about?'

Bodhi nodded.

'Your father though wasn't able to able to make any sense of it at. He looked at a picture of your mother on the wall above Marcelyn's desk, he said it was ridiculous, because Mimi was all woman, and he was all man; "How can this happen?" He was speaking calmly, as though the logic of what had been said was too much to argue against, but then he leafed through the stack of papers on the desk in front of him, shook his head at one page after another until with a desperate weariness he buried his head in his hands and said; "I don't even know what half of this means." Dr. Tzu said she could run the tests again, but there didn't seem much point. Your father asked about the chances of contamination, but that seemed very unlikely. Or a mix up in the lab. Again; very unlikely. He had to accept what was being said, but he didn't want to. Or maybe his brain had been so messed around with by the drugs Dr. Tzu kept giving him that he actually couldn't accept what was being said. Anyway he went out to dance some energy off in his exercise room, and then he caught up with me later that afternoon and told to make sure you, Bodhi always had macho clothes to wear and a manly haircut.'

'Okay.'

'Though I guess we've let the haircut slip recently,' I said, smiling.

Bodhi smiled back.

'But then your father added something else. "From now on," he said to me; "I don't want you to hire any more young men as Bodhi's companions. Once their contracts expire, only hire girls, young women his age." I tried to remind him of all the work you had done in his Dino dome, and all the time you liked to spend outdoors, but he wasn't interested in negotiating, he just said; "I've got such a fucking headache. Don't question me, just hire girls. Just hire actresses, I have an idea." And that was that.'

We had reached the place of Joshua trees. They dotted the scrubland that ran along the freeway, making it seem bizarrely exotic by the side of mundane signs for the approaching town of Mojave. The traffic was heavier now, and more urgent.

'So, he told you to hire girls. But where did they come from?' Bodhi asked, 'and what was the deal with their weird names, like Diamond, Ruby and Emerald? They didn't have those names to start with, did they?'

'I got the girls from cheap talent managers. Proper agencies wouldn't work with me, I couldn't tell them exactly what the work would entail. I could tell them their clients would be working with Michael Michael, which made them very interested, because that was true, but I didn't know what they'd end up having to do. They had to be willing, that was about it, basically, and that wasn't good enough for proper agencies.'

'Why did you do all this?' Bodhi said, staring at me.

'I was starting to wonder,' I said. 'But Marcelyn wouldn't do it even though it was what Michael wanted because she said; "We'll end up having to deal with the sort of low-life's who promise girls in L.A. fame and fortune, and then hand them over to sweaty pornographers." She was used to finding dancers and backing singers; that she could do she said, but she wasn't going to deal with rip off agencies. So if I hadn't, you'd have been alone, and your home was starting to look more and more like a prison anyway. You wouldn't have been the first young person to be hidden away in a private prison in the wilderness.'

The fuel gauge was showing empty for one tank, and the other was low. We'd have to refuel in Mojave.

'Their names?'

'Your father insisted that the girls we employed used stage names. He said; "A lot of friendships are just a performance anyway," so he came up with the idea of calling them after jewels; "Bodhi's garland of jewels; his adornments; a precious necklace of even more precious stones...and wherever he goes in Pleasurelands day or night, he will have the finest, most gorgeous companions any young man could possibly want." That was his idea.'

'So that was how Suzie became Diamond...'

'And Leisha, with skin like mine, and sparkling eyes became Ruby. And Uliana, the Barbie doll from the Ukraine became Sapphire. And Trishna, with the lisp became Jet. And Kerry, with red hair and porcelain white skin became Emerald, which was suitable enough because she was Irish. And Aylya became Amber, and Daryl became Jade,' I said. 'But what made Michael the happiest was that we could give the girls contracts in their own right and not have to deal with parents anymore. He said; "Hal can draw it up. We can say that they can't bring their cell phones in, or computers or cameras. We can tell them that they can't make outside calls while on duty too; then I don't need to worry about non-disclosure agreements and security arrangements, and I don't need to worry about Bodhi being lonely. I'm glad I thought of this." I told Michael; "I can't make Bodhi call Suzie Diamond, you know," but Michael only cared that I called her Diamond. "You are going to do that, aren't you, Shaun?" he said. I hesitated, but eventually I gave in, and said; "yes", and he said; "good, because she won't object to it because she's signed the contract." And he looked as though he knew exactly what he was doing.'

'Is that why you gave in and agreed to do what Michael wanted? Because he looked like he knew what he was doing?' Bodhi said.

'You weren't a child by then,' I said back, 'you could have asked him yourself. You could have disagreed.'

'You called her Diamond, Shaun.'

'I said to you that if any of the girls you had were bothering you, you only had to tell me and I'd get rid of them.'

'I asked you why you were calling Suzie; Diamond. And you said to ask my father.'

'Yes.'

'So, I did,' Bodhi said. 'And you know what he said?'

'No.'

'He said; "Just because." And that was all I could get out of him. So, what was I supposed to do?' Bodhi said, shouting at me, 'I didn't want to get her into trouble, I didn't want to get you into trouble. So, I just went along with it. Like an idiot, like a fool.'

'I know,' I said, 'and I'm sorry. But they were helping you. You were still working in the Dino dome, planting Pitcher plants and Venus flytraps, and shit like that so Michael's dinosaur skeletons would look like they were roaming through your own Jurassic park...The girls were all agreeable, they wheeled barrows of soil between them, they poured buckets of water for you and they dug little holes for your plants, and they came with you around the grounds to find more plants when the old ones died, because it was too hot in the dome and there was no irrigation.' I looked at Bodhi; 'they weren't being cruel or unkind to you. You were nearly eighteen years old by then and you were surrounded by beautiful young women. In what sense was that something that I should have been worried about?'

We arrived in Mojave. I turned into a gas station and parked at a gas pump. Bodhi was looking at me with hostility, and I was upset by that. I couldn't find my wallet on me, so I took my shoulder bag into the store to pay. I must have been more distracted by my disagreement with Bodhi than I'd realised, because for some reason I stood at the wrong side of the queue. It was some ten drivers long and wound towards a little Vietnamese woman who stood by the till. I had started trying to find my wallet, when a sudden silence and stillness descended on the store, and made me freeze. In front of me a stocky fellow in fatigues fixed my eyes with his and reached his hand into his jacket pocket, pointing a small pyramid of his coat towards me. He thinks I'm reaching for a gun to hold up the store, I thought to myself. I slowly put my hands in full view, allowed my shoulder bag to close itself, looked at the line of folks staring back at me, and took my proper place in the queue. American men don't carry shoulder bags, I reminded myself. And they know which end of the queue to stand. And if you piss them off, they'll shoot you. And it doesn't help, being Black.

Just then the ground shook again. Customers looked nervously around at each other, and I was relieved—at least they weren't looking at me anymore.

Back at the pump, I filled up. Both tanks, because after I'd dropped off Bodhi in L.A. I was going to need to drive back to 'Pleasurelands'. Sure, I've pissed off Michael, I thought to myself, but Michael's not American, so that's alright.

'How far to L.A.?' Bodhi said.

'Ninety six miles,' I said, getting back in the truck.

'Is there going to be a big earthquake,' Bodhi asked.

'I don't know,' I said. 'I haven't heard anything, but who knows.'

We pulled out and headed onto Highway 14. There was a lot of traffic now, L.A. was sucking the life away from the mountains and the deserts, and we were pouring into it through its voracious tarmac orifices. I wound up my window, despite the heat, turning the fan on high. Bodhi wound his window up too. He was quiet, but we both knew there was no time for silence any more.

'You still didn't say anything when my father made me marry Diamond.'

'You're accusing me of letting that happen?'

'Yes.'

'She was pregnant, Bodhi. It seemed pretty reasonable. I could have done something, but why should I? I was thinking to myself; well, he can't have it both ways any more than Michael can. If he's going to sleep with a girl, he needs to be prepared to make it legal. And you know, the fact that Michael was willing to see you marry her, even though you were only, what; eighteen years old...that was a major moment in his life too. He's immensely rich, don't forget. He could have gone out of his way to keep you both apart. He could have defended you against her, but he didn't.'

'Why didn't he?' Bodhi said.

'Why would he? He was immensely proud of you, Bodhi. He thought he had every reason to be proud of you; I imagine he saw you there, as the prospective father, and he realised he could look at Marcelyn, and he could look at Dr. Tzu, and say to himself; "You were wrong, weren't you. I was right; Bodhi is indeed capable of being a man, he is indeed capable of becoming a father, even if he doesn't look entirely like a man. He's my son, and his own baby will be my grandchild, and Mia would be so proud and happy." So, when he found out he was overjoyed.'

I had to change lanes to overtake a long grey Lincoln with an elderly lady driver. Bodhi had remained suspiciously quiet.

'Are you going to tell me that the boy isn't your son?' I said.

'I don't know whether he's my son,' Bodhi sighed, 'he could be I suppose.'

'What does that mean,' I asked.

'Diamond used to fight the other girls way from me at night. She'd literally throw her hands around and slap off Ruby or Emerald. I got so tired, it was my house, or so I was told...I only wanted to sleep, but they'd fight and scream and shout and try to get on top of me, to sleep with me. I'd lie there, and usually Diamond won.'

I was trying hard not to laugh.

'It sounds funny, I suppose,' Bodhi said. 'But it wasn't. All of a sudden, there's a wedding, and I've got no choice; I have to marry her. There's a handful of cleaners and gardeners watching from the back of the hall in my house, while the Pastor does the ceremony. And Diamond's holding my hand, squeezing it whenever I'm supposed to say; "I do," or whatever it is, because I can hardly concentrate on what's happening. It's all so out of control its like I've got nothing to do with it, I don't even know the name of my wife anymore—but you think it's funny.'

'I'm only laughing a little bit,' I said. 'In two hours' time, you're going to have to fend for yourself. So you may as well know what you're up against.'

Bodhi wiped his face with both his hands and exhaled audibly. I shook my head and looked back to the road.

'He started crying,' I said, 'when he heard that Diamond was pregnant. I was standing beside him in his dressing room. There had been a costume designer's assistant fussing around with one of his sleeves when Dr. Tzu came in, and Diamond too. He had flapped her away, and then Dr. Tzu said; "Michael, I asked Shaun to gather everyone here, because this young lady has a very important announcement to make." And then Diamond made it, and your father said; "I'm so happy." He welled up, he put his hand to his eyes, and, with the silence Diamond and Dr. Tzu carefully left him for his emotions; he cried his eyes out. "This means so much to me," he blabbed; "My baby boy...Mia's baby boy." He gestured for Diamond to come closer to him; he hugged her waist as she stood beside him, and he put his hand on her abdomen; "My grandson," he said, and Diamond put her hand on top of his.'

'I get it,' Bodhi said, disdainfully.

'No you don't,' I said. 'It was so bloody corny I wanted to throw up. There was something staged about it and it was just plain wrong. Everything about Suzie; the way she related to you, the way she got on with Dr. Tzu...the whole thing set the hairs on the back of my neck on end. I knew there was something wrong, I just didn't know what. But then Ruby said something and I finally realised what it was.'

Bodhi looked surprized.

'I was clearing up after the girls in your house; discarded laundry and the like—it was only a bit more than a year ago, only a few days after the announcement—and then Ruby, who was laying on the couch in her underwear, said to me; "Don't you find it a bit strange, Shaun, that Diamond has managed to get pregnant, when Bodhi has had at least two girls sleeping in his room with him every night since we all got here? I mean, don't you think the other girls would notice?" And that was all it took really...'

'For what?'

'For me to realise that it was Michael who was being "played", not you. What did you have that was worth having? With all due respect...'

'I don't know what you mean?' Bodhi said.

'Michael has money. More money than he knows what to do with. But never enough money for what Suzie and Dr. Tzu, and half a dozen other people want to do with it. That was when I started to realise that you were in real danger. It was like I was waking up from a long sleep.'

On our right, more nodding donkeys marked the presence of oil fields in the distance. Oil was money too. Dirty and compelling.

'When you were getting married,' I said to Bodhi; 'Suzie was holding your hand, and yes, at appropriate moments I could see that she tugged at you gently, persuasively, until you looked around at her, and then she could touch your face or kiss you, and you, being polite would smile and seem as happy as she was herself. I wasn't blind to that. But then, why wouldn't she have been happy? She was now, apparently the bearer of the grandchild of the great Michael Michael, the bearer of the child who stood to inherit, through you, all that the Great Man had earned and accumulated through the course of a long and immensely successful international career, even as Michael himself was looking ever more gaunt, underweight and old at the same time. There was no reason for Suzie not to have been happy.'

'So, why didn't you help me then?' Bodhi said.

'To do what, Bodhi?' I said.

Bodhi stayed quiet. 'Then why didn't you tell my father?' he added.

'Again, what was I supposed to say to him? "Oh, Michael, you shouldn't trust Diamond, she's just after your money?" Everyone was after his money, he knew that.'

'So, you didn't do anything then? Dependable Shaun. Faithful, trusty Shaun.'

'Shut your mouth,' I said, slamming the steering wheel with the palm of my hand. I took a deep breath; 'I'm sorry. But you have no idea how much I owe your father,' I said. 'Didn't I tell you that this morning, as you were hiding in the scrubland at the edge of the property, pressing your face against the mesh of the fence your father built to keep the world out, begging me to help you leave?'

'I don't know anything about what you owe my father,' Bodhi said. 'It seems to me that he owes you.' He looked ahead on the road; 'Let me out here,' he said.

'We're not in L.A. yet,' I said, 'we're nowhere near Nicki's place.'

'I don't care where we are. We're somewhere, there's a rest stop ahead. Pull into it. Let me out. I'll start here.'

'Bodhi, don't,' I said, 'you don't know everything yet.'

'Why?' he said, 'because you haven't finished telling your stories? Tell them to somebody else. I know everything I need to know.'

And so I pulled into the truck stop on I-14, fifty miles or so outside L.A. and as I drew the Chevy to a halt, Bodhi threw the door open, grabbed the pathetic sack of possessions he had with him and leapt out.

'Bodhi, Bodhi, please! There's so much you don't know yet,' I shouted after him. I couldn't believe that he was going to run off, after everything we had been through. I leaned after him to try and catch his jeans as his legs shot out the door, but my seatbelt held me in place uselessly. I took it off and got out the truck myself. 'Come back!'

But he didn't. He ran off without a sideways glance.

I chased after him for twenty minutes, looking around the rest stop, knocking on the doors of trailer trucks, trying the Diner in the middle, shouting his name. But there was no trace of him. I figured he'd hitched a lift.

It was so abrupt. So painful.

Chapter 5.

'So Bodhi was off,' Hailey says, 'and I'm not that surprised, hearing everything you'd said to him. That was a lot for the young man to take in.'

She makes me lunch, and helps me eat. 'I don't think you need to worry about whether anything you said made him go wrong though,' she says, clearing up. 'You only told him the truth. It clearly wasn't your fault, anything that followed.'

She doesn't realise that wasn't the end of it though, and I tell her so; 'Hailey, I ended up in the Diner again with a cup of coffee, beating myself up for the fact that a journey that mattered so much to Bodhi had been left half done. I was exhausted and full of self-doubt. I wondered to myself what I was even doing, driving this young, immature man away from his home. But I couldn't help thinking that Bodhi must have really believed the reasons he'd given me for wanting to leave 'Pleasurelands' in the first place. After all, he was still welcome in Michael's house. He hadn't had to leave. He could have just as easily remained there and made everything good. But I couldn't dare say to myself, sitting in the Diner with my coffee, that I should have helped him remain there...'

I was sitting on a bench seat by the wall in the Diner. The sun was coming through the wide windows in the wall opposite me in three shafts that rode closer and closer towards me along the chequered vinyl floor. Time was passing quickly and I needed to keep a grip, there was so much at stake.

I settled myself down with a second lunchtime burger, fingering my way through my fries because I was only half interested in eating them. I was thinking about what I could possibly say to Michael when I got back. Should I say how difficult the circumstances were, when Bodhi had persuaded me to help him leave, earlier that very morning? Or should I say that there hadn't even been time for him to tell me the reasons properly?

I thought about what had happened, running through it in my head to try to get it to add up.

What had happened was that Bodhi had headed out alone into the north of the estate. It was where the Sagebrush and Cottonwood trees were growing wild, where there was Mountain Mahogany, Juniper and wilderness. He had reached the fence by the edge of the property, the fence with the cameras mounted on their posts that surveyed everything, and heard everything. I had known he was there because I'd been in the Security Office, scanning the output from those same cameras in order to find him. Once I'd seen him, his Orange silk trousers covered in snags and his green silk shirt sleeves dangling loose and self-consciously, I had left the room straight away.

I'd driven part of the way along the forestry roads towards him, then walked as fast as I could, following the distant sight for several minutes of someone else striding with determination in front of me. It had been Leisha. She had waded across the shallow river that flowed there, scampered up the dry bank ahead of me and forced her way, with her jacket as a shield over her shoulder, through the Sulphur Buckwheat and the Ponderosa Pine that hid the boundary fence from view. She'd peered closely at the ground with her bare legs still exposed, scanning to avoid being stung by poison ivy and poison oak, and as she'd picked her way through delicately, I'd come close enough to her to hear what she'd said as she reached him:

'Oh, for goodness sake, Bodhi. You're so dumb. You're walking out on the ridge? It's wilderness; there's old mine workings and all sorts, you could get yourself killed. And we wouldn't want that, would we?'

Bodhi had been sitting silently on a ridge of pink earth that rose into the cold early morning sunlight with his head in his hands.

'It would have taken me ages to find you, Bodhi, if I hadn't been told where you were by my friend in Security.'

That was when I learned how easily those boys would take a bribe.

'Just as well I found you too,' Leisha had continued; 'Last week I heard there was a Bear out here.'

Bodhi still hadn't moved from where he was sitting, in his posture of resignation.

'A mother Bear will tear you to pieces if you get between her and her cubs—what a way to go that would be—but everyone's looking for you right now. They might think you didn't have a good time last night with us in the club, if they don't find you soon. And that'd be ridiculous; because I mean you did, didn't you?'

I'd seen Bodhi shake his head without looking up.

'What? We had a great time last night? The car coming off the road and crashing—that didn't upset you did it? Because that was nothing.'

I caught up with them, noisily tripping over a loose clatter of stones. Leisha had turned quickly when she'd realised I was beside her.

'God, you must have been running,' she said to me; 'you're panting like a puppy.'

I sat next to Bodhi, and put my arm over his shoulder, as Leisha had kept talking; 'David and I just want you to have a good time, Bodhi,' she said, 'If there's somewhere you want to go again next time we all go out for the evening, just let us know; we can set it up, no problem.'

I told her to leave us alone, and after a moment of reluctance she'd stood up, brushing the dirt off her thigh.

'Thanks for everything yesterday, Shaun. Thanks for taking us to my brother's place in South Central; it was great to see DeMarco again. That was a great day. I'm going to go and let Michael know Bodhi's fine now.'

'No, no don't,' Bodhi had said, rising sharply. Leisha had looked confused. I'd shaken my head at her, urgently.

'Mmm, I'll just go then,' she'd said. And after a second or two's hesitation, she'd headed off in the direction she had come from.

'Do you not want to get some sleep, Bodhi?' I'd said to him. 'Last night was very tiring. You must be exhausted now.'

Bodhi, in his ridiculous dancing clothes had answered me. He had spoken though in a voice I had never heard from him before. It had been the voice of an adult. In it I could hear the ghost of a child shedding like a chrysalis, never, ever to be seen again;

'I'm tired, yes. But in some ways I feel more awake than I ever have, Shaun. More awake than at any time in my whole life. I can smell the oil in the spruce trees and the dry dust, burning in the sun. I can hear the insects twitch and stir, I can feel the breeze on my face; the same breeze blowing the long grasses around and the branches on the trees. I'm more alive than I've ever been before.'

'What does that mean?'

'It means I know why Ruby, or whatever her real name is...'

'Leisha,' I'd said.

'I know why Leisha came to find me.' Bodhi had paused until I'd looked at him; 'She doesn't care about whether I'm safe—she'd rather I was dead, and David too.'

'No. That's not true, Bodhi,' I'd said.

'Don't patronise me, Shaun. I understand now; my life is a mistake, there is no way around it.'

I had looked away from Bodhi, trying to change the subject; 'Where were you heading, Bodhi; when Leisha and I both tracked you down?'

'Away,' Bodhi had said; 'away. As far as I could go. Beyond the fence, beyond my little world.'

'Haven't you got a good life here,' I'd asked.

'Don't say that, Shaun. I'm living in a fantasy world.'

'There's Diamond, all the girls, your son, what more could you want?' I'd said.

'Look, Shaun; I've got to go, that's all there is to it.'

Bodhi had started striding away from me.I jogged the few paces to catch up with him;

'Wait Bodhi, wait. I guess these last six months or so have been difficult for you, but you can't just go. I mean, don't just walk away from me. Things can change for the better, you'd be surprised.'

There had been a desperation in Bodhi's voice; 'It's me that has to change, I have to change myself.'

As he'd spoken, there had been a grinding noise away from the ridge we'd been standing on, by the forest road across the river. We'd both turned our heads to face the source of it; it had been the sound of a vehicle slowing, starting again and then stopping. We'd hunkered down behind the ridge, hiding amongst a thicket of blossoming Manzanitas. It had been Michael, driving his special edition Hummer. David had been with him, following him around the back of the Gold coloured truck. We'd heard him working away on his uncle;

'So, Michael what I'm really saying is; Bodhi had a great time out with Suz' last night...with Diamond I mean, and I think these trips out are really cool, no big deal, and Bodhi's handling them fine, and...'

Michael had cut him off; 'And I thought you said Bodhi would be out here? I haven't seen him anywhere at all, and we're right out by the fence.'

Peering between branches I had seen David squirming and wriggling as he spoke. He'd been oiling his moves in front of a flustered looking Michael, who having cut short his sleep had still been dressed in his striped cotton pyjamas. Pyjamas, cowboy hat and boots, and sunglasses. It had been a combination of clothes that Michael was wearing as disordered as the day in front of us was going to end up being.

'Look, Ruby was near him,' David had said, 'she called me. They've probably made their way over to the nursery to see Stirling, or, I don't know, Diamond's been around maybe and they've left together. Anyway, everything's cool.' He'd paused to change the subject; 'And I mean, since I've got a chance to mention it...' Michael had been ignoring him, 'don't you think it's time Bodhi and Diamond got a place of their own outside "Pleasurelands" Michael? Because you know; I think that's what Bodhi wants.'

Beside me Bodhi had shaken his head.

'No I have not,' Michael had said, brushing David roughly aside. 'Get out of my way and don't interfere. Bodhi stays here, he lives here. He's my son and I know what's best for him; and you can mind your own business.'

'Sure thing, Michael. You bet, you bet,' David had said, surrendering with his hands.

Bodhi had tried to shuffle away from our perch. I'd pulled him down again and pressed my finger to his mouth to keep him quiet, but even though Michael was semi-deaf from years of stadium tours, he must have heard the noise we'd made;

'Bring me the shotgun from the boot, David. I thought I heard a Bear,' he'd said.

David had fumbled about in the back of the Hummer. He'd started unlocking the gun box I'd built for Michael. I knew how little time there'd be to think up a distraction for them both, before the gun would be ready in Michael's hands. Out of desperation I'd tried dialled Michael's number on my phone.

David had been taking his time with the locks, mumbling to Michael as Michael's phone had started to ring; 'Do we really have Bears?'

Miraculously I had managed to get a signal for my phone. I'd spoken to Michael in a stage whisper; 'Michael, just to let you know Bodhi's near the dome with the Ice rink inside. He's probably cooling down.'

Michael had span round, turning back towards his S.U.V.; 'He is? Are you sure?'

I'd reassured him, just as my tenuous network connection had failed.

'Good, I'll be there.' As he had jumped back into the driver's seat he'd called out to David; 'At last; some sense from someone. Get back in the Hummer, David.'

David had shut the trunk and had stared out over the undulating ground in front of him and across the ridge that shielded us. I guessed he had known we were hiding from him. He'd paused for long enough that I'd bristled uncomfortably with sweat. 'You really should think of another driver for Bodhi, Michael. Shaun's getting a bit past it I think,' David had said.

With the sound of doors closing and road dirt being kicked up, the Hummer had sped into the distance. I'd stretched out and lain on my back on the warming earth allowing it to dry my bones. I had been plenty tired and I could have stayed there and slept.

Bodhi had been staring into the sky; 'I've got to get away from this,' he'd said.

'Bodhi I don't understand,' I'd said, 'get away from what?'

'How can I say, so it makes any sense to you?' Bodhi sighed. 'Or to anyone?' He creased from the waist into a hunching squat; wrapped like a ball with his arms around his calves. 'What did my mum look like, when she died,' he asked; 'just before she jumped from the eighth floor of that hotel?'

'Bodhi, don't,' I'd said, 'not now.'

'I shouldn't be alive, Shaun, because David said she was carrying me in her arms. I think I understand now, it's all a mistake; I should have died there too.' Bodhi had uncoiled and stood up. He ran off, sliding, slipping and scrambling his way down the incline we'd been resting on, bending down to avoid the whips and thrashes of the low branches on the scrub Madrones.

I'd chased behind him but without a hope of catching him; he had been far too fast. Over the loose rocks of a stony outcrop he'd jumped and stumbled, balancing himself with his outstretched hands until at last, the ten foot fence had restricted him again. He'd squeezed his face against the tiny squares of open space between the linking wires. His fingers had grasped the mesh above his head and he'd looked up at the three taut lines of barbed razor wire that leaned out threateningly from above the fence into the land beyond. As I approached, my lungs heaving from the exercise, I'd seen the young man stretching himself out against the fence as though he were a recaptured slave, ready to be whipped for his audacity.

Turning his head from the cameras on top of the concrete posts, he had cried.

I gasped for air, bending forward and resting with my hands gripping my combat pants, watching as the sweat beads dripped from my nose onto the ground between my feet.

'How do I get past the fence, Shaun?' Bodhi had asked quietly, still crucifying himself against the unyielding barrier.

'Bodhi, the fence is watched day and night, the whole perimeter is, it has to be. You've got no idea how much hassle there'd be if it wasn't in place.'

'It keeps me in,' Bodhi had whispered.

'It keeps everyone else out,' I'd said.

'I've got to get away,' Bodhi had said; 'Please help me, Shaun. Please help me.'

'Bodhi, Bodhi; I've watched you grow up from a boy to be a fine young man. I love you like a son, like the son I've never had. I'll do anything for you, but please don't ask me to help you leave,' I'd said, but Bodhi had released his grip on the impassable hurdle and had walked, as fast as he could away from me.

'Then leave me alone.'

I'd followed him. 'You don't understand,' I said, 'I'm not your father. Michael is, and Michael pays my bills. He pays for everything and always has.' Bodhi didn't look at me. 'I just can't help you leave.'

'Then don't ever talk to me again,' Bodhi had said. The words flew at me like nails from a carpenters nail gun.

'Look me in the eyes, Bodhi,' I said; 'If I helped you leave, your dad would shoot me dead. Bang; that quick.' I was still chasing after him; 'You don't know how lucky you are, believe me. I'd cut my arm off to be in your shoes, at your age; surrounded by girls handpicked to do whatever you want them to...'

Bodhi stopped, turning to face me; his eyes drifting to the ground.

'Hey look,' I said; 'the girls at "Pleasurelands"—they've all had medicals, if that's what you're worried about. You're safe, have fun. Don't hold back, do whatever you want; anything.'

'Well, Shaun; you're not in my shoes.'

'Can't you get it while you can Bodhi, and lighten up?'

Bodhi had slowly straightened up, he looked relaxed and detached; 'How much time do you think we have, Shaun?' he said. 'We grow old like actors at the Oscars; we get sick like homeless people on Sunset Boulevard sleeping rough; we die, sometimes horribly like the man in Griffith Park. But there is more, even in the midst of chaos there can be serenity; I know because I've seen it, last night in Compton, but I don't know how to find it for myself. That is why I want to leave, and that is why you must help me.'

I tell Hailey that the waitress had topped up my coffee again; 'It'll be a dollar for any more top ups,' she'd said, and I had nodded.

'What was he talking about dead people for,' Hailey asks, 'your boy, when he said why he wanted to leave?'

'We'd had some trips out of "Pleasurelands",' I tell her, 'it must have been those, that Bodhi had been referring to.'

'They must have made an impression on him,' Hailey says.

'Yes, but we had never spoken about them together, so I couldn't have been sure. They were things I'd seen alongside him, that I had witnessed, that I had participated in; but the effect they had had on us, inside...they couldn't have been the same. There were four trips out of "Pleasurelands," the first one had been to the Oscars ceremony in Los Angeles...'

It was supposed to have been a trip to Los Angeles for Bodhi's twenty-first birthday, but he'd been so uninterested in celebrating that milestone in life himself that several months had passed by before I'd ended up organising it for him...and it just happened to be the Oscars' time. Michael was going to be there anyway to perform a medley of his hits in the middle of the show, so I'd figured it would work to go there, but Michael had still been reluctant to let us;

'The only thing that matters to me,' Michael had said, 'is that Bodhi is happy. That is all. For, so long as Bodhi is happy, then I am happy. But if Bodhi is not happy,' he said with menace, 'then I am not happy.' He had been stretching his neck against the back of a tall leather seat in his studio, twisting, exhaling and popping gristle. 'So make sure, Shaun, if you take him to the Oscars', that Bodhi is happy when he gets there, happy when he is there, and happy when he returns.'

'I will,' I'd said, and then I'd organised it.

Michael had a handful of complimentary tickets of course, so there'd been enough for Suzie, David and Leisha to attend the ceremony along with Bodhi. But then, before he'd travelled on ahead of us, Michael had insisted Bodhi have a chaperone, and so whether David and Suzie—or Diamond as we were calling her—had liked it or not, I had gone too, with my girlfriend Shanice.

We'd flown in on Michael's Gulfstream 550...a nice little plane. We'd landed at Bob Hope airport, north of Downtown L.A., and we'd been limo'd through Los Angeles to the Oscars venue at the Kodak Theater, right in the heart of Hollywood. There'd been Champagne flowing all the way, even while we'd been flying, so by the time we'd got there David and the girls had been a little bit drunk. Diamond in particular, as her new-born baby had been in the care of Marcelyn and her nursery staff back at the ranch, and she'd been free to play.

We had been seated in the theatre, and I'd started talking to the guy next to my girl and me. It had turned out Vince had been the producer for a movie nominated for Best Make-Up, or whatever, but he had been really interested to meet Bodhi, who had been sat one row behind us. He'd leant across and said to him; 'This must be a great moment for you, seeing your father on stage on such a magnificent occasion.'

'It's a real privilege,' Bodhi had said, 'I understand that...'

'You seem a bit uncertain, though...' Vince had said, waiting for a reply.

'I just, don't think I've ever seen so many old people before,' Bodhi eventually said.

This guy next to me had laughed. We'd been a long way from the stage, high up in the third tier of the balconies, but looking down on everyone, it had been true; there were a lot of grey haired heads on show.

'All the beautiful young stars are down near the front rows,' Vince had said, 'the rest of us get kept out of sight of the T.V. cameras.'

'Sorry, I didn't mean to be rude,' Bodhi said.

'No offence; you'll be old one day too,' Vince chuckled, with a huge grin. I smiled too, and as the show had gone live I had settled down to watch the evening unfold, thinking how lucky I was to be watching it. We'd cheered along with everyone else for the award winners, we'd watched Michael perform and then receive his second Oscar for Best Original Song, and we'd revelled in the attention that complete strangers paid us for no reason other than that we were there as Michael Michael's guests.

And then we had all got the flight back. Except that we hadn't, because David had ignored the rules and had started taking photographs with his iPhone, and then he'd refused to comply with the security guards because he was drunk, and had got himself arrested. So we, meaning Bodhi, Diamond, Shanice and I had had to leave him and Leisha, who we were calling Ruby, to find their own way back, while we had returned in Michael's jet.

The white leather seats had been hugging us as the city lights below glinted in the darkness, but Bodhi had gone quiet. I said to him; 'You know, if you're still thinking about what you were saying to Vince back there, the actors are always older than they look because the entertainment industry is very hard to break into.' He'd kept gazing outside, looking through his airplane window. I tried again; 'They spend their whole lives in the industry, like your dad, working their way up through the system...' I'd thought I was educating him. I said to him; 'For many of them, this one night of the year, at the Academy of Motion Pictures Annual Awards Ceremony; that's the culmination of their careers.' But Bodhi had been unmoved. He'd glanced at me, then had turned back to the window and the night sky. I heard him say finally, in a strained whisper;

'There were so many people with skin that looked like melting plastic, so many old women with lipstick sinking into their wrinkles.

There were so many smells everywhere; perfumes, sweat, stale food...it was revolting.'

'An evening like that would have an effect on anyone,' Hailey tells me, 'he was probably just tired, wasn't he?'

'I'm sure he was,' I say to her. 'And anyone else might say that Bodhi couldn't have been disturbed by suddenly encountering the fact of old age there anyway, because he must have encountered old people before, not least because I'm thirty years older than him myself—even though I am so good looking and youthful...' Hailey laughs. 'But there had been more to it than that, I'm sure of it.'

Yes, such an exaggerated effect it was that our first trip out had had on Bodhi that when David had proposed another trip out I hadn't wanted to agree to organise it. It had been only a month after the trip to the Oscars and it had seemed too soon. But Michael had had a photoshoot to do for a fashion magazine—Vogue or GQ or something, so he had been tied up and somehow David had managed to persuade him to let us use the Plane again. He had been reluctant, Michael had said to me, but he'd permitted it, because he trusted me. It would be a 'works night out', that was how David had billed it to him; we'd fly down to L.A. again and go to a music club on Sunset strip.

Charlie had helped me, to make the trip easier to handle. We'd taken all of the girls; Ruby, Emerald, Sapphire, Amber, Jade and Jet, as well as Bodhi and David, though Suzie, who we were calling Diamond hadn't fancied it, and neither for that matter had Shanice, so I had gone with them on my own.

I had ended up spending most of the evening sitting by the bar with my earplugs in, watching a couple of corny, make-up covered rock bands in the reflections on the bottles of spirits dangling opposite me. Bodhi's girls though had all had a good time—that was the main thing; drinking, laughing, chatting and dancing. Bodhi had seemed to as well.

Everything had been going great in fact, until Charlie, who had looked really out of place in the club had grabbed my shoulder suddenly; 'Bodhi just got pushed out of the club through the exit door by the Restrooms at the back, boss.'

At first I assumed the alarm would have gone off and the clubs 'Security' would have to deal with it. But then I'd realised it couldn't have done or I'd have heard it, or seen some movement. So then I'd thought; where the heck is Bodhi? I'd jumped up and pushed my way through the hordes of dancers to the dingy toilets, following my nose past the urine smells and sick to a red light above one door, then through a corridor with posters and fliers peeling off, towards an exit with a push bar. I'd forced my way out through the door. Pins and needles had been stabbing my forehead and I'd started thinking; how the hell am I going to explain this to Michael, if Bodhi goes missing? It had been dark and hot and noisy and I hadn't been able to breathe. I'd held the door open for myself but I felt like I was going to be sick. I bent down to let my head clear, but then the door slammed shut and I'd been trapped outside in the dark with just a sliver of light from the passageway to the street to illumine me.

I'd stepped away from the rusty exit door to recover, but I'd only stepped back a few feet before I stumbled and fell onto a pile of plastic sheeting that someone had stuffed between two overflowing wheelie bins. I'd jumped up, but then the sheeting had kept on moving. From the heap, an old woman had risen, shouting a jumble of disconnected words. They'd echoed off the tall walls surrounding us. She stank, and I'd flinched. Then she tried to grab me and I'd told her to get away from me, but there had been fingers missing on her hand. I'd pushed her away but then two other bodies had started rising like zombies from the ground too. They'd been as scary as hell—so I ran away. I'd run towards the car headlights streaking across the end of the alleyway, running until I had been back in the normality of the crowds on the Strip.

'Mental illness is a disease,' Hailey says, 'you've got to feel sorry for people like that.'

'The hospitals in L.A. dump people on the streets when their health insurance runs out,' I tell her. 'it shouldn't happen, but it does. I mean, where are these people supposed to go? There isn't anywhere, so they end up begging for food, and sleeping in rubbish piles.'

'What happened to the boy,' Hailey asks.

'Oh, he'd found his way back into the club himself,' I tell her.

I'd realised that as soon as I'd got back in myself. He'd been surrounded by Uliana and the rest of the girls, standing in the middle of a conversation being shouted over the beats—there'd been a D.J. playing. There'd been some young guys with drinks in their hands hanging around him by the edge of the stage, they were trying to get their hands on Trishna and Kerry, begging for attention. I'd left them to it, and bought myself a drink. A big one, and as I drank it I was wondering how Bodhi had ended up outside the club in the first place. It was a mystery.

And it had to remain a mystery, at least until we'd got out of the cars on the last leg of our journey back; 'Why did you go out the back of the club, Bodhi,' I asked him, 'you know; half way through the evening? I just wondered, because you had me worried there for a moment. Can you imagine what your father would say if anything bad had happened to you?'

Bodhi answered me while looking at his feet; 'Ruby and David told me there was a woman outside who'd known my mum before she married Michael,' he said, 'and she wanted to tell me about her. But when I'd gone through the door, it shut on me.'

Oh, God, I'd thought to myself. 'Bodhi, don't believe everything they say,' I'd said to him, 'you can't trust those two.'

'But if you won't tell me anything about my mum, Shaun, then who am I supposed to listen to?' Bodhi had said. 'Was she as ill as those old people hiding in the piles of rubbish?'

I paused. Maybe I should have said something straightaway, before he'd walked off and the moment had been lost. Maybe I should have asked him how he was doing...because of course; he'd seen the same things as I had outside the club, crazy old women and homeless folk. But he'd seemed to be coping with it okay in the car back to "Pleasurelands," so I'd just let it ride.

And he'd seemed to be coping with it okay in the days that had followed. Perhaps he was even growing up and maturing? How was I supposed to know, one way or the other?

So another month had passed and needless to say I hadn't spent it thinking about Bodhi. As it happens I'd mostly spent it wondering about how to deal with Ruby, or Leisha, because after she'd hooked up with David she seemed to think she could ignore anything the man signing off on her wages said to her, i.e.; me. And there'd been no easy answers to that one.

But then Michael had had another day of meetings to work through in L.A. and knowing that, Suzie (Diamond) had asked if she, Bodhi, and I could fly in too. Presumably Michael hadn't heard that much about the previous trip out—it had been in everyone else's interest to keep him sweet on it. So he had said yes.

We had landed at Santa Monica airport and been limo'd in to Lose Felis, to one of Michael's producers' houses. Lionel had owned a lovely place in a gated community not far from the Hollywood hills. We had had lunch, we'd messed about in Lionel's pool while he and Michael had talked, and then Bodhi and I had popped out to Griffith Park, to stretch our legs and catch a Frisbee or two.

We had wandered up to the old Zoo, where there were usually lots of people around, but it had been quiet. After a while the Frisbee had drifted from a throw I'd done. It had been a bit of a stupid throw, I'd been getting tired and it had almost been like I was throwing a ball for a dog and I'd just wanted the dog to disappear for a bit and leave me alone. But, yes it had drifted. Bodhi had gone to get it, it had gone over the edge of one of the ravines and had lodged itself in the undergrowth.

And that was when the screaming had started.

I hadn't see anything to do with it, but I had heard it. There'd been a man screaming from the old animal cages on the edge of the Zoo buildings. It had just sounded like some idiot letting off steam, so I'd ignored it. But an hour or so later, just as Bodhi and I had been walking out of the park, the Police presence became very obvious, and passers-by had been muttering something about someone getting killed.

I'd been concerned of course, but I'd thought to myself that Bodhi hadn't said a word, and we'd even kept playing with the Frisbee after the screaming had stopped, so it couldn't have had anything to do with him—but I should have known he'd know more about it than I had, even though he'd been as quiet as usual. Always so bloody quiet...

It had taken Suzie to tease it out of him later, when we'd got back to Lionel's. Fortunately Michael had still been tied up with business, but while Suzie had been showing me the best parts of Lionel's house, Bodhi had been sitting on his own in Lionel's garden. Eventually we'd caught up with him and she'd asked us both what kind of a time we'd had in the Park. I'd started to try and tell her, but then Bodhi had interrupted;

'There was blood everywhere,' he'd said; 'A man killed himself.'

'Oh, no,' Suzie had said; 'did you see him do it?'

'No. He was just lying on the floor of a cage, in a pool of bright red and black stuff.'

'Why didn't you tell me about it earlier?' I'd said.

'I didn't realise what had happened,' he'd said. 'It sounds stupid, but I hadn't put what I'd heard and seen into a story. I just heard what I heard, and I saw what I saw; the screams had ended; it was someone lying down; there was red stuff, and a long sharp looking piece of metal.'

The situation had been bad, and I'd thought to myself; I hope to God Michael doesn't hear about this, but then Bodhi had put the empty glass he'd been drinking from on the table and had walked back towards the house. 'You're coping with it very well,' I'd said, or something like that.

'What else are you supposed to do,' he'd said, 'when someone kills themselves...after that, what else are you supposed to do?'

'Yeah, that would be upsetting,' Hailey says. 'That sounds horrible. The poor boy. Do you think that's what pushed him over the edge?'

'Not sure,' I say to Hailey, 'but back at "Pleasurelands" Bodhi slowly went more or less catatonic. He became withdrawn. I'd noticed it, of course I had, but hey, I'd been busy, or preoccupied, not least because Shanice and I had been going through a tough patch, she was an old girlfriend...'

'Yes, you've had a lot of them,' Hailey mutters, thinking I can't hear her.

'Anyway, everyone else had had something better to do than think about helping Bodhi, but he'd had his wife, he'd had his son; he'd had his hobbies and he'd had his time to himself. Really, he'd had everything he could have wanted. He'd seemed okay, if not too happy, but he had seemed okay. So when David and Ruby had urged me to arrange another trip into L.A. to another club on Sunset strip, even though I hadn't wanted to, they'd been too energetic and too scheming for me to do anything about it. I'd lost control of them, and Suzie too...'

We drove there in two cars, Charlie and me driving so that the rest of them could party. Suzie had wanted us to fly—I guess it made her feel special. But we'd driven. That particular decision had been Bodhi's. He'd insisted on it.

The evening had been loud, raucous and much the same as before. But when it had been time to leave, we'd taken a detour at David's request. It had been to visit Ruby's parents in South Central L.A., or at least it was supposed to have been her parents place. It turned out to have been her brother's place. Anyway, it was late at night and it didn't seem like it was going to add that much to the travel time in the broad scheme of things, and since Bodhi could always have slept in the back of the car, it didn't seem like it was going to make all that much difference to him either.

After we'd got off the freeway we'd driven on slow roads past derelict rows of shops, blocks of cheap motels and doughnut parlours. Eventually we'd reached the side street we wanted and parked up. We'd scraped back the chain-link gates to enter the yard beside the yellow painted house that Ruby—that's Leisha of course—had told us her parents lived inside. It didn't look very friendly or family oriented, what with the bars over the windows, the loud music and the sweet smelling tobacco smoke drifting into the street, and my suspicions were raised straight away, but I gave her the benefit of the doubt. Next door there was a mission church; the spaces for the windows had been bricked in crudely and boarded over, rubbish was blowing around in tight circles in the yard. It was a rough area in a rundown neighbourhood.

The door had opened to us, but not by Ruby's parents. It was her brother DeMarco instead. He was younger than Ruby, in fact he barely looked old enough to have left school, and the tattooed and grimy friends inside looked young too. They made me feel old, anyway.

DeMarco had pulled me inside with big smiles and a man-hug. He had a gold tooth and gang tattoos on his knuckles.

'I've heard all about you bro' come on in,' he said. So in we went.

'Did something bad happen there?' Hailey asks. 'I get the sense you're going to tell me a horror story...'

'No, that's the thing,' I say to her, 'it was rowdy and aggressive, noisy and chaotic, and, okay there was a fight at one point and someone pulled a knife, but nothing actually happened, no one got hurt. It just hadn't been like anything Bodhi had ever seen.'

I can hear Hailey relaxing again back onto the sofa she's sitting on.

'We stayed there an hour or so, and then we got back in the cars and left. It had been an interesting end to the evening, it had been very tiring though.'

We'd driven back through the night. All had gone well until Charlie had missed his turn off from the Interstate. Then, an hour later, a few minutes after we had entered 'Pleasurelands' and the great gates had closed behind us, I had crashed the Mercedes SUV I'd been driving into a tree.

It had been a low speed crash. Everyone had been alright, Suzie (Diamond), Ruby, David and Bodhi; they'd all been fine, it had been just a slow slide and a bump. But because there was no phone signal we'd had to walk the last six miles in the dark. And at some point, in the early morning chill, Bodhi had disappeared.

It hadn't seemed a big deal. He'd known the routes back to the buildings better than   anyone. If anything, I'd only been annoyed that he hadn't led the way and saved us all the trouble of having to follow the winding entrance road for miles and miles instead of cutting off the twists and turns and going cross country. We could have shortened Michael's scenic detour by walking through the woods and across the fields, saving ourselves time and blisters. But Bodhi had disappeared.

'So the car crash was the fourth of the reasons Bodhi gave you for wanting to leave "Pleasurelands"?' Hailey says.

'No, not exactly,' I tell her. 'Bodhi had said; "in the midst of chaos, there can be serenity"...'

'And he had uttered those words when you had caught up with him. You'd looked on the security cameras, found out where he was, and gone to get him, but Ruby what-ever-her-name was had got there first...'

'Yes.'

'Then you had shooed her off, and the boy had said what he said...'

'Yes.'

'Then you had felt sorry for him, and had driven him away...'

'Yes...No, it was more complicated than that,' I say to Hailey:

We had split up, walking at different speeds on our way back from the car crash. Suzie and I had reached the maintenance buildings five miles along the six mile entrance road. She was muddy and fed up. That was when she'd said that if we'd flown in Michael's jet none of our difficulties that morning would have happened. She had tidied up her make-up and smoothed out the creases from the party dress she had still been wearing, and meanwhile I had phoned the Security Office.

Michael himself had driven up the last mile to meet us. He had been wearing the tightly drawn trench coat that Bodhi and I were to see him wearing later that morning, covering himself from neck to ankles against the cold. Suzie had got into the car straight away, Michael though had looked at me intensely, demanding I explain to him how we had come off the road; 'Shaun, what am I paying you for?' he'd said.

I had told him the road was icy, and sure enough, in October, in the foothills of the Sierras it wasn't unusual for snow to cover the hills and roads overnight. But Michael hadn't been happy about it;

'Where's Bodhi now,' he had asked.

'I haven't seen him for a while,' I had said.

'What about Diamond, has she seen him? Does she know where he is?'

'She doesn't know Michael. He's around somewhere,' I had said, pacing between the work benches.

'Did he bang his head,' Michael had asked, following me.

'No. He's fine,' I'd said. 'It was a bit of a shock for a moment, but then we just laughed, got over it and started walking.'

'I knew this was a bad idea,' Michael had said, glancing down at the floor of the workshop. 'Get in the car. I want you to find Bodhi. I want to make sure he's alright.'

As we left, David and Leisha had been making their way towards the maintenance buildings. I had told Michael that, but he had said that they could find their own way back, and had kept driving.

When we had got back, the first thing I had done was to go to the control room to scan the camera outputs. The first screen I had looked at was the one covering the maintenance building, I'd put the headphones on and toggled the volume switch to hear what Leisha and David had been saying after I'd left them.

I guess they hadn't realised the surveillance equipment extended to where they were;

'Shaun is so funny,' David had sniggered. 'I mean, what is it to him, all this business with Bodhi?'

'So he works for Michael, so what,' Leisha had asked, sarcastically.

'All the same, we'd better be careful, Leisha; you see, he's not on our side.' David had sneaked a peek down the length of Leisha's drooping blouse neck while she had been bending over putting her shoes back on.

'Oh, we can forget Shaun, he's got no guts,' Leisha had said.

'Yes, but last night Bodhi finally got to hear the whole story of how his mum tried to kill him when she killed herself. Things could really blow up soon!'

'That was really cruel of you, David,' Leisha had said, jokily, 'but okay, I'll go and find Bodhi, and I'll be super nice today if I bump into Shaun.'

I had growled at the image of Leisha and David on the screen, flinging the headphones down on the desk. I'd scanned the rest of the camera outputs and eventually I had seen where Bodhi was from the control room.

So, taking the old Chevrolet Pickup truck I'd used for maintenance tasks I had headed out onto the forestry roads myself, following them until I had disembarked and had tailed Leisha ahead of me on foot. After we had reached Bodhi, I had told Leisha to leave us. And after Michael and David had nearly caught us, after Bodhi had run away from me and I had chased him; after Bodhi had stopped and had told me his reasons for wanting to leave "Pleasurelands"...after all that, what Bodhi had said was this;

'Last night, Shaun, in Leisha's brother's house in Compton, in the midst of the chaos there; in the midst of the chairs getting thrown around and the glasses getting smashing on the floor, and people pulling knives; someone was standing completely still, unfazed, unmoved, un-shocked, unworried. And I thought to myself; that person knows something that I don't; that person has something that I need in my life. But I can't find it here, Shaun, and I never will. I can see a longing for it in everybody's eyes; a reaching out, from the heart wordlessly for something deeper than the surface appearance of things, a reaching out for love, or truth or wisdom—but when you're living without that; you're lost, there's just despair.'

He had put his hand on my shoulder; 'I have to go, Shaun. I have to find eyes that can shine out with that knowing, with that wisdom and with that love. I have to find it for myself.' He had paused, gently shaking my shoulder again until I'd looked at him, man to man; 'It was you standing there, Shaun, last night, in amongst the chaos,' he'd said.

Nearby a pair of Shrikes had disturbed the air with a flurry of wing beats, landing between Bodhi and me, and then departing rapidly. At a distance, Chickadees had called out to each other, flying together in acrobatic flocks.

Bodhi had put his hand down from my shoulder. There had been a silence that reached the very depths of my heart, and I couldn't have denied him. I didn't know how Bodhi could possibly have meant it had been me who had inspired him—that had made no sense, but despite that, I had agreed to help him;

'If it's really what you want,' I'd said, 'I will help you leave, but only because I love you.'

We had hugged, then I had told Bodhi to follow the fence and meet me as close as he could to the gates. Then I had trekked back along the dirt paths that wove through the outskirts of Michael's land, stopping to pick up the old red Chevy. From breaks in the cover of trees on the forestry roads I had seen the panels of Michael's domes shining in the distance, reflecting the sunlight, and the silver grey metal frames that supported them coming ever closer into view.

I had parked out of sight and had watched as bodies in the distance scurried between buildings, slamming car doors and running along the footpaths that joined the domes, frantically searching for Bodhi, and frantically searching for me. Then, as the central area quietened down I had started the red beast up and trundled it down one of the access roads, stopping only to pack a few things in an old bag and, then hopefully looking like one of the gardeners, I had headed towards the main gates in the Chevy.

I hadn't seen where Bodhi was when I had arrived there, and for a few minutes I had had to leave the Pickup by the side of the road and hide in the undergrowth that hid the estate from the view of the public road beyond. Each time the roar of an engine approached my heart had raced; how would I explain my presence there? What could I say I was doing with the old Pickup, when Bodhi was missing and Michael was worried sick? My life had flashed before me; my thirty years with Michael; all that we had been through. But the decision had been made, and I had known that the consequences would be unavoidable.

'Over here,' I had called to Bodhi, as I'd seen him emerging suddenly from the darkness of the tree cover. He had run over to the truck. 'Take off those clothes,' I had said to him, pointing to his orange and green silks, 'you'll need more sensible ones than the designer stuff Suzie buys you. Here's a pair of jeans and a T-shirt, there's more in this bag.' I had given him the rucksack of clothes and maps and money that I had put together for him, the best I had been able to find in so short a time. Even so poorly fitted out, I had figured Bodhi would have had enough kit to at least help him start out on his life away from "Pleasurelands". If he hadn't got far before I had had to pick him up again, that would have been okay; he would have been happy and Michael wouldn't have been too upset.

'Thank you, Shaun. You've always been like a father to me,' Bodhi had said. I had dumped his old clothes under the dense branches of an ancient Manzanita and had hauled myself into the Pickup's cab. Bodhi had leapt into the passenger side and with a pair of slamming doors and the rumble of a six litre engine, we had started driving the last three hundred yards to the gates.

'I've got so many questions for you, Shaun,' Bodhi had said. But I had told him to duck down below the dashboard, out of sight and wait until we had passed the final cameras and the gates had safely closed again behind us. Then, as we had headed along the public road, leaving 'Pleasurelands' behind, Bodhi had sat up and had started asking me the questions I have mentioned already, beginning with why I had given him his name.

'Are you sure you're not making this up?' Hailey says, 'because the four reasons you say your boy gave you for leaving Michael Michael's place sound just like the four reasons the Prince gave for leaving the palace, in the story of the Buddha. I remember that one from school.'

'That's just a story,' I tell her. 'This was for real. Besides, the story of Prince Siddhartha leaving the palace doesn't say anything about what happened immediately afterwards.'

'Nor have you,' Hailey says.

'But I will,' I tell her, 'I will.'

'Okay. Take your time though,' Hailey says, 'don't become agitated.' She daps my cheek with a paper towel and strokes the sweat from my forehead with her silky touch.

Relaxing my head against the vinyl neck support of my wheelchair, I remind Hailey that after Bodhi disappeared from the Chevy at the rest stop north of Los Angeles, I had taken my time to think in the Diner, and had eaten some more lunch...

Chapter 6.

The Eatery was busy. A couple across the walkway opposite me waddled towards the last empty seats and eased themselves down. Near the windows a waitress was hovering.

I was filling up four seats on my own as no one was going to sit next to me, and there were no other seats available. So I finished my milkshake, left a ten dollar tip and got up stiffly. With no less a sense of disappointment at the way Bodhi had disappeared, I headed back out into the afternoon sun.

I felt like throwing up. Partly it was from having eaten too much, partly from the belief, slowly crystallising that I was achieving nothing after all by driving Bodhi away from 'Pleasurelands.' My head was swimming. I needed to find a place to vomit. Two galvanised skips half concealed the back door of the restaurant, the rancid odours of old cooked food flowing out of their overstuffed bellies—I pushed my way between them to find some privacy. Bending over, I retched, spewing a stream of thin bile down the side of one of the skips. Between heaves a ketchup smeared pizza box toppled out of the furthest skip, falling towards the wall. Where it fell, to my intense surprise the figure of a young man revealed itself, crouching silently. As our eyes connected with each other I stood back up.

'Bodhi, is that you? Thank God you're still around,' I said to him, wiping the sick off my mouth.

'Are you okay?' Bodhi said.

'I'm better now.'

'Shouldn't you be heading back,' he asked, sitting casually against the base of the wall; 'Michael will be missing you.'

'I said I'd take you to L.A. Why don't you let me finish what I promised?' I said.

'Well, I guess I just need some more time to think,' Bodhi said, 'to make sense of everything.'

'I know you do, Bodhi,' I said, 'but you can think in the truck.' I beckoned him towards me. 'It's as good a place to think as anywhere. But I can't just leave you here. I won't disturb you if its quiet time you want.' He sighed, shook his head and threw his gaze heavenwards. Then standing up, he lent me his unresisting shoulder, and we walked. Shortly, we were by the old red beast itself. Bodhi threw his bag back in and climbed up to the cab. I was glad we were out of the sun even the though the cab was hot and smelled of plastic.

I was reaching to put the key in the ignition when, out of nowhere a deeply sun-tanned white man appeared at Bodhi's window; 'Hey guys, can I have a word?' he said, spitting out some gum.

Here's trouble, I thought to myself, but before I could say 'no' to him I could feel the hard twist of a metal gun barrel screwing against my neck behind me; 'Get out of the truck. Don't make a scene,' another man said. I tried to turn round, but a hand landed on my neck with rough, fat fingers and a strong persuasive grip. I took my hands from the steering wheel and felt my leg being pulled backwards towards the ground. I was dragged back through the driver's door which was now open again.

The heavy jawed bone head on the other side of the truck thrust his hand onto Bodhi's T-shirt neck, turning it into a knot to pull him with. 'Do as he tells you,' I said to him, as Bodhi tried, unsuccessfully to struggle.

'Get out the cab quietly and you both won't get hurt,' the voice behind me whispered hoarsely.

'You're making a big mistake,' I said to him.

The two men smelled like serious. We'd been taken by Pro's. They knew it, we knew it. Or I knew it anyway.

'Joel, thread the cable ties on your one. This brother's gonna behave and put his hands behind his back; isn't he. If he knows what's good for him.'

'Gotcha, Randy.'

I figured we were up against bounty hunters. Plain thieves wouldn't have used their names, and plain idiots wouldn't have held us up in public. Not that anyone noticed us. We were quiet. With a gun against my neck I wasn't going to shout. I put my hands behind my back and sure enough the cable ties strung my thumbs together tight enough I couldn't move my hands.

'Why are doing this guys?' I asked. 'I can pay you off; I know someone big...'

'Shut up and get in the back,' Randy said, taking my phone from my back pocket and pushing me away from our old Chevy towards the shiny white Ford F150 that I now realised was parked conveniently right beside us. 'I know who you are, so just keep your mouth shut.'

Bodhi had his hands tied in front of him. I guess they realised he was going to be no trouble. He climbed in obligingly, while I had to slide in bum first. The covered rear bed of the truck was a hard camper shell. There were rigid benches along both sides and pads everywhere. I felt like expensive cargo and I wasn't going to get bruised unless they wanted me to. At least Bodhi was safe from obvious harm, but where the hell were these guys going to take us. I was dripping with sweat.

Joel and Randy shut the tail gate and I could hear the lock turning. We weren't going to get out of this with guile that was clear.

'Shit, shit, shit,' I shouted, stamping my feet.

'What's happening?' Bodhi said.

'I don't know. But if we head north I'll bet we're going back to "Pleasurelands",' I said.

The truck started up and we swayed sideways on the benches as the speed increased harshly.

'Why would we be going back there?' Bodhi asked.

'Oh, grow up,' I said, losing my cool. 'You father thinks the world revolves around him, he's been living in Michael-land for a long time.'

'Don't tell me to grow up,' Bodhi shouted, kicking my leg and falling off his bench at the same time.

'Fucking Jesus,' I shouted, doubling up with pain.

'Fucking Jesus?' Bodhi said, to surprize me. 'Fucking Buddha you should be saying.' And then he kicked me again.

I shuffled down the bench I was squirming on. Bodhi got back onto his sideways seat.

'You think Michael's been living in Michael-land for a long time?' Bodhi said, 'Well let me tell you; I've been living in Michael-land for a long time too...and so have you. And the last thing I want to do is go back there.'

I banged my head backwards in frustration against the fibreglass shell we were captured inside, as the truck veered onto the freeway and through the dark shaded glass the signage pointed to I-5 north. 'We're going north,' I said out loud, to myself.

Bodhi stamped his feet on the bed of the truck, 'What the hell, in all honesty, are you doing keeping working for this man? I know he's my father, I know he's the most famous man in the world...whatever shit piece of logic that is. I know he pays your wages. But are you an idiot? Do you have no life of your own, no sense; no moral compass?' He looked at me with a glare so harsh I couldn't keep a stare at him. I was embarrassed and encouraged at the same time, for if he could stand his ground with me, well, maybe he'd be alright in Los Angeles after all. If I could still get him there, that was.

But would Michael have been able to get together bounty hunters this quick? I was wondering to myself. Joel and...what was his name? Randy—yes, it had to be Randy, a better pair of redneck names you couldn't come across. Or maybe that was a smokescreen. Maybe those weren't their names, they were just aliases; something to let them communicate with each other without giving anything away. Maybe they were kidnappers looking to win a ransom, like with Getty's son in the '70's. But hang-on, Getty didn't pay the ransom, so that never worked, and why would they take me too. God, Michael wouldn't pay a ransom for me that was for sure! They must be bounty hunters.

But how could they be bounty hunters? I wasn't a criminal, I wasn't on the run. Not from the law, anyway, and neither was Bodhi. You can't hire bounty hunters to do your dirty work. You can't hire bounty hunters at all—that's the point; there's a bounty on someone's head because they're running away from justice, so the county courts puts a bounty on someone to bring them to justice, and if you're feeling brave and needing the money enough you can go and find them and bring them for the courts to deal with.

But shit; Michael might not know how to hire a pair of guys like this, but David certainly would. Shit. And then again, you can hire anyone to do your dirty work, if they're up for it, and that's what this must be. But why I-5? We hadn't come down that way. Surely they weren't going to try to take us back to 'Pleasurelands' over the Tioga Pass?

'How can a person be a good person, but work for someone terrible?' Bodhi suddenly said, breaking me out of my thoughts. 'My father made me into a prisoner; he kept me in ignorance; he married me off to a girl I didn't care about. How could you have worked for him for so long?'

'Michael is not a terrible man, and anyway, you don't know anything about me,' I said.

'No, that's just the point; I know nothing about you, except that you've spent your whole life helping a man who only thinks of himself. How am I supposed to understand the world I'm walking into when I can't even understand you?'

It seemed ridiculous that Bodhi could say he knew nothing about me, but as we bounced over the uneven tarmac of the highway to...wherever, I slowly realised it was probably true. Yes, he had met my girlfriends and yes, he had seen me hiring and firing staff over the years, but had I ever been his friend? No, I hadn't. Had I ever opened up to him? No, I hadn't. It was a risk, but what had I got to lose—I figured I'd lost my job anyway from what I was doing.

'It was 1980 when I met your father for the first time,' I said. 'It was at a private warm-up show he was doing in London. He had a tour coming up and he had some new material and he wanted to preview it to a friendly audience. I didn't know that at the time, and it wouldn't have made any difference to me. It was ten years or so before you were even born, and I was younger then than you are now. Your father back then was the king. King already. He'd come on stage and sung such an amazing set that I was blissed out by the end of it. Completely lost in my own thoughts.'

Bodhi had gone quiet. I didn't know if he was listening, but he should have been.

'There were encores after the show, okay? They began and I was like a zombie on a mission. I went through a side door nobody was watching, away from the audience. I could hear the thumping of feet in the distance and the roar of the fans as I felt my way through the backstage corridors in the darkness. I could hear more doors opening, and excited voices whooping with each other and I followed them to the dressing room. It was open slightly and I eased inside. And then, just as your father and his bandmates were turning to see who the stranger was who was entering the room—and to probably tell me to fuck off—there was this flash of light, and Michael's jacket caught sparks from a lighter and just exploded into a sheet of flames.'

Bodhi was listening, I was sure of it.

'There was a split second before anyone moved; stunned silence. So I threw myself at him, slapping my hands down on the flames, smothering his body into my chest and arms until the flames were out.'

'Okay.'

'Okay. So, your father pushed me away in shock, swearing and looking into a big bright mirror, running his hands over himself, checking he was still okay.'

'Okay,' Bodhi said.

'"Get this kid out," someone shouted, but Michael wouldn't let them; "Leave him, you bunch of shits. You didn't do anything," he said, easing off a wig which just hung there in his hands; "this little one really saved my skin." Then he looked down and saw some raw scarlet rope burns lined up on my forearms and wrists...' I paused, for effect.

'What was that all about?' Bodhi said, rocking with the motion of the truck. 'Was that from putting out the fire?'

'That was just what Michael asked. He said; "God, what happened to you, pretty one?" but I pulled my arms away from him.'

'Pretty one?'

'Yes,' I said to Bodhi, 'I was young once too, okay? And I looked good.'

Bodhi snorted.

'I pulled my arms away from Michael because I was embarrassed by the wounds I had on them. I hadn't thought about them. I hadn't want Michael to see them, I'd forgotten I had them. I was embarrassed that he'd noticed them, and embarrassed I hadn't been more careful to disguise them.'

'How did you get them,' Bodhi asked.

I shook my head and smiled; 'You're so like your father. The same look on his face...Yeah, he wanted to know that too, but I couldn't say a thing. I was speechless. I was in the presence of an androgynous God, someone who to me shouldn't have been an ordinary human being, because he was an image from a T.V. screen. But now he could be smelled as well as heard because he was a real person; a real person responding to me, touching me, being in front of me, not just a moving picture.'

The truck was bouncing around on the road. We were too light a cargo for this monster truck. It was going to be a queasy, uncomfortable ride.

'Michael broke me out of my star-struck silence. He held my arms above my elbows and squared me up to him, bringing my face until it was inches away from his, whispering hypnotically with a broad smile; "Speak. To. Me!" He was kind. He made me feel at ease. Behind me the band were laughing and glasses were clinking...whiskey and cigarettes, you know, the usual thing, but then there was another smell coming through; a perfume, an aftershave. It was a distinctive one. It made me feel sick instantly. It made me tremble.'

'Tremble?'

'Yes.'

'What are you talking about, Shaun?'

I wondered to myself at the time; do I need to tell Bodhi all my memories to help him see his father in another light? How a softly masculine voice had whispered sarcastically; 'Mm, kinky…' from the corner of the dressing room, and I had instantly known who it would be? How I had knocked over a chrome and padded stool, spinning round and shaking myself free from Michael's gentle hold, lunging like a mad thing, tearing through the arms and legs that had instinctively sprung up like done toast to slow me down? How a guitar had crashed to the ground, discordantly screaming and scraping on the gritty floor, a bottle of Jack Daniels' toppling from the make-up strewn counter and smashing beside it?

He was sneering at me and the laughter had evaporated into annoyance. Stronger arms than my own had reached over my shoulder, restraining me and pushing me down to Michael's feet.

'I'd met him before.'

'Who?'

'The man wearing the perfume.'

He'd stopped sneering at me and had shrunk into a ball on top of the stool he was perching on, one hand thrust out towards me like a jousting pole. He had held his chin up defensively, looking sideways and flinching with his upturned lips clamped shut. I could see the end of his pony tail behind his shoulder as he tensed.

'What the fuck, boy, what's all this about,' Michael had asked.

'Who was he?' Bodhi said.

'Turned out it was Michael's manager. Anthony…something. Can't even remember his name now.'

Tears had rolled effortlessly down my cheeks, flicking onto Michael as I shook my head, fighting to break free from the hands holding me down. My heaving sobs had silenced the room. Michael called out and a woman had come in, kneeling awkwardly in her high heels beside me, her hand on my back.

'What was the big deal,' Bodhi asked, 'what did he have to do with the rope burns?'

'He said he just wanted to talk, Michael,' I'd said. 'He said he was lonely and shy and he said he played in a band and could get me tickets.'

'He raped me, Bodhi.'

'Michael, this is bullshit,' the man in the corner had said, standing up and kicking out at me. 'He said we could have a pizza,' I'd said to Michael, 'and that he only lived nearby.' But the memory of the night before had hurt too much and I had gone silent again. 'Then what,' Michael had asked, leaning down till his head was no higher than mine.

'He had drugged me, and the next thing I had known was; I'd woken up shackled to a chair facing a wall with my clothes off. The chair was too heavy for me to move, and my head was held in place, and I was gagged with a ball in my mouth.'

I had broken down into tears again, and in the space Anthony had said; 'Michael, don't listen to him.' But Michael had told me to go on.

'My arms were tied with rope at my elbows and my wrists to the chair, and it was itchy and rough and the knots were too tight. My legs were tied at the ankles and the knees.'

Bodhi was silent. The truck swayed and rattled as we moved over the cats eyes from one lane to the next.

'He's a fucking rent boy, Michael,' Anthony had said. 'I'm not,' I'd said to Michael.

Bodhi was searching for his words; 'why? I don't understand how...what were you doing?'

'I was homeless. I was sixteen. I had no money, my mum was in as insane asylum; my dad was a drinker. I sold keys...'

'What does that mean,' Michael had asked.

'I'd find square looking guys on the underground and I'd push past them. I wouldn't make any eye contact, I'd just brush past them and whisper; "Looking for some action?" that's all.'

'What have the keys got to do with it?'

'If I hooked them, I'd tell them where I'd meet them and then sell them a key. It was fifty quid a time, just for starters. If they wanted more, I'd tell them they'd pay later.'

Bodhi sat looking at me. I caught his gaze with quick glances of my own.

'Yeah, they'd pay later. See?' Anthony had said to Michael. 'But there would never be a later; that was the point!' I'd shouted. 'Once I had their money that was the last they would ever see of me!' I had pulled at my jeans and a couple of keys had fallen to the floor, skittering across the concrete.

'I gave this little shit a hundred and thirty quid,' Anthony had said, 'and it wasn't just for a key.'

'That's a lot of money for a bit of metal,' Michael had said to me.

'He only gave me thirty,' I'd said, 'but then he told me he'd get me more, but he had to find a cash machine, so I showed him where it was on the street outside.'

'And I gave you a hundred more, you little black shit.'

'Why didn't you just run,' Michael had asked me, still holding my hands.

'I was tired and I was hungry, and he looked like he was okay, and then we were going to get Pizza. But then he must have drugged it.'

Anthony had laughed; 'it was just a couple of "roofies", it was no big deal.'

'You gave him Rohypnol?' the girl by Michael's feet had said, outraged.

'Then he left me there,' I said to Bodhi, 'for three whole days.'

'Three days,' Bodhi said, 'how did you get free?'

'A friend called Luca found me. He'd smashed the door handle off the room I was in and untied me. Then I'd had a wash, got dressed and wandered out into Soho in a daze. It was only when I'd checked my pockets for some cash to buy a drink that I'd found the ticket for the show. I hadn't even thought about how I'd come to have it in my pocket, or who had given it to me, I just held it in my hand and went to the show.'

Michael had sat back on his stool, drawing in a deep breath; 'Anthony, you're a perverted piece of shit,' he'd said.

'He's just a little black tosser,' my torturer had said. 'Michael, lad, come on.'

'No, not "come on". You've gone too far. You're a sick bastard. Anyway, why did you give him a ticket for here? Did you think he liked it or something? Did you think he was going to come back for more? You could have killed him.'

'Oh, fuck off, Michael. They always have a get-out, they always do, this sort!'

'What did my father say,' Bodhi asked.

'He said; "Get out, Anthony. Do you think I'm going to have you manage me after this? You're done; leave now, and never contact me again." And that was that, Anthony stood up off his stool and shrugged his shoulders, pleading with his eyes. But Michael was adamant; "Out, that's it." he'd said, with an otherworldly calm. And so Anthony had left the dressing rooms, shouting, just to rub my nose in it; "He's not worth it, Michael. He's just a useless little arse-wipe!".'

The small crowd of onlookers had parted and the dressing room door had slammed shut behind him.

'What happened to your friend...Luca?'

'It was Luca who had got me into it in the first place. He was no friend. He saved me, I guess. But I didn't say a word to him, I just walked out in a daze.'

Bodhi thought about it. 'What happened then?'

'Michael asked me what my name was, and then said; "We'll make it better for you, Shaun." He whispered to the woman kneeling by his feet; "Get him sorted out, take him home, clean him up, whatever you have to do. I'll see you both tomorrow."'

'Who was she?'

'That was Louise, his Personal Assistant.'

'So, what...did she take you somewhere?'

'She took me back to her place. She had a small flat in Camden, with her boyfriend. I've got no idea how I got there, I was more or less delirious by then. But by the time I woke up the next day they were making breakfast. I'd slept on a fold out sofa in their living room. Louise pointed me to the shower, and her boyfriend found me some fresh clothes. I was still confused and sore, to be honest, but as soon as I'd eaten, Louise took me down the stairs to the street and opened her car for me. Her boyfriend kissed her goodbye and I could hear him ask her; "Are you sure you'll be alright?" because though I was skinny and young, I was still a little bit wild too.'

Bodhi smiled and suppressed a small laugh.

'We drove through Camden to Regents Park, and when we reached the middle of a big crescent of tall old houses, Louise reached over me for a permit in her glove compartment, and parked outside. She sat me down in the posh basement and left me to fill out my details on a form.

I'd looked at the ceiling of the office. It had been painted in a deep matt blue, and gold stars the size of the palm of my hand had been painstakingly added to it one by one.

'Funky, huh?' Michael had said, striding through the door, and I had shrunk back into the plush leather chair I had been given. 'There's no need to cower,' he had laughed.

'Your father introduced himself formally; "I am Michael Apollo Haywood," he said, "better known, for obvious reasons as Michael Michael." He asked me again who I was, and I said; "Shaun Milligan Adefumi."

'And why were you hanging around my dressing room last night?' he'd asked, smiling and raising a carefully plucked eyebrow at me. 'Don't go clamming up again, I'm only asking.'

'I just wanted to meet you,' I'd said.

Michael had nodded and sat down on the table in front of me, one leg spread over the papers I'd filled in, the other on the floor. 'So, what are we going to do with you?' he'd said, looking straight through me to the shelves of box files stored against the wall. 'Can you drive?' I'd shaken my head. 'Are you any good at cooking?' I'd shaken my head. He'd thought about what he was going to say for a moment. 'Well, I'm looking for a new bass player. I don't suppose you can pluck strings in order can you?' I'd shaken my head.

'Louise came back into the basement laughing. "What you could do with Michael, is a cleaner," she said, "this place is always in need of a freshening up, and Terry could use another pair of hands with maintenance."

'So Michael took you on as a cleaner,' Bodhi asked, with his face screwed up into a question mark.

'Yes.'

'Why?'

'Well, looking back, I guess Louise had warned Michael how easy it would be for me to sue him, and if the papers had found out what his manager had done to me it might have damaged his career for ever.'

Louise had picked up the form I had filled in, examining my answers. I had waited nervously for her judgement of me.

'Are you really sure you want to do this, Michael,' she'd asked.

'I think we'd probably better, all things considered,' he'd said to her.

Louise had pulled her glasses down her nose and spoken severely; 'Don't think for a moment that you can do what you like here. You may think that Mr. Haywood's house is a free for all, but I can assure you it isn't. The slightest sign of disorderliness and you'll be back where you came from. Got it?'

I'd nodded.

'Where did you live? You were still homeless?' Bodhi said.

'There was a small room in the roof space she said I could use. She said she'd pick up the few things I had from the hostel I'd been staying in and bring them back.

She'd paused, adjusting a hair clip that had held her long secretarial bob firmly in place. 'Do you have much stuff for me to load up?'

'Just some clothes in a bag under the bed and a few books,' I'd said.

'What sort of books,' Michael had asked.

'Just some books on religions,' I'd said.

Louise had looked at Michael, raising her eyebrows. 'Well, you're a surprizing one, aren't you,' she'd said, before adding; 'Don't go back to that room, you understand?'

I'd agreed, and the meeting was over.

'Okay, so my father's not all bad,' Bodhi said. 'But still, I've made my choice and I'm not going back. So how are we going to get out of this?'

'See if you can find something sharp or hard enough to break the plastic cable tie that's holding your thumbs together.'

Bodhi looked around, but there was nothing left exposed beneath the padding we were sitting on that would have worked.

'Try the eyelets on your shoes,' I said, grasping for some hope. Bodhi tried. He breathed heavily as he ran the plastic over his shoes again and again, gasping as the bouncing truck pushed him out of balance. He lifted his foot onto the bench seat and used his other foot to stabilise him. It seemed to work, for ease at least, but the rubbing did nothing. He gave up, leaning back against the shell of the cabin.

'So, Michael made you free?' he said.

'In a sense,' I said. 'He gave me a place to live, some work to do—even if it was only cleaning things to start with, but yes, he gave me work, a purpose, a second chance.'

'And instead he made me captive, and gave me anything but freedom.'

'People change, Bodhi. That's all I can think to say.'

'What made him change?'

I paused. Hadn't I told him already? 'Your mother's death,' I said.

'Don't tell me that,' Bodhi said, 'I don't believe it. My mother didn't just wake up one morning and decide to kill herself, did she...'

'No. No...'

'What had happened?'

The truck slowed, and whichever redneck it was driving sounded his horn, long and hard. We sped up suddenly, and Bodhi and I swayed violently from side to side. But I thought; hey, if we get into an accident any time, there might be a chance to escape. Bodhi and I settled back on our benches.

'Your mother was crazy to start with,' I said. 'Not crazy bananas, but crazy with life, energy, enthusiasm, call it what you want. She knew how to live more than most people ever do. I don't know if she was manic, but she was beautiful, and anyone with looks like hers has every door open to her. You couldn't blame her if she chose to go through too many doors, too quickly.'

'Keep going,' Bodhi said, trying to cut the plastic that bound him again.

'She saved Michael, just like he saved me. He'd have gone off the rails in not much time at all if she hadn't come along. Yes, she was hunting him down, I suppose, or if not him, then some other Superstar. She didn't need money, not her or her sister either, they were both rich anyway with a banker for a dad, so she cruised around where she fancied with her sister in tow. And wherever Marcelyn went there was sympathy, and wherever Mia went there was desire. It suited the both of them in some funny way. And of course there was the drugs; the heroin that they bought so easily from the dealers in Long Island who came over from New York.

'My mother was a drug addict?'

'No. Not exactly. She'd used it as a crutch. Marcelyn told me about it. There had been an affair at her school. She had fallen in love with her Chemistry teacher—the kind of thing that must happen in a thousand places. He hadn't been married so he'd seemed fair game, but she'd assumed he'd love her back as much as she loved him, and even though they'd stayed together for a few months...'

'It didn't work out like that,' Bodhi said, finishing my sentence.

'No, instead he got scared and told the school board, which was really stupid because they sacked him, and then he got arrested and sent to jail. They had to leave the school, both of them; Mia and Marcelyn.'

'That must have been difficult.'

'It was, it was very difficult Marcelyn said, because the word got around whatever new school they went to afterwards. And that was why she started playing with heroin...'

'She got off it though...'

'She did, she had enough money to try other things, and she had enough money to find herself a reliable supplier. Which is where Dr. Tzu came into her life.'

'Okay, so it was my mother who introduced Michael to Dr. Tzu? I though it had been Marcelyn,' Bodhi said.

'Oh no. It was your mother who pulled in Dr. Tzu to Michael's life. Michael had always got sick from traveling you see, and Mia told him that her little Chinese doctor could get him Melatonin, for the jet-lag, and that was how it started. But then Michael knew she'd get him other things as well; whatever he wanted, in fact. So Dr. Tzu became his Doctor and his best supplier, both in one. Which, if I'm honest was a bit of a relief for me.'

I could see the thoughts connecting slowly through the expressions on Bodhi's face; 'You mean to say that you had been doing that before her?'

'Don't be so shocked. I hadn't wanted to, but there was always something your father had wanted; a little bit of blow, an ounce of hash. He had had me living in his house, he knew I'd seen the streets enough to have some contacts. He used me, yes of course he did. And I used Luca. I knew I'd find him round the back of stations somewhere, under cardboard, or in front of shops sleeping rough. He did the business for me and Michael paid me well enough...it just made sense.'

'That's not good.'

'Don't judge me Bodhi. I hadn't wanted to, I didn't use the stuff myself. But what was I to do? These were the years when I worked for Terry or Sam or whoever it was doing the maintenance on Michael's properties. What do you think I was doing for the first few years? Michael didn't know me, he didn't care about me. He knew it was sensible for him to keep me on, but I wasn't spending time with him. I hardly ever saw him. I was cleaning things then I was mending things. I was nobody.'

Bodhi looked away. He raised his eyebrows to himself, but I could see him.

I thought about the first time Michael had asked me to buy coke for him; He'd been looking for a new bass player and when the auditions had finished he'd found me turning over the compost heap at the bottom of his garden. He'd strode across the grass to the London Plane trees hiding it, just as the light was fading.

'We're having a party tonight to celebrate my new band member, Shaun. The drinks and food are sorted, but I'm short of Coke. Could you get us some more Coke, Shaun?' He tapped the underneath of his nose twice; 'Go large though, got it?'

Michael had peeled several high denomination notes out of a new Adidas tracksuit, slapping them into my muddy hands with both of his. A twitch of discomfort must have flickered across my mouth, because Michael leapt on it;

'Have you got a problem with that,' he'd asked.

'No, Michael,' I hesitated, 'but do I have to?'

Bodhi was shaking his head to himself.

Michael had huffed in frustration; 'Yes, Shaun, you do have to do the things I ask you to do for me. And if you don't want to do them, then, basically you can crawl off and die; it's as simple as that.' I'd lowered my eyes, and Michael had sighed. He'd bent down before me, almost kneeling at my feet; 'Look at me,' I'd matched his glare with my own, 'work always means compromises, that's just the way it is. Not everything's going to be easy.'

'Okay.'

'So, like me, you do whatever you have to do, to help yourself. Okay, Shaun?' Michael had been holding my wrists and I'd felt very much under his control. 'I have to come up with a new act every couple of years—I was quite happy with rock music and long hair but the trends change and I'm the one who has to change them, that's my job. In your case, Shaun, your job is to do what I want; and if you have to go Buddha to do that, then go Buddha. Cross your legs and go into a Zen-like trance, seriously. It can help you, and you should, because you're on to a good thing here and you know it, so, go now and get me my Coke!'

I felt like Bodhi was avoiding my gaze. 'You don't know what it's like to be poor, Bodhi,' I said to him. 'You don't know what the relief is like when instead of that, you find yourself somewhere comfortable, somewhere safe, somewhere that pays. You don't know how far you'll go to protect that. Until someone pushes you, that is. Then—well, at the very least you're alive; walking the tightrope between what's right and what's practical. You haven't been there,' I said to him, 'I have. So don't judge me.'

'I'm not judging you. But now you're making it sound like my mother was the source of all the bad things my father ended up doing, whether you were involved in them or not.'

'No, but they were hand in glove, they fitted each other like cables in a port, the right way up first time, the right way round. They enabled each other. You can't imagine the love they had.'

'No, I can't,' Bodhi said. 'So what was it that made it like that for them?'

I shuffled around in the back of the truck, squeezing my face up close to the small tears in the black plastic covering on the shell's windows. Randy and Joel, or whichever automotive yard had fitted out their truck, had done a good job of concealment; you couldn't see out, but for the small tears, and I was sure you couldn't see in either. I rubbed the top of my head against the plastic coating in case it would crack more and wear off, but it didn't, so I had to settle for screwing my eyes up and trying to make sense of the tiny flashes of information I could gather from the road beyond. I knew where the sun was—but it was obvious we were travelling north anyway, so that didn't tell me much. The traffic was what I might have expected; it was a weekday in California, the central valley, vast swathes of farming space and not much else; so we hadn't turned off the Interstate, we weren't going to be taken to a dusty desert road and shot. Not yet anyway. There was nothing I could do without a phone in my pocket, and that was the one thing I didn't have.

'Shaun...'

'Okay...So, after the business on the tour coach and the girl from Chicago, your father needed to settle down. He'd had his nine lives, getting away with that. Just so you know, his guitarist eventually died from AIDS, and his other band members drifted away or moved on to their own projects. Nobody talked about what had happened, nobody told Louise, his P.A., nobody told his manager, who was Steve at the time. But your father knew he couldn't take the same kind of risks anymore. And that meant I got a pay rise, as it happens. But then, as I said, he met your mother at a party in New York, and they hit it off, and she came back to England with Marcelyn. Things did settle down. Michael was able to focus on his music, he had some of his biggest successes, one hit after another. He was a hit machine, and he was happy and stable. You couldn't have asked for any more from life. But there was only one thing, as Mia and Marcelyn followed him around from tour to tour—and I followed them around too, helping out—Mia kept getting pregnant, and Mia kept having miscarriages.'

'I would have had brothers and sisters...' Bodhi said.

'Yes you would. But that didn't happen, and there was an inevitability about it.'

We passed under a bridge, the shade strobing us.

'What do you mean, inevitability?'

'Look, your mother had started out a real wild child. She could dominate any room she walked into, she was a handful; she was authoritarian; if she was around you she was in charge. It would have taken some force of nature to tame Michael, but that's what she was. Let's face it, Michael could have had any girl he wanted to, so he wasn't going to put up with some boring madam. No, Mia was fun. But it wasn't without controversy, those two getting together, let me tell you...'

Bodhi laid down on the bench seat on his side facing me, I guess he was tired. He had every right to be. He was listening though.

'There was a big charity concert soon after your parents got together. It was a massive event and Michael was definitely invited. Everyone wanted him to play; other artists, Steve, his manager...Louise expected it. But Mia said no; 'Who wants to stand on stage with a bunch of losers for some dumb show where the money just gets given away to Africa, or somewhere stupid? Do you think my dad got rich doing charity stuff? No, of course he didn't. If you want money, you've got to make money. And when you've made piles of money; this is what it's like! Don't sell yourself short baby.' That's what she said to him, at least that's what I overheard. They were talking at a party they were holding on the evening of the day the concert happened. It was in their house, their mansion in Warwick. The same house I'd worked on years before with the maintenance manager, re-plastering, redecorating. Now there I was looking after guests. It was a step up for me.'

When the summer sun had started to set on the warm evening the entertainments had got into full sway on the terrace outside the ballroom. A fire-eater and his tattoo covered assistants had spewed bursts of flame into the still air, and the volume of the music on the dancefloor had grown. The heat and the rhythms had shaken clothing down to the thinnest of the dancer's layers, and the conversations in the quieter rooms had become more intimate.

'At about nine o'clock Michael and Mia had come down from their rooms upstairs and the usual crush of eager guests surged forward to meet them. Mia welcomed everyone, told them all they couldn't leave until the bar had been drunk dry—lots of cheers at that—then she told everyone to take off two items of clothing to get the party really started and led everyone outside to the pool. She stripped off; she was never shy, and on it went like that. Although the more nervous guests started to gather up their things and leave, because there were some ordinary people there like restauranteurs from the local town where Michael and Mia liked to eat without being disturbed, and managers from the staffing agencies that Louise had to keep getting more help from after Mia had bawled out the old ones and sacked them.'

The truck cabin was getting seriously hot in the sun. The dark blue plastic covered padding we were surrounded by stank of old foam and stale piss. Sweat was dripping down my face, but my hands, still tied fast behind my back were no help.

'Michael tried to follow Mia, but before he could get too far Steve had collared him; "I thought you said you needed time to rest, Michael? I thought you said this was your decision, not playing at Africa-aid?" he said, holding on to the loose sleeves of your father's silk shirt. "Oh, fuck off, Steve! Not now," Michael said, struggling to get away from him. I could see it clearly, I was standing a few feet behind them, minding my own business. "So, are you going to let yourself be bossed around by this little madam? She's half of your fucking age," Steve said, which was true. That must have pissed off your father because he peeled Steve's fingers off his shirt roughly, but Steve continued; "Michael, baby; you should know better than this. What's she doing making decisions for you?" "Don't push your luck, you fat piece of shit," Michael said, "This is my life, Steve, not yours. I'm not going to get ordered around by anyone, least of all you. If you can't see how much Mimi does for me; that's your problem." And then Steve wanted to know what it was that she did, blocking your father's path again. Steve said to him; "She's authoritarian, she's a wild-child, she's spoilt, she's undisciplined; and she's going to damage your career. I can't stand by and watch that happen, Michael; you mean too much to me." "What do you mean undisciplined?" Michael said. "She's teaching Marcelyn proper management skills, and she's doing a good job. Do you have any idea how difficult it is for Marcie, with her disabilities? But you wouldn't would you, because you don't care anyway." "I don't know about any of that," Steve said, "what I'm talking about is Mia crashing into thirteen parked cars in town and then just driving off, leaving Louise to deal with the consequences. Do you have any idea how much work it was for her to stop the owners dragging it all through the courts?"'

'My mother did that?' Bodhi said.

'She did, yes. Driving on the wrong side of the road. She just lost control for a bit,' I said. 'Anyway, the ballroom was more or less empty by now, just a few staff clearing away the last of the food from tables along the walls. In the distance Mia was shouting; "Come on, into the pool!" and jumping into the steaming water, and others were following her, sending up plumes of spray. So Michael and Steve were pretty much alone. "You don't get it do you?' Michael said calmly; "This girl is good for me, we can tell each other secrets and half-truths that we've had to hide from everyone else; the lies that we've told ourselves so many times that they seem harmless, even though they eat us up at night. Can you do that with anyone, Steve? Can you?" "I'm happy for you," Steve said, "all I'm saying is, don't lose your head. Okay, you're joyful and you're in love, but don't let those little nudges and dares that she sets you up with, no matter how wonderful they feel, make you exclude the other people around you that actually help you the most. I've seen it happen before; don't forget I've been in the business a long time, okay? It never ends well." "I know Steve, I know," Michael said. "I'll talk to Mimi, we'll straighten things out; it'll be alright."

'You've got a good memory,' Bodhi said.

'I'm making it up a bit, but the point is Mia was made for partying, she wasn't made for long touring. Unfortunately, they couldn't keep apart; and so he's doing massive shows in Brazil or South Africa or Malaysia or Australia, and she's there too, supporting him, standing by him...'

'Keeping track of him?' Bodhi said, fanning himself with his hands.

'Maybe, but he only wanted her anyway. It's just...it wasn't good for her.'

'How do you mean?'

'The miscarriages.'

'Oh, yeah.'

'I didn't know about them at first, not for a long time. I was still just a gopher, albeit that I'd been with him for a few years by this point. Anyway, things came to a head eventually. You see, Michael's decision not to take part in that big charity concert had made him seem aloof and arrogant to the press, and if you do that to them, there's always going to be trouble. That was when the rumours and innuendo about him and young girls started to appear in the entertainment pages, which wasn't easy for either of your parents to come across, not least because Mia was a full sixteen years younger than Michael—so they both knew that the rumours the press were spreading had an obvious foundation. They could swat the pressures away easily enough, for a while. They could holiday in the Caribbean; spend a week skiing or take a safari, but sooner or later Mia would lose her temper with someone, push away a journalist before they'd even finished their sentence and they were forever heading back to square one. She thought she had levers on everyone; sure, her father had big investments in publishing houses, but it still wasn't a good idea to treat people the way she did; it just ratcheted up the pressures on them both. She'd say to someone; "Your editor owes my father a favour, think about it," especially if she thought they were going to ask an intrusive question, but it didn't help. Neither Louise nor I were going to complain to Michael about Mia's behaviour—that wouldn't have been a good idea—and anyway Mia was always giving us little gifts; a beautiful jade necklace for Louise; a monks' bag from a Zen Abbot in San Francisco for me...other things as well, so in the end, no one around them could do anything to help, and Mia and Michael were heading into serious exhaustion on their own with no one to slow them down. They had months and endless months of travelling through unfamiliar countries with shows in new locations every night; they had the adrenaline of the performances, the exhaustion of the promotional events, the inevitable heavy partying; and all that took a serious toll. And even though they stayed together through all of it, they rowed often enough, and rowed with a passion and it all became public. The   fact was, Mia and Michael had reached a point in their lives where they couldn't keep away from the press, no matter how much they might have wanted to. And in the end they decided they absolutely had to.'

Another bridge cut the light from our fibreglass prison momentarily, then another, then a longer break as we dipped downhill before rising again. Did I know this piece of road? Were we outside Sacramento already? Surely not, why wold we have headed as far north as Sacramento? Shouldn't we have turned off I-5 before Fresno? Maybe we had and I was reading the road wrong? It was too hard to tell, but we might be hitting traffic soon, maybe there would be a chance to escape? I didn't know where we were.

'It was a momentous decision they took, in a townhouse in the West End. Michael, Mia and Marcelyn had just flown in from Geneva. They could have stayed at their house in Regents Park, but this place had been lent by the singer from some band, a friend of a friend, and it was less likely to be surrounded by photographers. It was small but very comfortable, and secure too, tucked away anonymously in a cul-de-sac off a road near Portland Place. Michael must have felt right at home. Anyway, Louise had settled them both in from their journey, and Marcelyn too. She'd intended to sleepover in a spare room herself, but a family phone call had come and she'd needed to leave. That wasn't a problem as I'd just driven them all back from the airport and I could cover for her.'

'This was in London?'

'Yes, London. Typical London rain was cascading onto the windows, droplets reflecting light from the apartments opposite. It was late, and I was preparing some supper for them all in the kitchenette. It was an open plan one and flowed out from the living room, so I could see Michael and Mia talking together—Marcelyn was resting already. Michael pulled the curtains. "Do you really want to listen to this, Mia?" he said, turning the radio down. Mia shrugged her shoulders and sat down on one end of a settee, wrapping her arms protectively around her waist and focussing her gaze somewhere in the distance. "I shouldn't have told you I was pregnant," she said, "but I was so excited that the baby was moving and kicking me." "And I was so happy to feel her, Mimi. It was a joy," Michael said, wrapping his own arms around your mother. "There was no way that we could have known that the umbilical cord was twisted around her neck."'

'Is that what happened?'

'Hold on, I'm getting there. Your mother choked back her tears; "I should have kept the whole pregnancy secret from you," she said. "I've let you down, again. She was kicking, and I wanted you so much to feel her, but she was kicking because she was suffocating, she was kicking out for help, she was drowning inside of me." "Please, Mimi," Michael said, as Mia moaned, kind of like a wounded dog; "God had a special purpose for her." "She was fully formed. She was beautiful, I wanted to give her to you so much. Why does this keep happening?" Mia said. She was really emotional, she was gasping for air. "Babe, its' such terrible bad luck; to lose three babies in three years. I hurt for you, you don't need to hurt for me," Michael said, "but we need to get you some more care, some more tests, I don't know what. There must be something the doctors haven't looked at?"'

'What was wrong with her,' Bodhi asked.

'I don't know,' I said, 'but I guess the one possibility the doctors hadn't looked at was Mia's past drug abuse, and that, perhaps was the true cause of your mother's desperation.'

'Why?'

'Because she knew there was nothing she could do about it. She couldn't turn the clock back, what was done was done. Anyway, that was when it all got a bit personal because Michael asked me what I would do, whether I would; "keep dragging Mia around from gig to gig killing our babies," or find her somewhere that she could settle down in; "and hatch our little chicks on her own?" I was trying to stay out of it, but by then, Michael trusted me. Mia said; "Michael don't. Don't drag Shaun into this, please. It's nothing to do with him." Your father flapped his arms in frustration; "you just don't need to come with me on tours, babe," he said, pleading. "Come to the studio; yes sure. But you've got to look after yourself better. I feel so wrung out, like the whole world is crashing down around me. You're not eating enough." "It's just bad luck," Mia said, shaking her arms at Michael as though she was in a conversation she didn't need to have. "Please take some time to yourself, Mimi," Michael said, "somewhere warm. Why don't we get you a place on the West Coast so you can bunker down for a while?" Your mother didn't say anything. Michael opened a curtain again and leant his forehead on the wet glass. It must have been cold, and I guessed he needed to cool himself down, but then he stepped back quickly, as though he'd noticed something in the street below. "Babe, you're strong and young, but even if your body can cope with it, any more miscarriages are going to really get you down," he said. Mia leant out from her seat and held Michael's hand loosely; "You belong here, Bubba, in England, it's your home and I don't want to be away from you, ever." "'I don't need to be here, Mimi, it doesn't matter where I live, I don't care. I just hate to be any place that isn't with you beside me.'"

Bodhi rubbed his forehead with his hands, tapping them against his damp hairline.

'I'm trying to show you how much they cared for each other, Bodhi.'

'Thank you, Shaun. But if we don't ever get out of this truck, then what you're telling me will all have been a waste of time.'

'Don't worry, Bodhi,' I said, 'I'm sure we'll get out of here somehow, just be patient and wait for the opportunity. Something will come up, it always does.'

I blew beads of sweat off my eyebrows with a puff.

'You know, it was that night that Michael and Mia decided to move to America. That was why I can never forget it because as soon as I'd secured my 'essential worker' visa, I joined them, and started a new life myself.'

Bodhi started rubbing at his cable tie again.

'Every moment of that evening was etched in my memory,' I said, but Bodhi was ignoring me.

I remembered; that just as Michael had finished talking with Mia the doorbell had rung, and my heart had sunk at the sound of giggling teenage voices outside on the street. Mia had sighed, and had headed off from the sofa to join Marcelyn. 'I'll be along soon, Mimi,' Michael had said, before telling me; 'You'd better go and see, Shaun; might be somebody important.' But of course he had known who it would be, he'd probably spotted them already out on the street. Even without seeing them I had known who it would be too.

The doorbell rang again just as I had reached the bottom of the stairs and had stepped towards the door to open it. Outside, three girls had stood. They'd straightened up and backed away a little, quite politely, as I had smiled a half smile and greeted them wearily.

'Could we say hello to Michael,' a slightly chubby one had asked, her pink streaked hair held in a scrunchie and looking bedraggled from the rain.

'He knows us, we're his biggest fans,' the taller one had said, excitedly bouncing on the pads of her thin cotton pumps.

'Michael is very tired girls,' I'd started, 'it's a really bad time. I don't know how you found your way here but...'

'Let them in, Shaun,' Michael had called down.. I knew he'd do that, I had wished he wouldn't, but he usually did. He couldn't say no to his fans.

'Take your shoes off,' I'd shouted at them, as they had rushed straight past me and up the stairs. I had taken up my station again in the kitchenette, part watching out for Michael, and part baby-sitting these three girls.

'What are you going to call your next album,' the chubby one had asked.

'What would you call it,' Michael had asked back.

'Black, White and Gold,' one girl had said.

'No; Kisses for Christine,' the taller one had said, and they had fallen about in screams and giggles, and I'd guessed the taller one was called Christine. I figured this could go on for hours, so I had leaned back on my barstool, resting my head on a cupboard.

The truck bounced particularly hard over an inconsistency in the road and Bodhi lost his balance, falling over sideways onto the foam padded bench.

'I wondered whether I could tell the story to Mia from the life of the Buddha of the young woman called Kissa,' I said, as Bodhi was distracted from his escape attempts, 'who asked the Buddha for medicine for her sick baby.'

Bodhi was indulging me, his eyes more or less saying; go on then, I'm not going anywhere.

'The Buddha could see straight away that the baby was actually dead, but he didn't want to break it to her harshly, because she was so very young. So, instead, he told her to bring him five mustard seeds, but only from a house where no one had ever died. Off she went, asking here and there, but ultimately being disappointed, until eventually she understood the reason why the Buddha had given her this task; death is part of life...That was what I had wanted to say to your mother, I'd thought it might have helped her.'

'Why didn't you?'

'Because of course the story didn't say what happened next. Did Kissa have another baby? Did she become a nun? Maybe she grew up and became a merchant's wife, had eight kids, found out her husband was cheating on her, and then killed him. Who knows, but then I figured Mia must have heard the story before anyway.'

'Why, did she know about Buddhism?'

'She knew about Zen, back when it was trendy. She'd spent some time with a Zen Master in San Francisco. Marcelyn too. She'd probably heard the story. She'd have thought I was pretty stupid telling her something she already knew so, no, I didn't want to risk it. She had a good line in humiliation, your mother. It was better for me to stay out of her way.'

'Why did she move back to America?'

'With your father?'

'Yes.'

'That was the compromise, it was the only way Michael could get your mother to stop following him around on tours. I guess she didn't feel comfortable staying on her own in London, or Warwick at the other house, or wherever. She had money, but she didn't fit in. Not in England.'

Bodhi lay down again, stretching his back with his hands arched above his head before relaxing and leaving them draped across his chest.

That wasn't the only reason though, I thought to myself. Just as it had really seemed Michael would spend hours entertaining his teenage admirers, there had been a horrible, upsetting cry from the bedrooms. It had been loud enough to silence the teenagers; it was an adult cry, the sort of cry that could have been a shard of glass in a hand or a broken dream. It was a woman wounded.

Michael immediately left the girls, and I took the opportunity to herd them towards the top of the stairs, grabbing their coats and bags as I did, bundling them together in the hope that they'd leave as easily as they had been able to enter.

Michael had reappeared briefly, his face ashen and distracted; 'Think you'd better go,' he'd said, giving each teenager a peck on the cheek and a hug.

'What is it? What's wrong,' the sensible looking girl had asked me.

'I haven't got a clue girls, but you know what these performer types are like, they're always hamming up the emotional stuff, so I shouldn't worry about it too much, okay?' I'd said, ushering the fan club down the stairs.

'Maybe we burst in on an orgy,' the chubby one had said to her friends; 'or maybe someone just got killed.' The other two laughed, and I joined them, laughing at the absurdity of it.

'Goodbye girls, take care in the rain.'

As calm in the house had settled again, back upstairs Michael had taken me by the shoulder and whispered from behind; 'Bloody hell Shaun; Marcelyns pregnant.'

It had been such a surprize—knowing Marcelyn as I did—that it took several moments for what Michael had said to register. Even then, I couldn't think what to say in reply. But Mia had saved me from having to try;

'It's so unfair,' she'd cried, rushing out of the bedrooms.

Michael had comforted her; 'Its okay, babe, its okay.'

'But just as my baby's gone, she has to have one herself,' Mia had said, bringing her shaking hands up to her face to hide her tears.

'Good for her. Let's hope she can carry it too,' Michael had said.

'But I don't want her to,' Mia had shouted. I was shrinking out of the way of them both.

Marcelyn meanwhile had hobbled out of the study, snatching a coat and umbrella before walking down the stairs. She'd mumbled to her sister; 'Sorry, sorry. My timing was awful,' as she headed out of the front door into the courtyard; 'I'll get a hotel for the night, Michael.'

Michael had ignored Marcelyn.'You do want Marcie's baby to be born healthy, you do really,' he had said to Mia.

'I don't,' Mia complained. 'She won't even say who's fathered it.'

Michael had hugged her closer to him, his arms clenching her tighter and tighter, until trembling and sobbing she had sagged into his embrace.

I'd stopped tidying things in the lounge and had headed back into the kitchenette to give them both some privacy. Michael had supported Mia to her room and I could hear him set her to bed.

As he had re-emerged the phone had rung in the hallway and he'd answered it abruptly. It had been Steve, his manager. Michael had trailed the cord behind him as he'd carried the telephone away.

I could hear Michael arguing; 'Steve were just not doing it, it's as simple as that.' He had slammed a door behind him. In the half privacy he'd given himself the odd word had still registered above the staccato murmurings. I'd gathered that Steve was trying to persuade Michael to do some interviews at the BBC. Mia had evidently overheard the conversation too, as she'd shouted; 'I can't believe that guy, doesn't he realise this isn't a good time?' I had busied myself with the last little tidying's in the borrowed lounge, then Michael had burst back in;

'That bloody guy. I tell you I've had it with him. He just doesn't give a shit about what I want. What is the point in having a manager who doesn't listen? All he says is; you live in this country you've got to pay your dues. Well fuck him, and fuck this country.'

Mia had come back out of her room, walking up to Michael slowly and placing her head on his shoulder.

'I'm fed up with being told what to do by him, Mia,' Michael had said, 'he isn't my dad he's my manager; he's supposed to do what I tell him to do. I need to be free for God's sake.'

Mia had signalled her empathy wordlessly, placing her hands around his arm, and as she'd done so Michael's anger had dissolved instantly. He'd paused, as though his line of thought had been cut off. Mia had smiled. She'd swept her hair back from her face and rubbed away the tears from her eyes with the heels of her hands, saving her make-up from smearing more than it already had.

The doorbell had rung again, and this time the sound of men's voices could be heard outside. I'd investigated, and to my dismay had discovered a group of leather jacketed paparazzi gathered, cameras in hand on the pavement;

'No, no photographs. Go away, you're not welcome,' I'd said.

'Just one, come on; we know Michael's here,' one had said.

'How,' I'd asked.

'She's a good girl; my daughter,' a scruffy guy in glasses had said.

'Michael, come on down will you, let us get a quick snap, that's all we're after. Michael!'

'Go home, he's not coming down. Get lost or I'll call the Police,' I'd said.

'We've got to get out of here,' I could hear Michael say to Mia, 'we're going to have to leave the country, there's just no other way. They'll follow us everywhere if we don't.'

'Your father had decided to get rid of his manager, Steve, and have your aunt Marcelyn take over as his manager,' I said to Bodhi , who turned his head towards me, while still laying down on his side of the truck. 'It was on the evening of the day they'd returned from

Geneva, although I didn't find out until the next morning. Louise had reappeared after spending time with her mum, who'd been having a panic attack for some reason, so between the two of us we were able to clear a way through the scrum of media people hanging around outside the flat, and bundle Mia and Michael into the Bentley. I drove us out, getting us away through London, through the greenbelt and the countryside, back to 'Oak House' in Warwick. It was a relief after all that high drama, to put my metaphorical chauffeur's hat back on and just drive.'

Marcelyn was making her own way to 'Oak House', something she could do because no one would recognise her. She could travel around England on her own, she had said, because people were only too happy help a disabled women with a glamorous American accent.

The truck slowed down, and for a moment I thought it might be worth throwing myself at the tailgate in the hope I could kick it open and we could jump out onto the freeway without being run over by cars behind us. But then we accelerated again and the chance was gone.

'So, I'm sitting in the Bentley,' I said to Bodhi, 'and behind the glass partition, which they hadn't asked me to shut, but which I more or less had, the conversation that the arrival of the paparazzi had sparked the previous night was still continuing. I could hear through the glass, the rising tones of Louise's incredulity and frustration as Michael outlined to her the plan that he and Mia had worked out through the long sleepless night they'd had. He had intended Louise to follow them to Los Angeles, but Louise said that Marcelyn, being only twenty four, or thereabouts, was far too young and inexperienced to be managing someone as famous as your father, to which Michael replied that she had been learning from him for years already and that she knew everything she needed to. Louise couldn't understand why your father was doing this, she said; "Are you trying to save money or something?" To which your mother said; "Don't be jealous! We're going to pay Marcie the same as Steve used to get," and your father added; "that way we keep the money in the family, which makes sense if you ask me." "Oh, God. That's just ridiculous," Louise said, sitting with her hand on her forehead; "Michael, Steve is good at his job, he's got years of contacts in the business," she said, but Mia said; "So has Michael, don't forget." "It's not the same," Louise said, exasperated.'

'Whatever happened to Louise,' Bodhi asked, 'I never met her did I?'

'No, you didn't, and that's just the point,' I said. 'Michael   told her; "If you join us in Los Angeles we can make a fresh start, it'll be great. It's a great climate, you'd get a tan. You'll love it," but Louise huffed in frustration and said; "Michael, I'm not going to Los Angeles. I mean, for God's sake; I'm married—I can't just say okay I'll move, just like that, I've got Peter to think about." She shook her head and gave it one last go; "I'm happy to keep working for you here in England, but you know, Marcelyn's only twenty-four...you've got to realise, Michael; if you seriously make her your manager instead of Steve, you're making a huge, huge mistake." After that it just went quiet in the car, and after we'd arrived at "Oak House" and I'd unloaded, Louise waited for me, then grabbed me into a big motherly hug, and said; "Shaun, you're a really nice guy, take good care of yourself and above all, be careful." Then she cleared her office, made the rest of her goodbyes, loaded her things into one of the estate's spare cars, and drove off back to London, out of Michael's life, and out of mine. And that was the last I ever saw of her.'

Chapter 7.

'So mum and dad moved to America,' Bodhi said, 'but they didn't move straight to "Pleasurelands" did they.'

'No, because "Pleasurelands" didn't exist back then,' I said. 'When they arrived in the U.S. they bought a place on the slopes of Laurel Canyon and the three of them set up home there. They were the three "M"s; Mia, Michael and Marcelyn. They were a team.'

'Where's Laurel Canyon?'

'In the Hollywood Hills, northwest of downtown L.A. It's a privileged neighbourhood—if I ever get you to Nicki's place, you can go and see it.'

'I'd like that,' Bodhi said, looking around the small prison we were in; 'We went to the place near Griffith Park, where we played with the Frisbee. To Lionel's place, in Los Felis. Was it anything like that?'

'It was, although your parents place was on a hilltop so it had great views down over the smog and the city in the distance as well. It was a nice area, very relaxed. There'd been hand painted "Peace" signs on trees and fences by the sides of the roads when we got there, it had been a hippy paradise in the sixties. But they were faded relics; sure enough the real estate values had shot up to the point where all of the old hippies were selling out to people with the kind of late eighties money your parents had.'

Bodhi nodded.

'As for the building itself, it was white concrete mainly,' I said, 'long terraces with rooms that flowed out into gardens, and gardens that flowed back into the rooms. It was the sort of place you could only do in

Los Angeles. They'd just come over from rainy England, so why wouldn't they want to make the most of the Californian sun.'

'It must have been really different for them both.'

'Yes it was, it was a time of great changes for them; in Marcelyn, your father had a new manager for his career instead of Steve, and in Konrad, who I told you about earlier, he had a newly hired manager for his house and diary.'

'Instead of Louise?'

'Yes, so that was all different. But at least there was one person Michael and Mia hadn't needed to replace...'

'And that was you,' Bodhi said.

'And that was me, because I'd decided to accept their offer to join them, made the few farewells I needed to, and took the flight over to LAX.'

Bodhi pushed dripping strands of wet hair out of his eyes and flicked beads of sweat off his brows with his fingers. Sunlight strobed over his bound hands through the slightest of gaps in the fibreglass canopy we were trapped inside. Sweat damp patches were darkening his t-shirt under both arms and he didn't smell so good. Though, I supposed, neither did I.

'I was asked to arrive a few days before Michael and Mia,' I said, 'to settle into my rooms and to give Konrad a chance to get to know me. He was a funny guy and I didn't like him much; very proper, very slim, immaculate, always wore a grey suit, never seemed to sweat. He was really in control of everything, especially himself. But he was good at what he did, and I never had to worry about anything. I was just there to do what he wanted me to, which was fine by me.'

'How old were you?'

'I don't know, about twenty three, twenty four.'

'That's very young isn't it, to travel across the world and start a new life?'

'I had my work permit. It was exciting,' I said, 'and it was exciting for Michael too I think. Because, at least for the first few days, until word got around that he was really living there, he was free; he could enjoy himself. I'd see him freewheeling downhill to the Canyon store to buy cigarettes and whiskey, and then pushing his bike back up in front of him on the way back. And he'd have spotted the homes of some of the neighbourhoods other celebrities as he explored the winding roads; Carol King's place on the left, Michael J. Fox on the right. But of course, before too long people recognized him on his bike, and then they'd stand gobsmacked on the sidewalk waving to him, or worse than that; leaning out of their cars and shouting after him.'

'Why?'

'He was Michael Michael, that's why, and his fame meant more in L.A. than anywhere else on earth.'

Bodhi sat hunched on his bench seat, rocking from side to side with the truck as the gear changes shuddered and the truck rode slightly uphill on the freeway.

'So, your father had to remind himself how to drive on the right hand side of the road,' I said, 'and once he had, he'd take an anonymous looking S.U.V. out in the early afternoons and travel wherever he wanted to—recording studios in Brentwood or West Hollywood, short drives to 'The Village' for a jam session, or Paramount for some serious recording time, or to a private bar somewhere. At least, that was what I picked up on.'

'What about my mum,' Bodhi asked.

'She was okay. I'd to drive her around to places. She'd sit on her own in the back of the Bentley. She could have sat up at the front, we could have talked; it would have been friendlier. But maybe that was the point; she didn't want to be friendly anymore, certainly not with me, and anyway, if you're in a grand car and it looks like you've got a chauffeur, I guess you might as well play along with it. So, no, she sat in the back stony faced.'

'Where would you take her?'

'She had a few close friends, I'd take her there. Tania Visconti was one of them, she lived out in Malibu; Colony road, or movie star mile as they call it. We'd cross the 405, she'd have coffee in her beach front house and they'd watch the gulls fly by together, or watch the waves roll in and hear the surf crashing down. Your mother would tell me to leave her and pick her up later in the evening. I'd go out to the coast myself and watch the world go by. Or other times there'd be errands.'

'Where else?'

'I'd take her to her medical appointments, and I'd take her on her shopping trips of course.'

'What did she shop for?'

'To start with it was everything wedding related, because this was when your father had proposed to your mother, and your folks were preparing to get married. I'd take Mia to "Nelson's", on Wilshire Boulevard. There were fittings for her wedding dress. It was a frock shop, but your mum would call it what Mr. Nelson himself did; a "Couture Bridal Atelier." She'd go with your aunt, Marcelyn. I'd help Marcelyn in, because she was pregnant with David still, and that meant she'd stopped using her meds and she was even more unstable on her feet than usual, and using a crutch...well, she really didn't like to use a crutch so she'd hold my arm instead.'

'And, mum was happy?' Bodhi said.

'Yes, I suppose she was. I mean, why shouldn't she have been, she was in a place she knew well, she was getting married to the most famous man in the world, they had no end of money. Why shouldn't she have been happy?'

'It doesn't always work like that,' Bodhi said.

'No.'

'And I was born, what, a year later?'

'Nearly two.'

'So what happened in those two years?' Bodhi said. 'What went wrong? What led her to do what she did, with me, just a few weeks after I was born? Did she hate what I am so much that she just looked at me and felt sick?'

'No, Bodhi, no. You looked just fine as a baby. No one said anything. You looked normal.'

'To you maybe, but she must have known, she must have suspected, she was my mother.'

'She never said anything. I would have heard, or I would have picked up on something. But there was nothing said, not by her to Marcelyn or to Michael, there were no strange silences at inappropriate times, there was nothing in the air. Your parents were overjoyed you'd been born. That was all.'

'Until all of a sudden she jumped off a balcony with me...'

The air in the flatbed of the truck was close and claustrophobic, but even if it had been as cool and fresh as mountain air, I would still have preferred to have had us crash, than to have to tell Bodhi what had happened on the day of his parents wedding. But he had left me with no choice;

'Of course there were things that happened,' I said.

Bodhi sat staring at me impatiently.

'It was a big high pressure wedding your parents had. It wasn't like yours, with the cleaners and the gardeners sitting there listening to a country bumpkin pastor. It was the social event of the year, it was the entertainment industry's social event of the year. Anyone who was anyone was there, they had been fighting for an invite. You know, your aunt made the invitations for your parents, she handled it. I heard her talking with your father, she was having lunch on one of the terraces of the mansion in Laurel Canyon.'

The road noise was increasing and I had to speak up for Bodhi to hear me.

'"Its only self-preservation really Michael," Marcelyn said to him. "You never know who'll be big next year, so we've got to make sure we don't make enemies. If they know they're not going to be invited they can arrange something else for the day in advance; that way they don't lose face," that was her way of dealing with lesser celebrities. She took a lot of care.'

Marcelyn had left her office on the mid level of the house and had been having a light lunch on the terrace by the swimming pool. Michael had been shaved and dressed in a very loose white shirt and tight blue shorts, but he hadn't been ready to eat yet, as his day had just been beginning.

'He wanted the heads of the recording labels there,' I said to Bodhi, 'he wanted them to compete for a new recording contract with him, his old one had run its course—five albums I think he said, and now they had to re-sign him. And that of course is where the money came from to build "Pleasurelands," because they wanted him. They all did, and they paid, because they knew he'd make much more money for them, than they'd have to pay to him.'

Bodhi swayed gently with the rhythm of the truck, his shoulders resting against the fibreglass shell.

'Michael invited the President,' I said. 'The President of the United States of America. At least he wanted to. Marcelyn thought he was joking, she'd already told him the Governor of California couldn't come because he had a prior engagement. She was sitting there picking about at a green salad and laughing at him. But he wasn't joking; "I performed for him and the first lady at a Press association event a few months back, we had a chat offstage. I'm sure he'd appreciate an invite, even if he's too busy," he said.'

'Did she send him one,' Bodhi asked.

'I don't know, I suppose so. He didn't come obviously, and neither did any of the royal family that he invited. Marcelyn was laughing at him again saying; "do you want me to invite the Queen?" She was being sarcastic, but your father was straight faced, he said; "no, that would be rude, she definitely won't come. But you could ask a couple of Prince's, maybe a Princess?"'

'Did any of them come?'

'There were a couple of minor royals, but it was Hollywood royalty mainly that came, every famous face you could think of. Konrad had us all working frantically to get ready for it, cleaning everything he could think of, cars, clothes, furniture. It did seem a bit pointless because the venue for the wedding and the reception was the Greyfriars Mansion estate in the Holmby hills, and they had their own staff. Still, there were deliveries of gifts for the guests to book in securely; Swiss watches and so forth, and they all needed locking away in safety deposit boxes, so there was plenty to do.'

'Did something happen at the wedding,' Bodhi asked. 'Did something go really wrong?'

'No, it wasn't that,' I said. 'It was great day, a beautiful occasion, I can see it now.'

The guests were checked in by private security guards at the entrance gates, they drove up the hill to a parking area on the same level as the mansion. There was a short walk for them through generously watered grounds along a wide path bordered by bright, fragrant flowerbeds. Then there was an avenue of slim Cypress trees leading to a sparkling rectangular lily pond that mirrored the cloudless Los Angeles sky, and beyond that there was the grand medieval style building itself. From its honey coloured stone, a large lawn of emerald velour flowed on, sweeping the eye towards the majestic view of Century City below.

'Two hundred of Michael and Mia's guests, family and friends were there. They had drinks and finger food in the courtyard of the mansion while the lawn was prepared with rows of white chairs lined up precisely, and an alfresco altar for the wedding ceremony to take place in front of. Your mother looked sublime for the exchanging of vows; she was wearing flowers in her hair and the broadest of smiles, along with her spectacular dress. Her father was in his morning suit, his silver hair combed over the bald but dignified crown of his head. He led her between the chairs towards the minister in front of his altar, and as he did so her dress spread itself dramatically along the manicured lawn. And cameras clicking hungrily all the while.'

'Did they say anything to each, as they were standing there in front of everyone, by the minister?'

'God, how should I know? I wasn't anywhere near them, I was standing with the waiters and the drivers and the other non-speaking extras you get so many of in L.A. My very presence was hidden by the layout of the gardens; I couldn't see a thing. It was all I could do to hear the ooh's and aah's of the gathered guests as the happy couple kissed. But that was all.'

I tested the strength of the cable ties around my thumbs again. They were still tight, but the twisting at least restored some more circulation.

'The day passed by so quickly; the ceremonies were finished, the photographs were taken and the formalities of the speeches came and went. The guests relaxed afterwards in the afternoon sunlight, and the Champagne flowed. The wedding band played covers of anyone but Michael's hits for everyone to dance to, then the night sky darkened; the fireworks following the band flashed and banged, and folk made their polite excuses and prepared to leave, heading off to enjoy the hotel rooms in Malibu and Bel-Air that had been pre-booked for them.'

I started wondering whether Bodhi would be able to cut my cable ties if I sat in front of him and held my arms where he needed them. But he'd need a sharp something and I just couldn't think of anything.

'It was late in the evening when I got word to find Michael and help him. He was outside a restroom in the lower ground floor of the Mansion. He was with his father—your grandfather,' I said to Bodhi, 'and I'd never met him before, not once, though I'd seen a few old pictures.'

'What was he like?'

'He was old. Maybe eighty. He had grey hair, though not a lot of it. And he had a stoop and a big old belly. A red face, and wrinkles, but a very alive smile and a twinkle in his eyes. "You've done us all proud boy," he said to Michael. He was in pain, he'd drunk too much, or that was what your father said. He told his dad he should have stuck to shorts not pints, he said; "your prostate can't handle pints, you know that but you drink them anyway..." and then they got into an argument. I asked Trevor...'

'My grandfather's name was Trevor?'

'Yes.'

'I never knew that.'

'Trevor and Mary; that was Michael's parents' names.'

'He never spoke about them.'

'No, he wouldn't. I suppose that wasn't an accident. Anyway, "do you want me to find Mrs. Heywood for you," I asked, meaning Mary. "No," he said; "she'll be enjoying herself trying to chat up some of Mikey's pop friends. You leave her be, or I'll never hear the end of it."'

Bodhi sniggered.

'"Dad, don't talk about mum like that," Michael said. "I don't like it." But Trevor said; "don't tell me what I can and can't do. I made you, boy. And don't you forget it." Michael was starting to look mad, so I tried to leave them both alone. "No, don't you go, Shaun'ie. I've heard all about you from my boy, and I'm glad you're here, son," Trevor said. And then he doubled over clutching his groin and groaning; "oh, shit." I could see he was pissing himself; "my catheters slipped out of its bloody drainage bag, help me over to the toilet."'

'Old age,' Bodhi said, cryptically.

'I supported Trevor under his arm while Michael opened the door for us. As we were struggling, he put his thick skinned hand over my shoulder and drew me closer to his face; "I'm glad you're here to look after my boy, Shaun. After all you've been through." Your father started laughing manically and shaking his head; "Just shut up will you that was private," he said. "Well, you shouldn't have told me then," Trevor said. I eased Trevor's pants down and helped him with the drainage bag that was held to his leg with elastic bands.'

'You mean Michael had told Trevor about what had happened to you the night you met my father?' Bodhi said.

'Yes. Probably other people too. But it was a long time ago, and that was what I said to them both then. And Michael was obviously embarrassed, so in fact it made me feel good.'

'You could have felt humiliated,' Bodhi said.

'But I didn't. In fact it was your father who felt humiliated,' I said to Bodhi. 'Trevor said; "Mikey, you've done yourself proud, my boy. All you and Mia need now are some kiddies. What's keeping you, eh? I thought you'd be elbow deep in nappies by now?" At that, Michael suddenly thrust an arm towards his father's throat, and started to strangle him. Trevor coughed, let go of the waistband of the trousers he was trying to push over his shoes, and punched Michael quite convincingly in the gut. Michael stepped back winded. When he caught his breath he launched into a full on rant; "You never fucking stop do you? I've had this all my life; when are you going to win a prize at school, Mikey boy? When are you going to get up on that stage and sing a song, Mikey boy? When are you going to make your first record, Mikey boy? When are you going to kick those losers out of your band, Mikey boy?" He was burning red in the face with rage; "You're not doing it anymore," he said. "Got it? I'm not putting up with it. You just mind your own fucking business from now on. I've sorted you out alright, haven't I? You're not short of a bob or two now, are you?" or something like that. Then Trevor said the strangest thing, he said; "Mary always said you'll be a bloody difficult man to live up to, so maybe its better you don't have children because they're going to have to be saints to cope with you." And then Mary caught up with us anyway before your father could say something back.'

'What was she like, my grandmother?'

'In her sixties, a sunburnt woman, with a high collared blouse that tried to hide the loose flesh on her neck. They're both dead now you know.'

'Mmm.'

'"Oh, you silly old goat. I knew this would happen," she said, stepping straight into the restroom and pushing Michael and me away. She took charge, and Michael stormed off. As I left, Trevor called out after me; "You're a good lad, Shaun." Then I could hear him say to his wife; "that's Shaun, Mary. You know; the one I was telling you about."'

The truck started shaking from side to side, vibrating as though it was running along the cats eyes between lanes. But it didn't feel right. It lasted half a minute and Bodhi and I stayed silent. As quickly as it had started, it finished and the usual rumble of road noise continued unabated.

'All of that had nothing to do with my mother,' Bodhi said. 'What was it that affected her?'

'I'm getting to that,' I said. 'It was the mood your father was in, that was why I just told what I did.'

Bodhi huffed.

'Konrad came up to me later and told me there was a change of plans. Michael's parents were going to spend the rest of the night at Greyfriars mansion but Michael was going to make a grand exit himself, with his new wife, back to Laurel Canyon. Only the Press were waiting in huddles outside the gates expecting just that, or anyway, expecting Michael and Mia to drive to one of the airports in Los Angeles and fly off for their honeymoon. So to fool them we switched vehicles, and sent the Bentley off ahead of us with Konrad as the driver and a group of backing singers in the rear, with a couple of bottles of rum for company and trailing strings of tins and cans tied onto the rear bumper. Half an hour later we quietly drove off on our way in a dark coloured Mercedes. Obviously I was relieved when no one spotted us, but—being unprepared, I may have got slightly lost in the late traffic because I was driving a vehicle I wasn't used to, and I was tired.'

'So what?'

'So, after I'd only been driving for a few minutes Michael shouted at me from the rear of the Merc, saying; "You're going the wrong way, Shaun." He sat sprawled over the middle of the back seat, his wife to his right and Marcelyn, baby bump prominent, to his left. "Pull over," he said, although it sounded like pullover because he was so drunk and your mother and aunt just burst out laughing. Only he wasn't joking, and having them both laughing at him just made him more determined. "I'll drive," he said, and I ignored him, even though he was probably right that I was taking the wrong roads. Mia slapped his chest playfully and said; "No, don't baby. You're in no state to drive." I flicked my eyes back and forth from the road to the rear view mirror. The three of them were crammed in together, uncomfortably close. Marcelyn was pressed against Michael; she breathed out wearily, resting her head on Michael's shoulder. Michael instinctively put his arm around her. Mia whispered; "don't," to Michael and tugged at his jacket to try and pull his arm off from her, but Michael just huffed, and resisted without looking at her. "Just leave him be," Marcelyn said to her sister, taking a sleepy hold of Michael's arm.'

We passed under an overpass, the few seconds of shade were a brief relief.

'At this point I tried to turn off Sunset Boulevard to pick up the local roads, but even at such a late hour the traffic was jammed and we slowed to a crawl. Checking my passengers I could see Mia reach over Michael and pull his arm away from her sister. Suddenly Marcelyn woke up, and lashed out, sparking Mia to retaliate. "Whoa, whoa, whoa, calm it down," Michael said, trying to stop the flapping and flailing arms from hitting him in the crossfire. "You need to get your own man," Mia screamed.'

'She said that?' Bodhi said.

'They were all drunk,' I said, 'it got worse, believe me. "He's my client," Marcelyn said, meaning your father; "you need to get yourself a life girl, instead of mooching about all the time." "Oh, you need to get a proper business degree" your mother shouted, "so you can do your job properly." "I know everything I need to know," Marcelyn said. "You don't even know who your baby father is," Mia shouted. I could see their arms reaching out slapping each other again.'

'Wow.'

'So, we were close to a turning we needed to take, but we were stationary and then, without warning Michael leapt out of the back of the car, opened my drivers' door and said; "We'll never get back at this rate, go and sit with the girls." Michael is very strong when he wants to be, he has the core strength of a dancer. I refused to get into the back, but I couldn't stop him from pushing me into the front passenger seat. As soon as he was clear of me, he slammed his foot on the gas and swerved out of the queuing traffic, speeding onto the hard concrete of our exit road. The car screeched through a few more corners to pick up the quieter local roads.'

I looked up at the roof of the shell a few inches from my head; 'I regret letting him take control of the car. I regret it, I regret it. I should have pulled out the keys.'

'What happened?'

'The car was pitching manically as Michael swung it around and Mia and Marcelyn were stunned into sobriety by it. I looked behind me to see that they were all right, to satisfy myself that they weren't about to start fighting again. They looked back at me like naughty schoolgirls waiting for a teacher to pass them in a corridor. It was all fine, but as I turned back silently to face Michael and the road ahead once more, there was a sickening thud and instantly my blood was shot through with adrenaline. I knew what it was even before my eyes could make sense of what they were seeing; it was the shocking sight of a body smashing against the bonnet of the car, bent double at an unnatural angle from the waist.'

'Oh, no,' Bodhi said. The enormity of what I had just told him stunning him too into silence.

'Michael was shocked, he said; "fuck, fuck, fuck," as the Mercedes rolled forward, stalled, and ran over the body. "He was in the middle of the road. I couldn't miss him," your father said, but I was furious that he was covering up for himself before we'd even worked out what he'd done. "Crazy old guy was jaywalking," your father said. Michael was gasping for air; both hands on the steering wheel, looking into space with his eyes wide open and focussed on infinity. I pulled the handbrake and jerked the car to a halt. There were rags and clothes from the bag the man had been carrying strewn all over the windscreen and the road. My breath was bouncing, my heart was pulsing in my throat.'

I looked at Bodhi, but he wouldn't meet my eyes. I was sorry to have to tell him this. I knew it would leave him thinking less of his father, but what could I do to explain to him the things he needed to know, the things he wanted to know?

'I leapt out of my seat and ran around the front of the vehicle to check the body. I pulled on a gaunt grey arm that hung out from under the car. I dragged the rest of the body out, checking for a pulse that I had no way to find on his filthy wrists. I checked his mouth for a breath, for some sign of life; but there wasn't any. Michael was motionless in the driver's seat, I had to call him to help, and he slowly stepped out of the car, just as Mia and Marcelyn left it themselves. "What are you going to do, Shaun?" Marcelyn called, and I'm thinking a hundred thoughts all at the same time. "I don't know," I said. "Can't we call the Police," Mia asked, innocently. "No, no, no. They'll crucify me," Michael said, suddenly sober again. Your father looked at me; "Shaun, you can say you were driving, can't you? You can say he just stepped out and there was nothing you could do." My heart sank. "Yes, it happens, sometimes homeless people do that, they get themselves into accidents for the insurance money," Marcelyn said. "We could get Hal Kardanglian to sort out the details."'

'That's not very nice,' Bodhi said, looking at the floor of the flatbed.

'I couldn't do anything but look at them both, hoping that my eyes were digging into their hearts; that they were asking themselves whether they could really live with themselves afterwards, if they let me take the blame for Michael's carelessness. Then Mia said, "You can't do that to Shaun." She was shaking. I was relieved. But there was no time to think; there was an incline down to a ditch across the tarmac, in the undergrowth by the side of the road, I pulled on the body. It was too heavy to move. I gathered my strength and braced my back; "We've got to do something with the body! Michael; take a hold," I said. "Oh my

God," he said, wrapping his hands around the old man's legs; "he stinks." Together we flipped the lifeless body down the slope until it sprawled untidily under a dense thicket of Manzanitas, out of sight. Marcelyn said; "Get the rags and the bag out of the road, Michael." He was in shock though, blank in the face. "Get the rags," she said again, half screaming and keeping her voice down at the same time. She hobbled round the car and prodding him. Finally he came to and did what she said, hiding the trash in the ditch. Meanwhile I scanned the road ahead of us, and the distant buildings in case someone had spotted us, but mercifully they were quiet.'

'Mercifully?' Bodhi said.

'Mercifully for us,' I said.

'But not for the old man...'

Randy or Joel hit the brakes and Bodhi and I lurched forward towards the hard divider of the shell that kept us separate from the two rednecks driving us. My breath left me for a moment as I thought we were crashing. But straight away the truck sped up, and in the exchange of honking car horns Bodhi and settled back down on our seats.

'No, not for the old man,' I said to Bodhi.

'And you just helped my father deal with it? Like there was no problem at all, just a mess, just something to clear up like a spill in the kitchen?'

'No,' I said firmly to Bodhi. 'We got into an almighty row over it, if you must know. Your father said; "'He was in the road. He was walking towards the car. I couldn't have missed him..." "How could you not see him," I asked, wiping my hands on my trousers and the sweat from my face. "I don't know," he said, "I just lost concentration for a second or two, that's all. It was probably you turning round to look at the girls, I was wondering what you were doing." He was still trying to blame me. "It doesn't take much concentration to spot someone standing in the road in front of the fucking car," I said. "Well we're not all super fucking meditators, Shaun; sitting looking at a wall for hours on end. You should get a life," Michael said, which I thought was really out of order seeing as it was his idea I'd got into that in the first place. I said to him; "You just took an old man's life," I was fired up by adrenaline; "and all you can think about it is insulting me?" At that point Mia started screaming wildly to herself. Michael ignored her and shouted back at me; "Is that what you go to the fucking Buddha place for, Shaun? So you can be the great holy one, holier than everyone else? So you can become a Zen Master? So you can become the next Abbot of some monastery? So you can have lots of little disciples running around doing whatever the fuck you want them to, eh?" I didn't know what he was talking about—it was so stupid. "You..." I said to him, "you write all these songs about sex and love that don't have any basis in reality; you earn a fortune fooling people into living with their eyes closed, and you think that gives you the right to keep your own eyes closed, eh?"'

'Serious argument...' Bodhi said.

"'What do you know about love?" your father said. "You live in your own little bubble." "And what do you know about wisdom and compassion?" I said. "You're just full of your own opinions." Then Marcelyn cut in; "Stop arguing, and get us out of here," she said, supporting your mother back towards the car. But Mia was still screaming, drawing in great lungful's of air, and then without pausing at all screaming again. "She's hysterical Marcie; for God's sake shut her up," Michael said, or something like that. "Come and help me then; she's your wife, I can't move her," Marcelyn said. Your father told me to get Mia into the car. We stepped away from arguing with each other and I went to help Marcelyn. I covered Mia's head with my hand and eased her body, which had gone suddenly rigid through the door of the car and back into a seat.'

'That was the end of it?' Bodhi said.

'No. Before I had finished buckling the seat belt, Michael grabbed my shirt at the collar and pulled me. He pulled me so hard he tore the buttons through the fabric; "If you want to sit on the moral high ground like a Buddha, Shaun, that's up to you," he said, "but don't you ever judge me. I have to make music for ordinary people, that's what I do, and if you knew what the cost of that was; you wouldn't be so fucking high and mighty." That really pissed me off. I took his hands away from my torn shirt and pushed him back—banging my head hard on the sill of the car door as I got out. I thrust my hands out against his chest in anger, jolting him backwards into the middle of the road. He staggered for a bit, then when he recovered he bounced forward and snarled at me; I punched him in the face.'

'You did?' Bodhi said.

'Yes, I did. He threw a punch back and I threw another punch and then we wrestled each other to the ground, thrashing about in the dust until we were both limp and exhausted. It was really ridiculous. Anyway, eventually we struggled up onto our knees to catch our breath. Our heads were downcast, and I don't know about him but there were certainly tears in my eyes. I guess slowly the adrenaline drained out of us, and the anger, and then your father said, softly across our little battle ground; "I'm sorry, Shaun. Okay. About all this; I'm sorry."'

Bodhi sat silently.

'I asked your father what we were going to do. He said; "Just drive, please. If we're lucky no-one will see us; its dark, it's late. We're not far from home. If we get caught, then we get caught." So I drove us all the last few miles back to Laurel Canyon, sweating every time I saw a car in the distance driving towards us. There was a deep blood stained dent in the bonnet of our pristine Merc, and if anyone had passed us they would have guessed straightaway what we'd done and driven away from. But the roads were still clear, still quiet. The only headlights we saw were from cars turning away from us.'

'Was my mother alright?' Bodhi said.

'She was silent. She'd stopped screaming. They were all silent. They stayed completely quiet until we got back. Michael sent the housekeeper to bed. I guess Konrad had told her to expect us, and then helped Mia and Marcelyn inside. Meanwhile, I took the car to the garage at the rear of the property and locked it in, knowing I'd need to deal with the damage as discreetly as possible.'

'That's all terrible,' Bodhi said.

'Yes. So you see, what should have been the happiest day of your mother's life couldn't have ended up worse. Except no; that's not quite true. It could have been worse—if she'd had to read about it in the L.A. Times the next day. If she'd heard about it repeated over and over again on CNN on the T.V. the next day, that would have been worse, a lot worse, because by then Michael would probably have been arrested and charged with manslaughter, while being no doubt surrounded by a scrum of flash popping photographers.'

'Which didn't happen?'

'No. The story of how an old man had died in a hit and run, a mile or so from Michael and Mia's home in Laurel Canyon didn't break on the news the next day, although the coverage of their wedding did. As it turned out, no-one cared much about the old man's death anyway, even when his body was discovered. Only a short passage appeared in the L.A. Herald appealing for witnesses, but the wording wasn't very hopeful, and the Police department were quoted saying they were unlikely ever to find out what had actually happened.'

'So they got away with it? You got away with it?' Bodhi said.

'I suppose so,' I said. 'At least, there were no obvious consequences for me, and not for Michael and Mia either. They went away on their Caribbean honeymoon as planned. But still, they knew what Michael had done, and it wouldn't have mattered if they were sitting poolside on a private yacht, or laying in the sun with no cares—whatever they were doing—that Michael had killed a man couldn't have escaped their knowing. And that knowing, their conscience...your mother's conscience; it must have undone their honeymoon—because when they returned from the Caribbean, it was clear for everyone to see that the dreadful depression Mia was carrying with her was more than sadness, it was downright catatonia.'

Bodhi looked at me as if to ask me what I meant.

'She was still silent—Michael was lavishing gentleness and care on her, but it didn't make any difference. Even as months passed by, her mood stayed the same...not her mood,' I said, 'her behaviour. It was more than a mood. It was terrible. I'd see your father walking behind Mia, carrying her jacket, trying to connect with her, reaching out ahead of her to open doors and steer her around obstacles that she didn't seem to even notice were in her way. I'd see him gently taking her head and resting it on his shoulder while she sat on the couch beside him, motionless and wordless.'

And there were times when it was worse than that, and I'd see Michael's confusion all too evident on his face, as Mia repeated manically word for word, small things he had said to her.

'Couldn't Marcelyn help,' Bodhi asked.

'In a funny way she did, but don't forget she was pregnant and the baby was nearly due. She'd moved out of the house in Laurel Canyon and bought a new place in Santa Barbara, an ocean front property with plenty of space for her to raise the baby she would soon have. Oddly enough, that seemed to help. After all, Marcelyn being heavily and obviously pregnant, while, for all her efforts Mia couldn't conceive; that must have been part of the problem.'

'Did she get any help at all?' Bodhi said. 'You make it sound like my mother was just left on her own, having to cope with everything without any help.'

'Not at all,' I said, 'there was no end of specialists coming to talk with her and ask her questions. I know, because they asked your father the same questions when they talked with him in the garden, after talking with her. '

'What did they say it was, that she had?'

'I don't know they ever found out. I'd hear Dr. Tzu telling Michael that it wasn't his fault; that the specialists were looking into everything, that so long as Mia knew that Michael loved her and always would, then time would be the healer and he would have done everything he could. But he didn't believe Dr. Tzu, he'd say; "how can she know that I love her, if she can't even recognise me?"'

'It was that bad?'

'At times. And there was no answer to that. Dr. Tzu would push her sleeping pills on your father and tell him to rest and he would get weirder and weirder himself. He'd panic if the specialists hinted that Mia's previous drug use might have been the cause of her illness, he'd say; "But she's clean, she's totally clean Dr. Tzu. She doesn't use." And she'd say; "They're just looking into everything, Mr. Heywood. Don't blame yourself." 'But I do blame myself," he'd say, "maybe it was me,

Dr. Tzu; I must have said the wrong thing to start her off, I just don't know what it was. It must be my fault."'

'How long did it go on like that?' Bodhi said.

'For a good while. Dr. Tzu would spend hours talking together with Konrad, in places where I couldn't overhear them, and about what, I couldn't know. But in the end he asked me to go and help Marcelyn with her daily living tasks, once she had given birth to a healthy baby boy. "The other Miss Seligman," he'd say.'

'She'd had David,' Bodhi said.

'Yes, she had, and so she was tied up finding nannies to look after him while she kept looking after your father's career. And I did the shopping and looking after her house, and drove her around. I said to her I was glad to be out of Michael's way, but she said I didn't need to be, that; "he had said he was sorry, hadn't he?" And hadn't I seen the big Buddha statue he had put in the garden?'

'For what?'

'As an apology, that was what she meant.'

So we'd sit there in her garden looking out on the sun setting over the pacific ocean, across the beach that flowed out from the ragged lawn, the palm trees that framed the view swaying gently in the slightest of cooling breezes, and the dark blue sky above us broken only by the elegant sweeping of gulls passing overhead.

'This is what I mean about Marcelyn helping your mother,' I said to Bodhi, 'the thing is, the arrival of David, even though the name she gave him didn't hint at the identity of the father, it was a turning point for Marcelyn, and it was turning point for your mother too. It lifted her mood. All of a sudden she could talk again and act reasonably normally. It was as though Mia's illness was cured, like an exorcism by the pain Marcelyn experienced in giving birth.'

And, conversely as though the pain of Mia's illness had found out a human form to inhabit, in the wriggling limbs and lusty wails of the boy, David that her sister Marcelyn had just given birth to.

'So then everything should have been good from there on,' Bodhi said, 'it should have been a happy ending, and everyone should have lived happily ever after. But it wasn't?'

'It almost was,' I said, 'because five months after David was born, Mia too, to her delight found she was pregnant again. It had been a cryptic pregnancy; the drugs she'd been on for her depression must have hidden it, even from her. She was delighted of course, but the toll her illness had taken on her hadn't been repaid. Not in your father's case. I mean; your mother's illness had taken its toll on him too.'

'He got exhausted, you mean?' Bodhi said.

'It was more than that, he got distracted. Yes, he was glad that Mia seemed better, and yes, he was glad she was pregnant. But he must still have been worried that the pregnancy would end the way all her previous pregnancies had ended, and that Mia would once again become unwell. So, to hope that he would become a father at last, to hope that Mia would become a mother; it was too much for him to contemplate. Instead he got into the habit of working in one or other of the studios in West Hollywood from the early evening onwards. He'd be working away through the night, through the sudden darkness that falls over L.A. until the first threat of the dawn.'

Perhaps the city felt more his, when most of the normal people crammed into the boring repetitions of their lives were fast asleep and out of sight, and he and his crew of technicians and musicians could jam together and record without inhibition.

'There were things I knew nothing about,' I said to Bodhi, 'I knew nothing about a lot of things. But I especially knew nothing about what else your father got up to during the long nights that he worked. And it wasn't until one morning, very soon before you were born, that I found out. He'd returned exhausted after one of those nights—yes, as you say; he was exhausted. I was preparing to repaint a garage floor. The same garage in fact, where I'd cleaned the Mercedes after our journey back from Greyfriars Mansion, although that had been several months before.'

'What did you do with that car,' Bodhi asked.

'I sold it cheap to a mechanic I knew. He handled it discretely after that,' I said. 'Anyway, Michael ambled over from the Chevrolet Pick-up he'd parked in the driveway. He'd been sitting in it, with a cowboy hat pulled over his eyes for at least an hour. He asked me after Mia, whether she was up and out of bed. I shook my head. He asked me where Konrad was, and I told him I didn't know. I told him he might have got caught in traffic, but just then Konrad pulled up in his very modest and efficient silver Toyota. He would have eased it around the side of the house to the staff quarters, as he usually did, but Michael had been parked blocking his way. So then they had this weird conversation, or at least it sounded weird to me at the time because I didn't know what the background was, I had to work it out.'

Bodhi looked at me quizzically.

'It turned out that Konrad had been following Michael, and Michael kind of knew he had been following him but wasn't sure, and Konrad kind of knew Michael wasn't sure he'd been following him, but also wasn't sure. So they were feeling each other out. "Lot of delays on the 405 today," Konrad said, "so I took the coast road. The sea air was lovely this morning." He straightened his glasses and adjusted the cuffs of his shirt. "Did you go to the beach?" Michael said. "I didn't have you down as a surfer, Konrad," I said, innocently. "Oh, there's lots of things

I like to do, that you don't know about," he said back to me. "He's no surfer, Shaun," Michael said, abruptly. "But I do like people watching," Konrad said. "I bet you do," Michael said. "Who did you watch this morning, Konrad?" There was a ballet going on between the two of them, Michael was leaning in towards the back windows of Konrad's car, trying to see what Konrad had been covering with his jacket, Konrad meanwhile was stepping into Michael's path, forcing him back towards the truck he'd been sitting in—come to think of it,' I said to Bodhi, 'it was this very truck that your father had been driving, only it was newer then.'

The strange road noise that had shaken the truck a few minutes before returned. The truck seemed to be skating along the road. We were weaving from side to side as though the driver was falling asleep. But there were no horns from other road users to warn us or object to us, it was a strange experience. The truck slowed for a moment, then sped up again.

'So, I said to Konrad; "You were watching the surfers?" I was puzzled. Konrad changed the subject; "Shaun, how is Mrs. Heywood this morning? Is she well and comfortable?" "She's not up yet," I said. 'What's Mrs. Heywood got to do with this,' Michael asked Konrad. It all went something like this,' I said to Bodhi, 'then Konrad turned his back on your father and walked away from his car, surrendering it almost; "Does she know you like to visit your; what would you call her?" he said. "My publicist," Michael said, "if that's what you mean." Konrad swivelled round; "Ah, that's what Mrs. Visconti is; your publicist. Okay."'

'This was my mother's friend?' Bodhi said. 'The one you used to drive her to visit?'

'Yes,' I said. 'So, Michael told Konrad that it was none of his business who he goes and visits; "if I want to visit her and discuss my future plans I'll do that," he said, "any time I want, Konrad." But Konrad said; "even while her husband's away? And it's none of my business, well, no of course it isn't. Of course it isn't." He was passive aggressive. That's what I meant when I said he was always immaculately dressed—he was a control freak, and he was trying to control your father. "What do you actually want, Konrad?" Michael shouted; "more money, or what?" But Konrad just walked off.'

'He sounds awful,' Bodhi said.

'He was. I just stood there, dripping paint onto the concrete driveway. "Shaun, he was following me last night," Michael said. "I thought I saw him out by the coast, but now I know I did. The bastard was following me. I took a drive out of Hollywood, after we'd finished for the night." I put my brush down to give your father the attention he clearly expected from me. "I just need to drive sometimes, you know, Shaun. Out to the coast, or wherever." I nodded along to him. "It's been difficult for me, with Mia so down a lot of the time." I was trying to be patient, standing there in my overalls with a paint brush hardening quickly in the heat. "I need company, you know, Shaun. My body needs it; I'm working hard. I need parties, I need to have a good time. I need to make emotional connections."'

'What was he trying to say to you, Shaun?' Bodhi said.

'I couldn't put it together at the time,' I said, 'it was almost like he was trying to get me to forgive him for something, and I couldn't bring myself to do it. I couldn't say, anymore; 'that's fine Michael. Hey, you're a rock star, you can do what you want,' so I just stayed silent, hoping that listening to him would be enough. And then the same day, later in the day, your mother went into labour, and on April 8th, 1990, to everyone's surprize and delight she presented to Michael, at Mercy Medical Center in Beverly Hills—a boy, healthy and energetic; you, which they both announced to the world, albeit without a name of course. They were both overjoyed, and in the haste to celebrate, your father decided suddenly to sack Konrad, on the spot, just like that. "You can look after things for the time being, Shaun," he said to me later; "until I find a replacement. You've been around for long enough to know what needs doing, and if you get into problems Marcelyn can help you out. Mimi and I just want to be together with our beautiful baby boy. Finding a replacement for Konrad is going to be a hassle, and I don't want to get into it now." So I took over his house and his diary...me, a lad from Hackney, who'd gone up in the world.'

'So you were all happy then,' Bodhi said.

'Yes we were, we were all happy, all at the same time. It was wonderful and I only wish it could have stayed like that. But you see, we weren't all happy; Konrad was seriously pissed off.'

'Oh, yeah.'

'And it wasn't long before we found out just how pissed off he was. You see, six weeks later the story broke of Michael's affair with Tania Visconti,' I said. 'Michael might have expected to have been able to deny whatever tale some scandal rag conjured up and printed on the basis of a tip-off, but Konrad hadn't in fact been providing tip-offs to a newspaper, he'd been doing much more; he'd been secretly filming Michael—and in fact the equipment he'd used had been on the back seat of his car on that day he had his argument with your father. It had been the video cameras he'd just been using.'

'He'd been filming my father...'

'So, when the story provided by Konrad broke, not in a newspaper but on the entertainment news reports on T.V., showing

Michael captured in an affectionate and compromising embrace inside the glass walled ocean frontage of Tania's Malibu house; the heartbreak that Mia felt at the revelation...'

'...must have been devastating,' Bodhi said.

'And it was, even though it couldn't have been entirely clear to your mother when she saw Michael and her best friend Tania kissing on the T.V., that what she'd actually seen was the sign of any kind of a passion likely to dislodge her prime position in her husband's heart. I'm sure it wasn't, and she shouldn't have assumed it was. But she did assume it was, and the husband and wife's fight which followed wasn't something I could get into and put my own opinions in without the clearest of invitations—which I didn't have. So, naturally, Bodhi I didn't involve myself in the drama that followed. I didn't attempt to reason with Mia, or with either of them. I didn't attempt to mediate, not between the two poles of the fury that I could see, but not hear, through the windows in Michael and Mia's home; not between the two poles of the fury I could hear, but not see, in the courtyard beyond the living rooms beneath the room I used.'

Bodhi looked down at the dusty floor of the truck.

'So many times I've wondered,' I said to him, 'looking back; if there was more I should have done, or said. Couldn't there have been a skilful hint or a prompt I might have made? Wasn't it an easy cowardice on my part to have allowed the boiling passions of two people—not just Mia but Michael too, to run on and on without saying something, until they reached the awful conclusion that they did?'

'My mother's death...'

'Yes.'

'But how could you have prevented it?' Bodhi said.

In the silence that descended over Bodhi and me, the strange rumbling of the road began again. It intensified, and then became an apocalypse. It was an earthquake; and as the oscillations accelerated the truck skidded, swerved, turned over and slewed to a screeching halt.

I should remember a cascade of petrol smells and broken windscreen glass as the truck crashed; first an eerie silence and then an eruption of screams, but I can't remember anything. What brought me back to my senses was Bodhi pouring water from a 24 ounce water bottle over me.

'What happened?'

'You'll be alright here,' he said, 'the bridge up ahead collapsed and a dozen or so cars piled up, but it didn't look like anyone was dead, and the freeway was full of helpful people.'

He cut the restraints from my hands. His own were already free.

'I found your phone,' Bodhi said, reaching into the bag I had given him only half a day earlier. I took it with confusion;

'How did I get here?'

'I carried you up,' Bodhi said, 'away from the freeway.'

'You've got your bag back,' I said. 'Does that mean those two guys in the truck are hurt?'

Bodhi stayed silent. I was lying on the bone dry ground, on an incline that pointed to anonymous hills in the distance. The sun was blinding and I sat up painfully to shade my eyes from it. The awareness of voices in the distance behind me filtered through the shock of my regaining consciousness. There was a small hill between us and them.

'Worry about yourself,' Bodhi eventually said, 'there are enough people around to worry about everyone else.' He helped me to drink and as I did I realised how fortunate we had been. We were free again, and unhurt.

'We need to get back to the rest stop,' I said, 'back to the old red Chevy. We can start again. We can go to Nicki's. I'll get you there.'

'No,' Bodhi said, 'the road's run out. We're here already; the end of the line, the end of the journey. I'm done, and you need to look after yourself.'

'What do you mean?'

'If you're well, I'm going to leave you here, and head off.'

'But why?' I said.

'To be free,' Bodhi said.

'But we are free,' I said.

'Bound up in superficial things...how can we be free?' Bodhi was kneeling over me. He wiped a wet cloth over my forehead. I took it from him and wrapped it around my neck. He sat back on his feet. 'I have my eyes and my ears, my nose, my tongue. I have my thoughts, my mind. It's enough.'

'You have to eat.'

'But not today, I've eaten enough.'

'Tomorrow, then.'

'There are any number of things I don't have to worry about,' Bodhi said, 'and you can sum them all up as; "tomorrow".'

I felt my limbs one by one, exploring my aches with my hands, making sure I was as complete as I first thought I was. Everything seemed to be where it should have been and in working order, but I was no closer to understanding Bodhi; 'What will I tell your father?' I said. 'I have to go back and tell him something. Whatever bullshit I have to say, I'll have to say it, I've been working for him for too long not to. I can't abandon him any more than I can abandon you. I have to tell him something; what am I going to say?'

'Do you think he'll understand whatever explanation you try to give him, for what I'm doing?' Bodhi said. 'Do you think he's even interested?'

'Of course he is,' I said.

'Why? Because of the effect it will have on me—that I'm leaving "Pleasurelands"—do you think that's why he'll be interested? Or because of the effect it will have on him; that it will make him question the control he has over the world, over you, over me?'

'I don't know.'

'So then think about it,' Bodhi said.

'I don't want to think about it,' I said. 'Look; can't you put up with things—even superficial things, Bodhi? Life doesn't have to be perfect, God knows; my life isn't.'

Bodhi eased his feet out from beneath him and sat cross legged in front of me. 'Why should any of us put up with suffering, Shaun?' he said, his face creasing into a frown. 'Because that's what it comes down to, that's what we're choosing to accept by not looking at the things that aren't right, that aren't true.'

'You just have to get on with things,' I said.

'But if we accept suffering for ourselves, then why not accept it for others too? Why not say the whole damn world can go to blazes, and everyone in it?' Bodhi was looking down on me and I felt embarrassed. 'You don't want that, I know you don't.'

'But you can't help everyone, no matter how much you want to; you can't even help the two rednecks in the truck back there,' I said.

'I know I can't help everyone. But I have to help me,' Bodhi said, looking into the distance. 'Whatever this thing called "me" actually is.'

I stretched my legs out one by one and wiggled my feet, clicking the bones in my ankles. 'You're young, Bodhi. The self you are is not yet fully formed. You can give it time and make it the best "me" you can possible have.'

'Do you really believe that?' Bodhi said. 'That there's some kind of a person inside of you somewhere that runs your body like a puppeteer? Is it your mind that does that; that pulls the strings? But wherever I look I can't find anyone; there's just a piling up of memories that I can't trust to mean anything; a piling up of thoughts that don't connect, of feelings that don't lead anywhere.' Bodhi shook his head at me; 'There is nothing anywhere to hold on to; no rock in the stream; no satellite in outer space that keeps spinning in its own orbit, un-related to anything. No constant thing. No "me" in fact.'

I checked my phone. There was no charge, the battery was dead.

'There is love, Bodhi,' I said, 'isn't there?' He looked over my shoulder. 'Don't throw away your chance of it. It needs what you already have; a good life, money, connections. You're better off than most young men your age are; richer than almost any young man your age could be.'

'You've been listening to too many of my father's songs,' Bodhi said. 'This is the lie he sells and pays the price for it; that there's some sort of over-emotion over the horizon, some fantasy called love that will make all of our selfish thrashing about in life okay, that will satisfy even the most unclear and confused of our desires. He can't not know it's all a falsehood, but still he peddles it.'

'It's not a lie,' I said. 'It can't be a lie to point to something higher than your own head in the mirror.'

'But to think it's something other than that; that is the lie.'

I twisted my torso back and forth, stretching out tense muscles in my abdomen. 'I know things haven't worked out with Suzie,' I said, 'and yes; your father's an idiot. But come back and talk it through with him, negotiate. Re-negotiate—that's what life is; a compromise, a game, a way to get the best we can and make the most of it. Michael won't live for ever and neither will your aunt; the whole place will be yours. The whole of "Pleasurelands".'

'The whole place is just what these eyes see, these ears hear and this mind thinks,' Bodhi said. 'The whole place is just what happens between this in breath and this out breath...didn't you teach me that?'

'When did I do that?' I said.

'Reading me meditation manuals, when I was a child.'

'I just read you the words,' I said, 'they didn't mean anything to me. They were from a book.'

'Well there is something right about it, wherever it came from,' Bodhi said. 'The rest is ideas built on top of ideas; a kind of madness that lets people think the things they do make sense. That lets my father think that spending his money on the prettiest ever prison will make his only son the happiest boy ever, when all it can do is make him the loneliest prisoner ever.' Bodhi took my hands and rubbed my thumbs, where the ties had bound them and a deep red ring still sat in the skin. 'Didn't you think any of these thoughts when you were tied up by my father's manager in London? You were my age, you said.'

'I was younger.'

'But didn't you question anything...everything? Three days you said...'

'Three long nights. But I am different from you.' Bodhi looked me in the eyes, it was as if he was older than me now, more mature, more willing to be in the place of the most ultimate of fears, and the most intimate of fears. 'I couldn't bear the thought of death,' I said, 'I wasn't ready for it. I wasn't ready for it to come, or even to entertain the idea of it. Every thought I had, one after another was of how I'd escape or what I would do to the man who had done this to me. The ropes wore away at my wrists. I cried and I cried and I cried.'

'Shaun, I am as good as dead right now,' Bodhi said. The words pained me and I put my hands up to his sweet face, taking a hold of him between my hands. He put his hands on top of mine though and gently took them away; 'but I will find life more easily because of it. I'm sure of that. There's no fear because there's nothing left to fear. This is the start of my freedom. This is where it begins.'

'Bodhi,' I said, 'I just thought you would spend some short time with Nicki and then come back. I thought you would use the chance to see the world from a different place and learn from it, and then come back home, to your father, to Marcelyn, to me. That's why I drove you away. I hoped you'd be a bigger person by the time you'd made the choice to come home, that you'd be able to stand up for yourself and not give in to the sadness's that overtake us from time to time. And there's still time to do that.' I reached for Bodhi's bag, but he pulled it away from me defensively, holding it close to his chest. 'I just want to get a pen,' I said, 'I just want to write down Nicki's address.' Bodhi relaxed his grip and I opened a pocket on the outside of the sack and retrieved the pen and notebook I'd shoved in there for him only a few short hours before—hours that seemed a lifetime ago now. 'Promise me you won't lose this,' I said, handing him the open notebook.

'Okay,' Bodhi said. 'But tell me, Shaun; does Nicki even know I'm coming?'

I was going to say; 'mind your own business, Bodhi—she owes me favour after favour,' but I was losing the argument with him. 'I haven't had time to do that,' I said, 'I'll call her.'

'So, she doesn't.'

I took the water bottle from Bodhi and swigged. 'She's really easy going,' I said.

'I can't lie to myself anymore,' Bodhi said, 'I can't tell myself that there isn't some responsibility I have; to make sense of what this life is myself. Life, death, old age, illness...I have to find what's true in amongst all this. No more lying; I can't keep telling myself I have to be a better person, when I can't find the person anywhere that I'm supposed to improve. There's just a bundle of things here that come and go,' Bodhi said, with his fingers on his chest, 'that change constantly, day by day, or even faster. My body keeps changing, my memories aren't solid permanent things. Can I even trust my thoughts? What did I think yesterday? Was it really me who did that thinking?'

The poor guy, I thought to myself, he's losing it completely.

'Don't humour me, Shaun,' Bodhi said, picking up on my body language. 'These are human thoughts, and I need to take my time to think them.'

'What are you doing this for?' I said.

'To find the truth, Shaun. To find enlightenment. To be truly free, to find an end to suffering.'

Like how many people before, I thought to myself, and where does it end up, except in disappointment, madness and an early death.

There were voices approaching, I turned to check them out. It was a young woman supporting a man her age with her arms tight around his waist and the weight and struggle of her effort obvious. His shoulder was limp and his long brown hair was matted with blood, which smeared onto his partner's blouse.

'Don't go back to "Pleasurelands", Shaun,' Bodhi said suddenly, looking back from the couple.

'What are you talking about?' I said. 'Why not? Why shouldn't I?'

'It won't be safe for you.'

'Don't be ridiculous,' I said.

'Do you think my father sent those two heavies as friendly escorts for us? He didn't, did he?' Bodhi said, with a coldness in his voice.

'It was probably David who sent them, for all we know,' I said.

'He won't take kindly to what you've done—helping me away. Now that you've told me everything I can see that more clearly. I'm sorry to have made you do this for me, Shaun. But you shouldn't go back. You don't need to anyway, do you?'

'What do you mean? Shanice is waiting for me.'

'Call her and tell her to meet you somewhere.'

'I don't think you realise that Shanice likes living at "Pleasurelands" more than she likes living with me,' I said.

Bodhi wiped his hand over his face, hiding a scowl.

'Anyway, I've invested half my life in that place,' I said. 'I can't just walk away from it.'

'You should.'

'I don't want to.'

I stood up. Across the highway there was a ranch gate leading through fields of yellow scrub to a barn with Dutch style roofs. There were hills in the background, dotted with Madrones like the swirls of black beard hair on my unshaved chin.

I turned around, and Bodhi was gone.

Chapter 8.

I tell Hailey with tears in my eyes, that the very moment when I lost sight of Bodhi after the earthquake proved to be the full stop in my relationship with him. As a single tear rolls down the side of my nose, my constant companion hugs my shoulders and presses her face against mine.

'But why did you go straight back to "Pleasurelands"?', she says. 'Didn't Bodhi just warn you explicitly not to?'

I don't know what to say to her, other than that my sense of duty drove me to:

'What had to be said and done after Bodhi disappeared had to be said and done, and that was all there was to it.'

After all, I was working for Michael, I had never been working for Bodhi and if there had been anything left over that Michael needed to understand—and of course there had been—then, whatever the cost to me, he had needed to hear it. Even if I hadn't understood yet myself why Bodhi had made me help him in the way that he had.

From the crest of the small hill Bodhi had carried me over, I looked down on the industrial wreckage the earthquake had left strewn over the freeway. Already in the distance there was the wailing of Police sirens stuck behind vehicles parked or abandoned, and an eerie absence of road noise. I made my way down, on my uncertain feet to the mangled white pickup Randy and Joel had imprisoned us inside, still hoping Bodhi might reappear into sight.

Peering warily around the distorted hulk of the engine hood, I saw our two kidnappers lying there. One of them was leaning against the upturned body of the truck, holding his right arm tenderly, an off-white Stetson covering his eyes. His shoulder was hanging unnaturally and it looked like his collar bone was broken. The other was flat out, his hands raised up to his face, his breathing noisy and strained. His left leg was twisted at a bad angle, albeit without any blood, so although he was in pain I figured he wasn't going to die on me and I didn't owe him any sort of good Samaritan act. He'd be okay.

I kicked the feet of the guy with the shoulder hanging badly and he raised his head and groaned; 'what the fuck, dude?'

'Who sent you,' I asked, squatting down to his face level to look him in the eyes. 'Who do you work for?'

'Hey, listen, we just get the jobs through an intermediary,' he grimaced, recognizing me. 'I don't know who you are, and I don't care. We were just told the vehicle registration, one black guy, one white, and to bring you to Fresno where we'd get paid.'

'Who's the intermediary?' I said, trying to sound menacing.

'Oh, jeez man. I'm not telling you that,' he said, and for a moment I felt like an amateur.

'Well, anyway,' I said, pulling myself together. I put one hand either side of his head, and rested them on the hot metal he was leaning against; 'you leave us both alone now, you hear?'

'Jobs over, dude,' he said. He propped his Stetson back further on his head and looked away from me, wincing. 'All deals are off, no problem. You go on your way...I never want to see you again. But hey,' he added as I eased away from him, 'listen, have you got some water for me and my buddy there?' He was looking sorry for himself; 'I know we did you no favours, but it was nothing personal, okay. It was just another job'

I was sorely tempted to tell him to crawl off and die, but my better instincts kicked in and I gave him the water bottle that Bodhi had given me. Joel, or Randy, or whichever one of them it was, gingerly eased himself across to his partner and helped him drink. Then I walked away from them both, out across the rubbish strew tarmac and the narrow median, leaving the pair of them to fend for themselves. I didn't know where Bodhi was, but at least I could feel reasonably sure he wasn't still going to be hunted.

My sore head cleared slowly as I walked to the other side of the freeway. There was no sign of Bodhi even though I called out for him, but there were still some vehicles moving on the south bound lanes and a small group of people milled around hitching for rides. I took my place among them. I figured Bodhi would have to join us if he wanted to get anywhere—but even though I waited he didn't show. Eventually a Latino guy called Iggy let me into his pickup, and reluctantly I accepted his lift and we drove away.

In amongst the free-for-all of broken down cars and fallen trees that made the highways into monstrous obstacle courses, switching rides a few times more, I made my way back to the rest stop where the old red Chevy had been left parked. Even with the keys in the ignition and the passenger door ajar, it was still there, which had been a nice surprize. But then again it was just a beaten up old truck that no one had wanted.

I was relieved, but it had been a hell of a long day, and standing with my arms draped over the rusty tailgate of the flatbed with its wooden frame still firmly bolted to it, I was tired like a zombie. Shaking my head to keep my eyes open, I pulled a tarpaulin out of the cab and threw it over the back of the truck. With the light fading into evening I hid myself under it, and with a few raggedy blankets from under my driver's seat as bedding, I fell very, very fast asleep.

The next morning, with the news on the radio full of road closures and stories of survival and stories of tragedy, I fired the red beast up. Maybe I was still tired, but I wondered how anyone could think that what I had done was wrong, or how anyone could misunderstand my intentions. Then, figuring that if I got the sack on the spot, so be it, I drove back to 'Pleasurelands'.

Michael of course saw things his own way; 'Why didn't you answer my calls?' he said, flicking the lapels of my chore coat.

He met me at the maintenance buildings. It was past midday and I was finishing off hosing down the old truck and topping up the oil. The double garage doors that opened up one side of the building were raised and the interior space was fully accessible; bright red tool chests on wheels sat on one side and a good solid wooden work bench on the other.

'There's no cell phone signal in the central valley,' I said, hoping that was true, 'and anyway my battery was dead.'

Michael looked at me like he was going to say; 'that was a lame excuse,' but instead he followed me around the side of the truck; 'Where's Bodhi?' he said, 'I've been worried sick. Even your girl Shanice, or whatever this one's name is, she didn't know where you were. Why didn't you call me?'

He peered into the cab of the Chevy, looking for clues.

'I was just so tired Michael,' I said, 'and Bodhi didn't want me to. He wanted to go on an outing on his own...' I was making it up as I went along, gauging how well I was doing by Michael's responses, while trying studiously to look like I wasn't. 'And then the earthquake happened, and everything got confused.'

'So where is he now?' Michael said. He was wearing bleached out skinny jeans and a faded comfortable Tee, paired with a loose shirt on top. He hadn't shaved for a day or two, but he had aftershave on. All in all, he looked stylishly scruffy rather than untidily distraught, though I could still see the end of his pyjama bottoms poking out the bottom of his trouser legs.

'I don't know, exactly,' I said, lying. 'We got separated.'

'You...you don't know where he is?'

'Hey, he's got money, I think he took my wallet. He's probably looking after it for me—but at least he's got plenty of cash, so he'll be alright, and he can make his way back here anytime he wants,' I said.

'I can't believe you, Shaun. You just look after the buildings, you don't make decisions about my family. That's three nights in a row he's been away from "Pleasurelands", and I never even wanted him to be away from here at all. What are you trying to tell me? That you left my son somewhere? Where? Where did you leave him?'

'I-5, south of Fresno.'

'I-5, what the hell were you doing there?'

I realised then and there that either Michael was bluffing me seriously, or I'd been right to think it had been David who'd hired the heavies onto us. 'Heading back here, as it happens,' I said, watching Michael's expression closely. He seemed to buy that.

'Go back and look for him,' Michael said, after a moment's pause. 'Just go and find him.'

Just then David appeared—he slithered around the side of the buildings, easing his way out of the shadows like a mongoose on the trail of a rattlesnake; 'why don't we hire bounty hunters to find Bodhi,' he said, tugging lightly on Michael's shirt sleeve.

I smiled wryly to myself as I studiously polished the glass of a side mirror with the cuff of my jacket.

'Oh, shut up, David,' Michael said, 'I want him to come back because he wants to be here, with me; to take over everything I've built for him. Not because some heavy's got his arm twisted behind his back.'

'No, sure Michael, but how are you going to know what really happened while he was away, unless he's here to tell you, I mean, Shaun might be making all this up.'

David looked me in the eyes, daring me to deny it.

'Bodhi will probably be back in a few days,' I said. 'Just give him a chance to get a few things out of his system and everything will come back to normal. He's just blowing off steam. He's just having a bit of fun...you know what I mean by that, Michael?'

I was getting quite good at lying—so much so that it suddenly dawned on me that if I chose my words right I might just get away with having taken Bodhi out of 'Pleasurelands' altogether.

'Yes, I know what you mean,' Michael said, stuttering.

'How are all the buildings,' I said, changing the subject, 'after the earthquake?'

'I don't know, you'd better check them out,' Michael said. I had never noticed before the care he was taking to cover the patches of suntanned scalp that his grey hair was failing to hide from the sun. He walked off, hesitantly, as though he wasn't finished talking but couldn't think of the next thing to say.

I picked up a polishing cloth from one of the tool racks in the dark garage, carefully polishing a pair of pliers that didn't need polishing.

David paused, I could almost hear the thoughts going on in his head; gears crunching to an inevitable question: 'Do you think Bodhi is going to come back?'

'It would serve you perfectly well if he didn't,' I said, 'wouldn't it?'

I turned round to face him. It struck me then just how small David actually was; he was a runt, a pixy faced, upturned nose little runt with a worsening stoop that made him seem even smaller than his half size too large clothes did. I scowled at him but he simply raised his eyebrows and pursed his lips, as much as to say; 'yeah, maybe...I never liked the guy anyway.'

'Where's Michael going now?' I said.

'Dr. Tzu's here. He's probably in the middle of things with her,' David said, miming a syringe being emptied into his arm. 'But do you really think Bodhi won't come back? Coz if Bodhi isn't here, I might as well use his house for myself. Suzie can live with her baby in the staff quarters, because that's all she is if Bodhi isn't here. What do you think?'

'The baby is Michael's grandson, David. For Christ's sake,' I said. 'And Bodhi's only been away for a couple of days, so chill out.'

David tutted, slinking away towards the domes, the central lawn and the houses. I threw my polishing cloth down and followed behind him, thinking about how best to keep him from making the situation any harder than it already was for me. I wondered if I could twist Michael's arm somehow and persuade him to force David out, just like he had when David had pushed Bodhi in the pond when they were both children. But then I realised that there were going to be all sorts of other changes that had to happen anyway and that there'd be no point in me trying to keep 'Pleasurelands' the way it had been.

I just had to let it all go, even the barren spots in the green velour of the central grassed courtyard, that I had spent so many years trying to eradicate. They made me think of Michael's scalp. I knew I might still be sacked at any moment, but I stopped and checked the sprinkler heads embedded in the dry soil anyway, pricking the ends of each one open as I walked onwards. I've been looking after 'Pleasurelands' for so many years after all, how can I just stop and leave if I don't really need to? The thought that I might have to, stung like a hornet.

In the distance Dr. Tzu's Prius was leaving Marcelyn's house. She dragged her suspicious eyes over me, then ignored me. It was as well; I had nothing to say to her. But then Marcelyn followed her out, limping with a crutch; 'Hi, Shaun,' she called, looking away from David as I caught up with him. 'Did you get through the earthquake okay?'

'Yes,' I said, waiting for a reprimand.

'Good. David says Bodhi isn't with you though, that's a surprize.'

'No, I mean; yes,' I said, glancing at David.

'Oh, okay, well—he'll be having some sort of an adventure, then.'

'Yes.'

Marcelyn hesitated as I hovered waiting for her criticism to flick out like a whip. But there was none forthcoming, she simply limped away, shaking her head to herself as though to say; 'what an idiot Shaun is.'

It suddenly dawned on me that only Michael seemed the slightest bit bothered that Bodhi wasn't around. I was surprized, relieved and disappointed all at the same time.

I stood there shaking my head to myself as David helped Marcelyn hobble back into the shade of her house, shutting the door behind him. There was a pair of hummingbirds zipping in to feed from the sugar drip hanging outside, hovering like miniature drones. Then Suzie, the mother of Bodhi's child and his supposed wife trotted unexpectedly into view.

As soon as she saw me she stopped, leaning against the stuccoed wall of the house with her arms spread out as wide as she could hold them. For a moment she looked like a pantomime villain just discovered by a pantomime policeman, but as soon as she recognized me herself she raced over.

'Where is he, Shaun?' she said. 'Why haven't you come back with him?' She was wide eyed and unsteady on her feet. 'What have you done with him?'

'I haven't done anything with him,' I said.

'You must have killed him. Is that it? You've killed him in an accident; it wasn't your fault, but you're covering it up now...'

'Suzie, what the hell are you talking about? Pull yourself together.'

She looked through me as though I wasn't there. Her auburn hair, styled into curls had fallen flat onto her brow, sweated into a disarray that stuck to her forehead and made her look like she'd stepped straight from a workout.

'You don't get it. He has to be here,' she said. 'I'm nothing but the mother of a child who doesn't mean anything unless Bodhi's here himself.'

'That's not true, Suzie,' I said, 'Stirling is Michael's grandson and he loves him.'

'He doesn't care a bit about Stirling, all he cares about is Bodhi. For God's sake, Shaun, you know that's how it is.'

I stepped away from Marcelyn's house, lest she overhear us unnecessarily, 'but that's not what's bothering you anyway, is it?' I said as Suzie followed me.

'What do you mean?'

'You can stay here, you're safe, your baby's safe. What's the problem?'

Suzie looked away from me as though our eye contact would shame her.

'The problem is you want to leave here and do your own thing,' I said, 'and you expect Michael to pay for it, but if you go on about this I'll get Sterling DNA tested to see if he really is Bodhi's son, okay. Now, just go and look after your baby.'

Suzie rubbed her forehead with a shaking hand and gasped for air.

'You're going to be all right,' I said.

I walked on, around the long covered cloister towards voices chattering and laughing in Bodhi's house. The smell of cooking seeped into the early afternoon as I clattered up the boardwalk that led to the front doors. I knew I'd find Bodhi's girl companions lounging there, but Leisha spotted me from a side window. She saw me as I saw her, dropping her lipstick from her hand as though it was the least important thing in the world. She was as cold as ice.

'So, he's gone then?' she said, pushing my shoulder firmly enough that I had to stop walking and face her. 'Leave the rest of the girls alone. They don't need to know anything. Not today, just give them a day off.'

She took me by the elbow, digging her fingernails like a claw into the back of my arm. I headed back outside with her, following Leisha's lead towards a secluded corner wall beneath a shady veranda. 'Tell me what happened,' she demanded.

'I haven't got time,' I said, trying to push her hand away.

'But Bodhi's not coming back...'

'Are you asking me or telling me?' I said.

Leisha gave nothing away, returning my stare dispassionately.

'You know he's not coming back,' I said, 'it's what you and David plotted.'

Leisha let out a short mischievous leer, letting go of my arm.

'I heard you both on the microphones,' I said, 'I saw you both on the video feeds; you weren't even bothered that I did. You knew this would happen, and you wanted it. And now, here it is, you win; you and David can have "Pleasurelands" to yourselves.'

I pulled myself away from Leisha, but she took hold of me again; 'Chill out, Shaun. Come on,' she said, 'you know yourself, he's only been gone a day, he might come back. I'm just seeing where we are with things...'

We stood facing each other silently for a moment. She seemed to have a hold over me in more ways than one.

'It's okay, Shaun. I really like you. I respect you. David's never going to do anything to hurt you. I'll never let him. You'll be okay.'

'Why shouldn't I be okay?' I snapped back.

'Because you took Bodhi away from here,' Leisha said. 'You know it, and I know it and David knows it. You on your own. But we're cool. The fact is, Michael couldn't care less about what Bodhi really needs to do with his life, could he? And if we try to explain it to him; he'll never understand. So it's cool. We'll just keep everyone happy; you, me, and David.'

'You wanted this to happen,' I said.

228

'And what would you rather have had happen?' Leisha said, 'that Bodhi spend the rest of his life like a child? You're not stupid, Shaun. You know this is for the best; it was the blue pill or the red pill for Bodhi and he took the red pill.'

Leisha stroked my shoulder. She had argued me into silence. The other girls continued chatting and screaming amongst themselves out of sight, and while Leisha left me to join them, I left the task of telling them all to pack their bags and leave, for another day.

It was a fortnight in fact, before I finally gave them the talk. I'd gathered them together in Bodhi's lounge. They were sat on the leather Ottomans and settees I'd kitted the room out with so many years before, seating now with stains and tears that reflected the mood of its users.

Sapphire, Jet, Emerald, Amber and Jade; the girls I had found when Michael had wanted Bodhi surrounded by jewels, all of them had been sat before me. I said; 'Uliana, Trishna, Kerry, Aylya, Daryl—you know why we're here this morning, don't you...' and with that Uliana had begun to sob.

I had to cancel their contracts and let them go. They had protested; Kerry told me that I'd misled them all by implying they'd had a future as dancers on Michaels' tours, but I denied that I'd ever promised them that. Trishna said that she could still do lots of things for Michael, with a wink, but I told her that there would be no need for that either.

'Can't we just stay anyway? It doesn't cost him much...' Daryl said, but I had told her; 'no.' I had told them all to pack up their bags, and with their inevitable tears rolling, they got up one by one to leave, and over the next couple of days, with their things all together they had done just that.

'Pleasurelands' became quiet without them, but there had been plenty to do. I made a point of tidying up my expense claims before submitting them to Marcelyn's office, swapping out some of the more excessive ones—just in case my character was ever to be questioned at a later date.

And I sent away in packing crates a few of my most treasured souvenirs for safekeeping, just in case my relationship with Michael ever deteriorated into pettiness, because, well, he was a pop star after all. And with my security in mind I put the most important of the video tapes we'd been storing into those boxes as well.

But Michael was busy too and not overly concerned with what I had been doing, for in the face of the obvious fact that Bodhi wasn't coming home, Michael had grasped for himself how useful social media websites were, especially the ones that Marcelyn had been managing for him.

I went to see him at his request, in his studio a few days after the last of Bodhi's girls had driven away in their taxis. 'Why isn't our web stuff fast enough?' he'd screamed at me. 'Why can't I get Safari to do what I tell it to do?' He flung his arms in the air in frustration.

Michael was hovering over a MacBook on a mixing desk with the screen pointing up at the ceiling.

'You'll have to get a studio engineer or someone to help you with that,' I said, 'I'm hopeless.'

'But all I want to do is ask everyone where he is,' Michael said. 'If everyone's on Facebook, somebody must have seen him. They can let me know. All those people out there; they call themselves fans, they say they love me and all that shit...'

He was grey in the face. The studio lighting was harsh and the wrinkles on his dried out forehead were throwing hard shadows that made Michael look older than I had ever seen him.

'You have to post something, don't you?' I said.

'Of course you fucking do, but how do I do that, that's all I'm asking?'

Michael ran his fingers over the keys, he was tapping, tapping harder, banging. He didn't know what he was doing, and neither did I.

'Fuck,' Michael said, holding the laptop in both his hands and smashing it down onto the console. 'This is your fault, you twat. If you hadn't taken Bodhi away, I wouldn't be looking for him.'

With the noise one of the studio technicians looked up from behind a keyboard in the acoustic room beyond the glass. Michael tried to look like he was in control of things, but the techie came into the mix room anyway.

'Everything alright, Michael?'

'Yes, fine,' Michael said, unconvincingly. He calmed down. 'Look, you probably know how to use this thing don't you...' he said to the young guy.

'Yeah, what do you want to do, Michael?'

'I want to post something on Facebook.'

'No problem.' He tapped away. 'You need to login,' he said. 'Do you want to put your password in?'

'I don't know what it is,' Michael said. He turned to me, 'Marcelyn does it all. How am I supposed to know...'

I shrugged my shoulders.

'Get Marcelyn over here.'

'You want me to call her?'

'Okay, call her then.'

I dialled Marcelyn's house on the mix room's phone, and put it on speakerphone when she answered it.

'What are you trying to do?' Marcelyn said.

'I want to find Bodhi. I want to put out a missing person thing on Facebook. I want people to let me know where he is. I just want to get him back here.'

'Michael, haven't we been through this?' Marcelyn said. 'We can't use your official social media accounts for this. It'll look stupid, and there's no way of knowing what people will end up posting back...they might even pretend to be him.'

'Don't tell me what I can and can't do,' Michael said, cutting off Marcelyn. 'Give me the fucking password.'

'You're out on a limb if you do this, Michael,' she said.

'Give it to me.'

'We won't write it down or anything,' I said.

'Am I on the speakerphone,' Marcelyn asked.

'Yes,' I said.

'Well, take me off it.'

Michael gestured to me to do what Marcelyn said, and I let her know it was just her and me.

'You know, Shaun, if he messes up with this I'm just going to wash my hands of it all.'

'Yeah, I don't know anything about it,' I said.

'Has she given you the password yet,' Michael asked.

'It's; Mia,' Marcelyn said to me, 'all in upper case, then; June 1, 1990. Have you got that?'

I hesitated.

'MIAJune11990,' Marcelyn said.

'Yes,' I said, 'I've got it.' It was the date of her sister's death that Marcelyn had set as the password.

'Do you want to just tell me what the PIN is...?' Michael said.

'I'll put it in for you,' I said, and before he could object to that, the screen changed and he was in.

'Shaun, there's nothing more I can do to help Michael if he ignores me like this,' Marcelyn said to me. 'He just has to get used to the idea that Bodhi has his own life now. You can't put out a missing person request for someone who isn't missing. Bodhi is just living his life. That's what you said to me isn't it?'

'Yes,' I said.

'Get off the phone,' Michael said, and I mimed back with a hand signal that Marcelyn was still talking:

'Shaun, Michael is getting this out of all proportion; Bodhi is gone and that's that. Anyway, doesn't he realise that David is still around, and there's lots David could learn from him. Michael should spend more time with David, don't you think? Shaun?'

With that I put the phone down.

'So let's type it up,' Michael said, gesturing to the studio assistant to disappear.

I sat down in front of the laptop.

'Has anyone seen my son Bodhi?' he dictated. 'He disappeared a week ago and he might have got lost. If you know where he is I can come and get him. I'll sort you out...'

'I can't keep up,' I said, prodding keys one by one.

'Get out the way then, Shaun,' Michael said, pushing me sideways and sitting down himself. I wondered if I still needed to be there, but I wanted to know what Michael was asking people to do, and in any case, I knew well enough that Michael needed an audience, and for the time being I was it. '...I'll sort you out, so just let me know, okay.'

'How will they know what he looks like?' I said to Michael, 'you kept him away from everyone. You kept him out of the limelight. They aren't going to know what he looks like at all.'

Michael thought about it. 'We'll put a picture up,' he said.

'But there's hardly any good ones, and anyway, he probably looks kind of different now, so who knows what he actually looks like.'

'God damn it. What the fuck are you talking about, Shaun?'

'Well, if he buys new clothes he won't look the same.'

'You're a fucking moron, Shaun.' He pressed the button. 'There, it's posted. Now, you get a photo and put that on too.' Michael span the swivel chair around as he got up to leave, 'and let me know every time someone gives us a lead...'

'Sure,' I said, 'but there'll probably be a load of people posting rubbish...'

'No, just tell me every time,' Michael said, kicking the door open in front of him.

Of course there were hundreds of messages and not a lot that made any sense to follow up. It was just as Marcelyn had predicted; jokes at his expense, sightings that were obvious fabrications, offers from detective agencies...anything but the actual contact Michael increasingly craved. It can't have been the cause of his deterioration, which, looking back accelerated so quickly after that, but neither would it have helped delay it's suddenness:

Two weeks after Michael's social media intervention fell flat, he was arrested in a bar in Stockton for molesting a young man.

'It was mistaken identity, Shaun.'

'What, they mistook you for someone else who had molested the kid?' I asked him. We were rehearsing the interview he was about to give to the San Francisco Chronicle. We were sitting in Marcelyn's office. It had seemed a more professional place to let the interview take place than in Michael's own rooms. He was reluctant to do the interview at all but, with a tour in the planning stages, Marcelyn had insisted on it. She refused to be present to help with the practice run though.

'No, it was my mistake...'

'What, there was someone else you were trying to molest?'

'What?' Michael said, looking back at me like I was mad.

'Well, Michael, Marcelyn said to throw you curveballs, to try and unsettle you...because that's what the journalist will do. They're like that...'

'Sneaky bastards. Yes, okay,' Michael said, brushing his untidy hair away from his face. He looked drawn and uneasy. Tired too. 'I was driving on the outskirts of the town. I was off I-5, I was getting some fuel. I'd turned out of the Gas station and took a wrong turn. There was a bar across the street I was driving along and I must have just glimpsed at it, I don't know why. But there was this kid going in, and for a moment it was Bodhi. I was sure it was him; the height, the colour of his hair, the walk he has...everything about him was just right. And I was so happy it was him, I couldn't contain my joy. To have found my son...can you understand that?'

'I can, Michael, but don't forget it isn't me sitting here, it's some newspaper guy...'

'It'll be a girl; they'll send a girl. She'll be pretty, really pretty. She'll have fought in the office to get the gig,' Michael said. 'She'll think she can seduce me, flatter me, take me into her confidence, get me to say anything she wants her audience to read, so she can make a name for herself and get famous.'

'Okay, but what was it about finding your son that made you stop the car and go into the bar?'

'Are you crazy?'

'No, no. But remember; it isn't me here.'

'It isn't you here...okay, okay.' Michael was shaking his head, scrunching his eyes closed and sighing. He sat on his hands, almost as though there was something he was trying to keep inside himself. 'I suppose I should have realised that the young man I saw going into the bar probably wasn't going to be my son. It was midday...'

'It was a strip club...'

'Yes, it was a strip club, but so what? Bodhi might have got a taste for the things in life he missed.'

'You mean you had a strip club set up here for him?' I said, with the kind of rising tone I imagined a journalist might have used.

'No? I mean he's a great young guy, with all the energies that go with it. What are you talking about?'

'What I'm trying to say is that, if you'd thought about it for a minute you might have realised that you needed to be a bit more careful about just going into a strip club and grabbing hold of some guy by the shoulder, because he might take offense more readily than if it had been in some other, less private place,' I said. 'That's all. And the interviewer will probably be trying to work out what your state of mind was.'

'I was fine,' Michael said. 'And anyway, I didn't grab the guy by the shoulder, I just threw my arms around him out of joy...'

'So then why didn't you let go of him when you saw it wasn't Bodhi?'

'It was dark in the bar, and I didn't have my glasses on...'

'You were out driving without glasses? Could you see where you were going?'

'No...Shut up will you. I took them off in the club and put my dark glasses on, because I didn't want anyone to recognise me.'

'Oh, god!'   I thought to myself, 'no wonder you couldn't recognise that the guy wasn't Bodhi.' 'So; you threw your arms around and greeted, what you thought was your son...'

'Yes. Well; "greeted". I guess I was in a hurry to get him out of there and talk things through properly in the car, because I was worried about being recognised, so I was sort of pulling him. I guess.'

'But then the guy did recognise you?'

'Well, no. Not straight away. He started lashing out, and swearing and it was only then, when I could hear his voice that I realised I'd made a mistake.'

'So you apologised, but the guy had realised who you were by then and started to make a big deal out of it?'

Michael sighed; 'Not exactly. I hit him back...anyone would. I mean, he'd smacked me in the face and it was bloody painful, so I hit him back. A few times.'

I couldn't stop myself slapping my forehead out of amazement. 'I don't believe it,' I whispered to myself.

'No, you wouldn't, Shaun, you piece of shit. I know you. You're the sort of fucking coward who just drives someone's son off into the distance and pretends like nothing's happened.'

I lowered my eyes to the floor.

'I mean, what's the difference between what I did and what you did...no answer, huh?'

I squirmed for a few seconds, but I couldn't resist the thought that had popped into my head; 'Well, I didn't get arrested by the Police, did I.'

'Oh, fucking clever you,' Michael said, sarcastically back. Then he snorted to himself; 'there was a cop in the fucking bar. Can you believe that? And he was on duty, too. What a bastard.'

'So, continuing the interview...if you want?'

'No. Forget it, Shaun,' Michael said, 'I'm not going to be doing it after all.'

With that, Michael got up and left Marcelyn's office. The wind blew the screen door to her house open and closed in his wake, but he didn't look back. He was gone.

I got tied up with Shanice leaving me. It took a month or two for our relationship to fall apart, and now—all I can say is good luck to her. But it meant I wasn't there for Michael as much as I might have been. I don't suppose it would have made much difference.

In the end Marcelyn did the interview. In the piece in the San Francisco Times she said that Michael had seen the young man going into the bar while he had been out driving around, searching, as any reasonable father might, for his missing son. He had gone into the bar himself to try to persuade the young man to come back to 'Pleasurelands', thinking, mistakenly, that he actually was Bodhi. That was what had caused the problems. However, Marcelyn explained, Michael had now apologized to the young man through his lawyers for his own misguided actions, and the case was entirely settled, and ready to be forgotten about.

But Michael had still been on the receiving end of a Police caution, there was no hiding that, and a random young man had earned himself a sizeable pay-out. So the end result was that, though the young man himself did keep his mouth shut, there was no stopping talk show hosts from making Michael the butt of their late night jokes, especially as Marcelyn was still adamant that the tour she'd been planning for Michael was going ahead.

Then, six weeks later, just as rehearsals had stopped for a break, Michael gave them more to talk about and made the papers again, falling out of a moving car on the freeway.

'How did you manage to do that?' was what I wanted to ask Michael. But as I picked him up from the private clinic that Dr. Tzu had sent him to, to rest in afterwards, all I could say instead was; 'Was it comfortable, Michael?'

I buckled up in the driver's seat. He sat in the back sprawling. He looked good, swarthy, pampered, clean shaven. His white silk shirt was open three buttons down and tucked tightly into his trim-waisted trousers. He fiddled with the controls on his door.

'You've got the child lock on the windows too?' he said.

'Doctors instructions, Michael. I'm just doing what they told me to. You can turn the air-con up if you want.'

Michael let go of the door handle and huffed. He relaxed in his seat and told me to drive on. We drove up along the Malibu coastline, the brilliant reflections from the Pacific arcing across our vision as we followed the twists and turns of the highway around the cliffs.

'Did she send you just to torture me, Shaun? Marcelyn. Did she?'

I couldn't look in the rear view mirror to gauge Michael's seriousness as the road was too snake like and the cliffs too steep. 'I don't know what you mean, Michael.'

'That wasn't a celebrity hide-out, you know. That was a psychiatric hospital.'

'Blue Lotus deluxe rehab?' I said. There was no reply, just a long painful pause.

'It's unreal. Everyone wants what they want of me, and if there's nothing left they just don't care,' Michael mumbled.

'I don't even know what happened...' I said.

'I see Bodhi everywhere,' Michael said, eventually. 'In my sleep, in my waking, in my dreams. In front of me, to the side of me. On the side of the road, on the off ramps, on the on ramps. Just a glimpse in the corner of my vision; but he's screaming at me, he's waving; he wants me to stop and save him from the nightmare he's living in. But its my nightmare, in the end, it's not his.'

It was awkward, and I wondered why Marcelyn had sent me if she thought it would upset Michael—Bodhi was still gone and had left no word of his whereabouts, how could I be other than the constant reminder of Bodhi's absence to Michael? But it dawned on me that Marcelyn had no interest in sparing me Michael's discomfort.

'I thought Bodhi was hitchhiking on the side of the freeway,' Michael said. 'By the off-ramp that we had just passed. I said to Charlie; "Stop!", but he didn't stop, so what was I supposed to do? I was sure it was him...'

'That was some nasty cuts you got there, Michael,' I said, 'you know we were all worried for you. Did you see us in the hospital after they'd cleaned up the lacerations on your back? Suzie came with Stirling. David too?'

'Like any of you cared,' Michael said, putting a pill from his hand into his mouth. Within a few moments he had become quiet, and for the rest of the journey there were no more than a few words that passed between us.

I had spent thirty years working for Michael, and it had been fun. But with Michael unwell, and Marcelyn only interested in David's wellbeing, I felt a sense of unease that greeted me on my waking and stayed beside me all day.

Perhaps it was as well then, that when Marcelyn arranged a holiday abroad for Michael, she didn't invite me. It didn't go well; even in the peace and calm of a Caribbean vacation, Michael had nearly drowned:

'He just dived in,' Leisha said, 'off the side of the yacht. There was no warning, nothing.'

I was helping her unload her things from the car after her drive back from the airport. David had shot off somewhere, but Leisha had a new found confidence about her. She had grown, with or without David.

'There must have been something,' I said, 'even if he didn't say what it was...a look, a vacancy...something?'

'He went quiet. That was all, then he just jumped. It was only afterwards, when the crew had hauled him back in, and I'd done the first aid with him that he said anything.'

'From what I hear you did well, Leisha,' I said, 'and for what it's worth; I'm grateful.'

'I know you are, Shaun,' Leisha said, hugging me, 'cheer up; he's still okay.'

'What did he say,' I asked.

'Well, you know what he said; he thought he saw Bodhi in the water. That's what it was.'

'How could he think that?'

'The water was very still, blue, lovely really. Maybe he saw a fish, or a reflection on the surface, or there was a dolphin. I don't know...but in he went, and with his clothes on and everything.'

'Then you went in as well?'

She nodded.

'You're a good swimmer,' I said, and hugged Leisha again.

'You know, Shaun,' Leisha said, releasing herself from my embrace, 'I don't understand why Marcelyn is still insisting the tour is going ahead. I mean, its true the press won't get to hear about this—so there won't be any bad publicity. But, he's not well. Michael's not well, and I don't see how just patching him up and sending him back out there again is going to do him any good at all. It's just unkind.'

'I know it is,' I said. 'But they've got their own agenda; her and Dr. Tzu, and they just don't care.'

bIf only Marcelyn could have had the heart to realise that Michael wasn't well enough to have embarked on yet another strenuous tour. If only Marcelyn could have seen that Michael was not receiving the care from Dr. Tzu that he really needed. If only Dr. Tzu herself, could have admitted that she wasn't qualified to give Michael that care, and had stepped aside. But they both were intent on it happening, because it served their purposes, and so it went ahead.

He nearly got away with it too. Sell out shows, big stadiums, big lighting rigs, big dance numbers, plenty of hits, not so many new numbers. Everything the crowd wanted and more. And that Michael avoided the press and interviews only made him seem more intriguing, not more aloof.

Until Vancouver. Sixty thousand people raising the roof and his set nearly ended. But then he stopped singing mid-song;

'Whoa, whoa guys, hold on. Cut the music, cut it.' There was a confused cacophony of instruments missing beats and pulling ahead, holding back, leading each other, following each other. Dancers colliding, choreographies collapsed.

242

'Bodhi, it's me. Can you see me?' People three rows back looked at each other, scouring the mass of people crushing forward around them for someone they ought to recognise, someone Michael Michael wanted to see, someone he wanted to be seen by. But he wasn't there, no one was, it was just them.

'Let him go, I'm coming for you...' Michael said, diving off the stage and into the arms raised aloft in front of him. Cheers went up, as though this was part of the show; audience participation? But it wasn't that, and the roadies who walked around the side of the stage slowly working their way into the crowd to rescue him, and take him, struggling against them, to the safety of backstage, saw his face change from 'edgy popstar' into a vacant shaking mask of confusion as they led him away.

Just as Michael was at the age where he should have been accepting lifetime achievement awards, instead he was having to fend off accusations that he was crazy.

'Michael Michael invests in space exploration so he can look for his missing son on the moon!' the jokes said on the chat shows and in the papers. And on and on it went.

So that was the end of his ill-fated tour, and there could be no touring after that. He returned to 'Pleasurelands' in the care of medics hastily arranged by the insurance company and settled back for the winter to the opulence and comfort of 'Pleasurelands'. Thus it was that, a few days later, as the first heavy snows of the season had begun to accumulate, I received a very peculiar call from Dr. Tzu.

The doctor with the suspicious glare informed me that Michael had decided he didn't want to dull his senses any more with her medications, but that he wanted to see me instead. I tried to get her to explain a bit, but that was all she would say. She was terse, and annoying as hell, but having no reason to be unhappy with Michael myself I went along to see him straightaway.

Michael met me outside his house. He strode towards me and threw his arm round my shoulder, spinning me on my heels and leading me back towards the rear of the building where his gold painted Hummer S.U.V. was sitting parked.

'Let's go for a drive,' he said, patting my shoulder as we parted.

'Sure, Michael,' I said, getting in. The soft pink leather of the seats still smelled new. 'Would you rather I drive?' I said.

'We're not going far,' Michael said, putting the wipers on fast to clear the snow from his view.

We drove along the estate roads until we reached a turn off. There was a wide metal gate padlocked shut, blocking inadvertent access to a forestry track which led nowhere except to other forestry tracks, and could easily be blocked by fallen trees after storms. I remembered putting it in years back when we'd first planted up the estate with extra trees.

'Do you want to get out and open the gate,' Michael said.

'I haven't got the keys with me, Michael,' I said. 'I wasn't expecting to be coming out here.'

'That's okay,' Michael said, 'I've got them here.'

He handed me the bunch of keys from the security office. 'When did he pick these up?' I thought to myself.

'Go on then, Shaun.'

I eased myself out of the passenger door, groaning a little as I landed with the ground further from my feet than I was expecting. I fiddled with the bunch of keys. There were at least twenty to choose from; anonymous looking, rusty bangles that hadn't been used for years. The third one fitted, and the lock released a corroded hold on itself.

I got back in the lavish Hummer, feeling silly that I had kept a hold of the lock. 'I'll grease it up when we get back,' I said to Michael. He ignored me and drove on through the open gate. 'Do you want to stop and I'll shut the gate again,' I said.

'No, I'm coming back this way,' he said.

'What does he mean; "he's coming back this way?"' I thought.

There was an awkward silence in the cab. 'Did you want to see me for something, Michael?' I said. 'Dr. Tzu said you didn't want to dull your senses...but, I don't know what she was talking about.' Michael stayed silent, his eyes focussing on the rough forestry track ahead of us. It gave the Hummer a chance to stretch itself, the pools of melting snow in ruts washed deeper by a dozen previous winters threatening to wrench the steering from Michaels grip, left and right. But he held on tight, driving fast into the dark tunnels of overhanging branches, slowly uphill towards the crest I knew we would eventually reach.

'The snow's quite heavy, Michael. It might bring some branches down on this road,' I said. 'And it doesn't go anywhere, you know...'

'I know where it goes,' Michael said, turning to look at me briefly. He kept driving, faster now; splatters of bright tangerine mud spat out ahead of us and over us, smearing the windscreen between the wipers rapid strokes. 'The road goes nowhere, and that's where my life is going.'

Michael had been looking straight ahead as he spoke, and for a moment I wasn't sure if I had actually heard him say what I thought he had said. There was a pause that needed filling, and all I could think to say was; 'No, surely not...'

'Oh, you don't have to be embarrassed, Shaun,' Michael said, 'it's true, it must be obvious.'

I played with the old lock on my lap, fiddling with the hasp.

'Only, the pills make it all seem like a fog; the day comes and goes, and I'm drifting through it like I'm hardly even here, and I wonder; "what's the point of this," because my life is drifting away from me.'

I was flattered by the intimate tone of Michael's confession, but it surprized me too that he had chosen this moment and this manner of involving me.

'Can't Dr. Tzu change the dose, or the type of pills it is, or something?' I said.

Michael stayed quiet, the Hummer going faster and faster.

'Or, can't you just come off the pills? I mean, you're safe enough here, I'm happy to help you out with anything you want to do, you know that, Michael. I always have been, haven't I...'

'So you could teach me meditation, for instance,' Michael said, eventually. 'Couldn't you, Shaun.'

'I don't do meditation,' I said.

'Come on, sure you do,' Michael said. 'I mean, you always used to, you used to go to that temple in Camden town, in London. Remember; years back? I know you did. And that place in L.A. You used to go there a lot.'

'It was because you said those places were cool, Michael,' I said. 'That was why I went there. Because if you said it was cool, I did it. Because, honestly...I mean, I worshiped you.'

Michael snorted out a laugh; 'But you did meditation a lot, and then you were a teacher too, I remember you telling me, you were proud of it.'

'It was just the once, Michael,' I said, 'just the one time when the proper teacher didn't come and there was no one to lead the retreat and so I made it up and did it.'

Michael smiled. I saw him relax his tense jaws and ease the concentration in his eyes.

'And that was why you taught Bodhi, wasn't it.,' he said out of the blue, 'all those years ago. I remember Bodhi said so. Don't you remember he said so, on the film, when the film maker came, you know, the one who slandered me?'

'Yes...but it was years ago, Michael' I said, 'fifteen years, maybe more. I can't remember. You told me not to teach Bodhi, ever again, and I didn't. I never did.'

The track was getting steeper, where the hillside fell away to our right. Trees growing on the side of the valley beneath reached as high as us but barely above us. I could see through the thicket of branches to white clouds and snow covered hills in the distance.

'But that's not exactly true, is it,' Michael said. 'How could it be, when Bodhi has just now gone and done everything the Buddha himself did; leaving home, leaving his wife, leaving his son, leaving his father, and with all he'd done for him? Funny how that happened, isn't it. So you must have been teaching Bodhi...'

I was stunned. I didn't know how seriously to take what Michael was saying. Was he really not taking the pills? Should he have been taking them? Had he taken too many? What was he talking about?

'...so now you can teach me.'

'What Bodhi did had nothing to do with me,' I said, 'if his life looks like the Buddha's...I don't know what you're talking about.'

'You do know what I'm talking about. It was your idea, remember?'

'What? No.'

'You told me when I was at my lowest ebb, after Mia had died, and I was so worried for the welfare of my baby boy...that I should build a beautiful place and fill it full of things for him to keep him happy, and never let him know what his own mother had done. And that way he'd stay happy, and I'd stay sane.'

'What is he saying?' I thought to myself.

'You remember...'

'But you took it literally...' I said.

'Don't blame me for what you yourself said,' Michael barked, 'I was down, as far down as a man can go into the depths of his own despair, and I listened to you, like a fool, like an idiot. You never said; "Oh, I'm only giving you a story to make you feel better, you shouldn't actually do any of this," did you.'

'No. But, Michael...'

The Hummer was pitching wildly as Michael threw it around the bends on the road, racing higher and higher up the hillside on the edge of the valley slope with the fall dropping away beneath us to the valley floor below. I looked at Michael, his fingers were wrapped tightly around the steering wheel, his mouth fixed in a taut grimace and his eyes staring intently into the distance.

'But you can teach me to meditate now, can't you, Shaun. In fact, you'd better teach me to right now, to take the pain away, to give me my life back.'

'I...I don't even do it anymore, Michael,' I said.

He twitched the steering wheel, and we barrelled headlong towards the cliff edge.

'Yes, okay, Michael, we can meditate,' I said, 'we can just breathe, and relax...'

The Hummer corrected its trajectory and the wheels fell back into the old ruts in the middle of the track. The breath had left me and I dropped the lock onto the floor of the Hummer.

'You can teach me meditation, just like you taught Bodhi meditation, huh?'

I gasped for some air in my lungs; 'Michael, I never did teach Bodhi. I never did, even in the beginning,' I said, 'I only let him sit with me. He was too young to understand anything I might have explained to him, I just let him sit in meditation with me. He learned all by himself, whatever it was that he learned, he learned it because it was a natural thing to him.'

Michael released his hands from the steering wheel one by one, stretching out the fingers and then returning them to the wheel.

'Michael, were there pills you were supposed to take?' I said, trying hard not to sound like I was patronising him. 'Medications to help you stay calm? I don't know what Dr. Tzu gives you, but wouldn't you rather have some more of them?'

'You just want to drug me up? Is that it, Shaun? So you can control me, take over my life, destroy my family?'

'No...'

'Are you trying to get your own back for something I did to you? Did I do you some great harm way back? Way back when you were young, and I took you from nothing and gave you a home and a job and a life?'

'No...'

'So why won't you help me?'

'I'll help you, Michael. I'll help you...' I paused, holding my posture contorted in my seat, trying not to shake. 'Help him do what?' I was thinking to myself.

Michael slammed on the brakes and the Hummer slid to a stop, the momentum forcing us both against the straps of our seatbelts. 'Help me understand why my son should have walked out from "Pleasurelands", like the Buddha walked out of his palace? It's not India we're in. It's the USA—the greatest place on earth. He had his girls, he had his wife. What was wrong with them?'

I laughed a hyperventilated snigger; 'But the Buddha didn't walk out of his palace did he, not according to the story—he flew out on his horse, and the four guardian kings carried the horse, one on each hoof. The whole story's ridiculous. It's got nothing to do with what Bodhi did!' Michael went quiet, and I dropped my shoulders with the relief. 'But I'm not Buddhist, I only went to the places you and Marcelyn told me were good; to the temples in Los Angeles, the one in London, near the Roundhouse. You told me they were cool, you told me to go there, and I did. And I did a bit of Buddhism and it helped me. But it was years ago and my life moved on, and I don't go there anymore, and I don't do Buddhism anymore. I said to Bodhi; "don't do this, what you're doing, go back home," I really did...'

'But he didn't come back, he stayed away and now he might be dead for all I know and you're the one responsible for that, because he's not going to become a Buddha is he, because this is the USA, not ancient India. '

'It's not India, it's not India, Michael. But Bodhi isn't everything you think he is, and he isn't everything you want him to be, and he can't be. That's the point, and the girls only made things worse.'

The car started forward again. We were driving slowly now, the tops of the trees on the hillside beside us gave way to unbroken views. We were near the crest of one hill and the ridge that led to the highest point on the mountain.

'Shaun, I've got something for you,' Michael said. His face was a cypher. I looked into the back of the Hummer, but there was nothing to be seen. 'I'll show you it at the top of the mountain,' he said.

There would not be much further that we could go, and whatever it was that Michael wanted to give to me, I would be getting it soon.

'Michael, I don't know what this is all about. I know I helped Bodhi to leave here, but it's complicated. He's an adult and I know you love him and only want what's best for him, but between the two of us, between all of us, the fact is; we can't stop him doing what he wants, and children...I know I don't have any, but children don't always do what their parents think they ought to, I mean you didn't, I didn't. When did anyone?'

Michael sat silently, manoeuvring the heavy Hummer to the end of the forestry track. He pulled up and carefully applied the parking break with his foot. He turned off the engine and for a short while that seemed much longer than it was, we sat in the vehicle letting the engine stop and cool in the winter brightness, cracking and pinging as the hot metal shrank in the cold.

'But, he might come back,' I said, hopefully.

'Take a walk, Shaun. Get some fresh air.'

I got out of the vehicle, slamming the door behind me and tentatively putting one foot down in front of the other in the virgin blanket of white that surrounded us. Michael got out too;

'Are you trying to teach me, Shaun? Like I should follow you and understand what you're teaching, even though you pretend you're not, and you won't say anything?'

'No,' I sighed, dropping my shoulders, and walking slowly away. 'It just doesn't matter what I say, does it.'

Michael reached the rear of his vehicle, and stopped.

I paused, looking over my shoulder. Michael opened the back side hinged door of the Hummer. I could hear him un-flick catches and pull something out with a scraping sound on the lining of the boot. He turned to face me, and I could see what it was that he had been freeing; it was his finely engraved Purdey rifle, which he had removed from the usual locks in place on it.

'You won't say anything, because it was your plan all along...'

'Put the shotgun down,' I said, firmly, 'there's no Bears around here, so you don't need that shotgun out.'

'You're jealous of me...'

'I'm not jealous of you...'

'Because, you had a vehicle,' Michael said. He was beginning to growl; 'you had a vehicle, and you helped him to leave...'

'You've no idea how much he begged me to...'

'...but you sneaked him out away from me,'

'What choice did I have...'

'...and then you came back here and lied, and lied, and lied to me...'

'I didn't lie,' I said; 'God damn it. I didn't lie because I said to you I had to do what I did. I did what's right...'

'Rubbish,' Michael said dismissively.

'I did what Bodhi pleaded with me to do...'

Holding the rifle in one hand Michael opened his arms wide, imploringly; 'But Bodhi has a wife and son.'

As he spoke, the barrel of the weapon crossed my path.

'A wife he didn't choose himself, because she was pushed onto him, by you,' I said, 'and a baby which couldn't possibly have been his—because he's sterile. And he knew that, and Suzie knew that, and all his "jewels" knew that!'

'Rubbish,' Michael said again. 'You've completely betrayed me,' he shouted.

'It's not about you,' I shouted, 'I've helped to satisfy the deepest, most heartfelt wish of the one person in all the world I care for most, if you have to know...'

I edged slowly towards Michael, I would never have turned away from him. But Michael shouted; 'You've let me down, Shaun.' He wasn't looking at me. 'You've robbed me of my heir! Damn it, he's not your son he's mine!'

'But he's not just your son, he's Mia's too and she's hardly ever talked about,' I said, 'you never mention her, you've cut her out of your life and out of his...'

'Leave Mia out of this; I'm warning you.'

'I can't leave her out of it, Michael. Bodhi knows what happened when she died. He knows she meant to kill him when she killed herself.'

'You told him?'

'He'd heard it...'

'But you told him it was true?'

'I just confirmed the things he'd heard but didn't know were true or not. He has a right to know.'

'You've ruined my life,' Michael shouted, looking up at the sky. 'I miss Mia so much,' he mumbled. 'I can see her beautiful smile, the joy in her eyes when Bodhi was born, the pain in her eyes when she worried that she wouldn't see him grow up to be a man. And she worried so much. I would have done anything to take that pain away from her. And I have tried, I have tried and I have tried.'

He raised his gun and pointed it towards me, one handed at first and then with both hands on the shaft and trigger.

'Michael; no,' I shouted; 'put the gun down!' But the gun was still raised. 'It wasn't me, it was David, and David's your son as well!'

Michael stared at me, open-mouthed.

'It's the truth. He's your son, your other son. Marcelyn's, by your own spare seed. He's the same as Bodhi...they're identical.'

Time stood still. There was eternity; the cold of the snow, the still air, the beginningless and endless rush of all nature paused.

If you can hear the sound of one gun firing, one bullet fired, you can't be dead.

But I didn't hear it. I felt it. The rip of barrelling air spinning into the side of my head, the shock of torn tissue on the left side of my face.

I fell to the ground. I put my hand to the side of my head. I looked at my fingers again and the mess of dripping red stuff on them. Then, with the reddening snow turning to an all-enveloping blackness, I lost consciousness.

It turned out Leisha and Charlie found me and helped me to my house. They had heard the gunshot, had seen Michael return, had sensed something was wrong and had searched for me. They had bandaged me up, given me some of Michael's heavy duty pain killers, and sat me in the reclining chair in the middle of my room until a private ambulance had come, sedated me properly and taken me quietly away.

A week later, Dr. Tzu had called and left a message on my answerphone;

'I've got to tell you Shaun, from Michael and Marcelyn; that you're no longer welcome at "Pleasurelands". Don't come back. That's what it amounts to. Michael's been as angry as hell these last seven days, and I'm finding every way I can to keep him calmed down and sedated. If you come back I'm worried he'll lose it altogether. And

Marcelyn and I wouldn't want that, nobody would. So do us all a favour, and stay away. There's money in your account—you'll be alright. But, stay away.'

That I had nearly died didn't seem to be a problem to either of them. Neither, I guess had Michael's own care actually been, for, three days later Michael was dead himself. Then, finding his lifeless body, Leisha had made the desperate phone calls to the emergency services that had so shocked the ears of everyone who had heard them, and then the ambulance had come, and then the Police, and then the media.

But I had not been aware of any of this, for once I had lost consciousness in the anaesthetising snow, I had not regained it until a month had already passed, and when I did, I was in a brain hospital, not in California but in the south of England, having somehow been flown over in a special air ambulance.

After that, I had spent several more weeks in rehab, slowly recovering my strength and slowly uncovering the reality of what had happened, not just to me, but to Michael as well. Yet, as soon as I could sit up and talk I'd been besieged by phone calls, emails and strangers visiting the hospital ward, and all they seemed to want was to blame me for the death of their beloved Michael Michael—as though I could have had anything to do with it.

'You rescued me,' I say to Hailey, 'I'd thought I'd be safe in St. George's, but I wasn't safe there for long.'

'Do you think David or Marcelyn tipped off the press?' Hailey says, and I nod.

'But then you stepped in,' I say, 'leaving your little sister with your other family, to stand by my bed and keep the journalists away.'

Hailey gently runs her hand across the tight grey knots of hair on my balding head.

I think back to how she helped me reserve a place in the care home in Belsize Park we're sitting in now, and how she helped me ship the flight cases I'd put into storage in Los Angeles over the Atlantic back to London too. Then, bless her, she came to look after me, and I don't think it was just because of my collection of Michael Michael memorabilia.

'When your strength is back, we can go to places and do things,' Hailey says, 'and you will learn to let the past fall away.'

I struggle to face her, twisting in my wheelchair, but before I can say anything Hailey tells me again to think of how well Bodhi is doing now, and just forget him; 'Don't you think he'll be doing great?' she says.

'But I wish I could ask him himself, how he's doing,' I say to her, 'and if he has found what he was looking for. If he is a hermit somewhere, or a monk in a temple hidden away. Surely he wouldn't be peddling drugs to get by, or thieving?'

'I guess we're never going to know,' Hailey says, and I can tell she's not that interested.

She doesn't know, I hope, how much I need her, so I dare not make her angry; but it matters too much to me to put it down, so I have written a letter to Bodhi, and one day I will deliver it:

I know it's your life, Bodhi, and I know you have the right to live it any way you want. And thinking back on what you've said to me, I can see that there were difficulties that must have changed your life just as they would have changed anyone's, even Prince Siddhartha's. How much it must have hurt you to know that your son Stirling, couldn't possible have been your son, and, that your wife knew that, and that the girls you were surrounded by knew that too. I can only imagine the pain you must have felt, and the humiliation. And to think that every night the girls around you must have pitied you or laughed at you, even though that was the last thing that I paid them to do on your father's behalf.

So I would leave you alone and let you live your life, but your father didn't leave a will. For all the advice he must have had from Hal Kardanglian and others, he didn't leave a will, and now that he is dead the rest of them are fighting like a pack of dogs for the largest share of "Pleasurelands". It should be yours, and you can do with it then whatever you want, but first you have to claim the place, and all that still exists in it.

So I have asked Louise...you'll remember her, I told you about her, she was Michael's P.A. when I first met him, well, my girlfriend Hailey has found her in London for me, and even though Hailey doesn't know why I was trying, having found her, Louise has agreed to help me search for your whereabouts.

So, we're coming for you, Bodhi, with the deepest of love, to make sure you get every piece of everything that's yours.

With all my heart,

Your best friend; Shaun.

Thank You!

Find out more about Shaun and Bodhi and the journeys they're still taking, and find out something about me too, with a free download from my author website here;

https://pjptuffrey.wixsite.com/free-download

If you enjoyed 'Leaving Michael', I'd really like to hear how it made you feel and what it made you think. Why not leave a review, and help other readers just like you decide on this book?

Warmest regards,

P.J.

www.ingramcontent.com/pod-product-compliance
Lightning Source LLC
Chambersburg PA
CBHW070904180626
46817CB00003B/912